Mrs. M. pushed Roan forward.

"One more," she said, somehow with his phone in her hands. Wanda Sue nudged Faith over and Mrs. M. cried out, "Smile!"

He and Faith exchanged a glance before facing forward for the photo of just the two of them. A hint of her floral perfume hung in the air. Her arm brushed against his and he had to hold his breath for a few seconds in order not to react to her closeness. Or—rephrase that—in order for no one else to notice his reaction to her standing by his side. Her laugh charmed him, and when her son, John, ran forward to take Faith's hand, he had to contain his disappointment.

"There's hot cocoa, Mama."

Faith inched away from him. Roan had to admit, the impromptu photo session had been fun. But then, he was learning that Faith made everything fun. Maybe his daughter's request that he make Christmas merry wouldn't be so difficult after all.

Dear Reader,

I'm thrilled to have written a Christmas story for Harlequin Heartwarming. I love this imprint and have totally enjoyed working on every book in each series, but to focus on the most wonderful time of the year? The book practically wrote itself.

When I think about Christmas, I get nostalgic. I love the traditions we had growing up. I can still sit around the table with my family and talk about the fun we had. Waking up at the crack of dawn to open gifts. My brother knocking down the tree three times one year when he poured water in the tree stand. My grandmother's silver artificial tree. Decorating the house outside while it snowed. We've shared plenty of laughs that come from cherished family memories.

Once I started my own family, I incorporated the traditions of old, along with new elements. I didn't want to miss a moment.

Single mom Faith Harper wants to make memories for her young children. Little does she know widower Roan Donovan, her hunky neighbor, and his daughters fit right into those plans. Does she dare hope for more with a man who makes her long for a future family?

I hope you enjoy Faith and Roan's journey through the Christmas season. Maybe you'll see a few of your holiday traditions play out in the pages of this book.

Tara

HEARTWARMING

Her Christmastime Family

—

Tara Randel

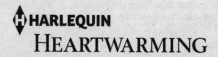

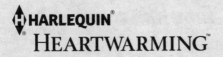

HARLEQUIN®
HEARTWARMING™

ISBN-13: 978-1-335-42652-9

Her Christmastime Family

Copyright © 2021 by Tara Spicer

This edition published by arrangement with Harlequin Books S.A.

For questions and comments about the quality of this book, please contact us at CustomerService@Harlequin.com.

Harlequin Enterprises ULC
22 Adelaide St. West, 40th Floor
Toronto, Ontario M5H 4E3, Canada
www.Harlequin.com

Printed in U.S.A.

Tara Randel is an award-winning *USA TODAY* bestselling author. Family values, a bit of mystery and, of course, love and romance are her favorite themes, because she believes love is the greatest gift of all. Tara lives on the west coast of Florida, where gorgeous sunsets and beautiful weather inspire the creation of heartwarming stories. This is her tenth book for Harlequin Heartwarming. Visit Tara at tararandel.com. Like her on Facebook at Tara Randel Books.

Books by Tara Randel

Harlequin Heartwarming

The Golden Matchmakers Club

Stealing Her Best Friend's Heart

Meet Me at the Altar

Always the One
Trusting Her Heart
His Honor, Her Family
The Lawman's Secret Vow

Visit the Author Profile page
at Harlequin.com for more titles.

To all who love the Christmas season.

May your hearts be filled with joy.

CHAPTER ONE

"Mama, can we get a puppy?"

Faith Harper paused while unbuckling her youngest child from her car seat and looked across the passenger seat at her son, John. His guileless expression met hers, awaiting an answer.

She clamped her jaw to keep her teeth from chattering. The temperature had dropped dramatically since the sun went down, ushering in winter and a little boy's Christmas dreams.

John continued to send her a pleading look. Lately he'd been on a please-get-us-a-dog kick, despite Faith's reservations about having a pet. Taking on one more responsibility. The closer they came to Christmas, the more his hopes rose that he'd receive a cuddly little puppy for a present.

She didn't have a response at this precise moment, so she dodged the question with one of her own. "What's gotten you so interested in wanting a dog?"

"You know Joey in my class?"

Faith nodded, lugging Lacey out of the seat. The icy wind crept into the gap between her jacket and scarf, crawling over her neck and down her back. Her hat went flying, snatched by a heavy gust sweeping through the trees. Faith reached out to grab it, but missed. Great, now her head was cold.

"He's been telling me about how Skipper is his best friend." John frowned, his little six-year-old face scrunched up. "I thought we were best friends, but then Skipper came to live at his house."

"Why can't you all be friends?"

"I guess. It's just that if we had a dog, I wouldn't miss Daddy so much."

Faith closed her eyes, inhaling deeply, wondering yet again how her ex-husband could so easily hurt their children. Lyle, with his big truck and fun trips, gone more often than in the kids' lives. He barely remembered to visit John on his custody days. Lyle was the fun parent. The irresponsible parent. The parent her son wanted to live with.

John still remembered his daddy and asked about Lyle all the time. Lacey, only three, hadn't spent as much time with her father. Faith still didn't feel comfortable letting Lyle take both kids on his visitation days, but Lacey had gotten into the habit of parroting her older brother like she did just now.

"Dada. Dada."

Faith lifted her into the air. Kissed her on her forehead. "Mama loves you."

To which Lacey responded with a string of repeated Mamas.

The car door slammed, alerting Faith that John had let himself out. He'd been extremely self-sufficient these days. She wasn't sure if it was because of his first year in school, but she said a silent thanks for his help, even in the small things like getting out of the car unassisted.

Instead of focusing on the dog dilemma, she said, "What do you say we go inside and unpack the goody bags Grammie sent home. We could have leftover pumpkin pie."

"With whipped cream?"

"You bet."

"Cream," Lacey said, tugging on Faith's shoulder-length hair. Reminding Faith that she really needed a cut and style.

"John, can you come stand by your sister while I get the bags from the car?" As she set Lacey down, John ran over to take his sister's hand. They talked about the floats they'd seen on television that morning during the Thanksgiving Day parade.

Faith quickly grabbed the handles of two generous-sized tote bags. There had been more than enough food at dinner, which meant Faith got leftovers. Which also meant she didn't have to cook for a few days, and for that she was grateful.

Juggling single parenthood was not for the faint of heart. Honestly, sometimes she didn't know how she kept it together. But then she'd take one look at her babies' precious faces and know she'd do anything to keep them safe and happy.

They hiked up the path to the porch, the children still discussing their favorite balloons. Here in the Blue Ridge Mountains, the days were short, and the nights were long if you didn't have a good furnace or a fireplace. Thankfully the house had both.

Faith placed the bags on the decking to unlock the door. As it swung inward, her gang ran inside.

Following behind, she dropped the food in the kitchen, then slipped out of her coat. The air in the house wasn't much warmer than outside. Had she forgotten to turn up the thermostat? Hurrying down the small hallway, she stopped before the display and tapped a few buttons.

"Sixty? That can't be right." She pressed

the heat button, hearing a weak groan, a thunk then silence. No loud rumble making the floor shake as the furnace fired up.

"Not again," she groaned.

This was the second time the furnace had refused to work since she'd moved into the house a month ago. Gayle Ann Masterson, her landlady, had sent a repairman to have the unit fixed, but apparently the heater was on its last legs. Who was going to come out on Thanksgiving night?

"It's cold." John said as he wandered down the hallway that led from the foyer to the back of the house. To the right, a staircase led up to the bedrooms. To the left was a spacious living room. The kitchen was located at the back of the house.

"Sorry. The heat is out again." She briskly rubbed her hands together, hoping to make the next few hours into a game. "How about I start a fire, then we can make popcorn, snuggle under a ton of blankets and watch a movie?"

"I want to play with my trucks."

She placed her hand on his shoulder and steered him toward the living room. "Get your toys out of the toy box while I call Uncle Deke."

"He's not my uncle yet," John informed her with great gravity. "Not until next month."

Her sister's fiancé and John had a strong bond that Faith was grateful for. A stickler for details, John wouldn't call him *uncle* until the big day, no matter how many times the family, or Deke, told John it was okay.

"Go ahead and play with Lacey while I give him a call. And keep your coat on."

In her mind, she made a mental to-do list: call Mrs. Masterson, buy a space heater, make sure the kids have lots of sweaters. Don't curl up in a ball and cry.

She got to the kitchen, realizing she'd left her purse, with the phone, in her car. She shrugged back into her jacket and rounded up the children.

"Let's go back outside while Mama gets her phone."

John ran ahead, Lacey right on his heels. When had she gotten so quick on her little feet?

Musing over how quickly her kids were growing up, Faith fought off another bout of shivers as the wind smacked her square in the face. Was it possible that it had gotten even colder in the few minutes they'd been indoors? If she couldn't find anyone to work on the furnace, they were all sleeping in front of the fireplace tonight.

She located her purse on the back seat floor of the small SUV. Just as she closed the car door, bright lights moved down the street, the arc of the beam sweeping over her yard as the car pulled into the driveway of the house next door.

"Policeman." John pointed.

She started to ask John what he meant, then remembered seeing the Golden, Georgia, police squad vehicle parked next door. There was no way to ignore the awareness that came from the knowledge that Roan Donovan lived only steps away.

The man had caught and held her attention from day one. Too bad she wasn't interested in dating.

"He can help," John said, streaking across the yard.

"John," she yelled, to no avail. His booted feet nearly flew to his intended target.

Scooping up Lacey, Faith planted her daughter on her hip and tried to keep up with John, Lacey laughing with each bump along the way.

John skidded around the car just as the inhabitant exited. They nearly collided. The tall form braced against the hit, steadying John with one hand.

"Whoa, buddy. What's the rush?"

Faith caught up, her breath coming in gasps. Roan, wearing a heavy jacket with GPD stitched on the chest, was bent down talking to John. When he stood, their eyes met and Faith's already spotty breathing lodged in her throat.

"Faith? Why are you out here?"

She inhaled through her nose. "Sorry, Roan. We were getting something from the car when John saw you pull up and… Well, we don't really need you."

He raised his eyebrows. "I don't know whether to be insulted or…insulted."

What was wrong with her? Why did her words get tangled and make her look like a fool whenever she spoke to him? "I didn't mean that like it sounded."

He cracked a smile. "Good to know."

The wind picked up again, howling between the bare tree branches. The thick evergreens bordering their properties swayed. The gusts snatched strands of her hair, swirling it around her head. She lifted her hand, remembering her hat was on the ground somewhere. Pride made her want to straighten the tangled mess, but she held back. Since becoming a mother, she hadn't had the time, or inclination, to bother with her appearance to attract the opposite sex. Until Roan had arrived in Golden.

She tightened her fingers to keep from adjusting her hair and said, "I should have stopped by to say hello sooner."

"I haven't been very neighborly either, since you moved in. I guess we're both guilty."

"It's been hectic," Faith said, ignoring her galloping pulse. Roan Donovan was one handsome man, with his thick, wavy black hair and soulful blue eyes. She didn't know him well. They'd first run into each other when Roan had done handiwork at some of the rental properties her uncle owned. Since then, they'd only seen each other in passing. She knew he had two daughters, was a widower. Even being stressed and overextended, she couldn't deny how his presence made her mind go haywire.

She clammed up, not trusting herself to speak around this man.

Which was weird. In high school, she'd run with the popular crowd. Never lacked a date to one function or another. Yet, she'd settled for Lyle.

Look how well that worked out.

She pushed Lyle from her mind, afraid her talk-before-you-think malady would create unnecessary problems. If this didn't clear up, she'd be living in a perpetual state of embarrassment.

After sharing some kind of complicated man-shake with John, Roan turned his attention on her. "Not the best night for a family stroll. It's freezing."

Was that censure she read in his eyes? The idea made her straighten her shoulders.

"Our house is cold," John announced.

Roan kept his gaze tangled with hers, waiting for an explanation.

"The furnace. It went out again."

Roan frowned. "We can't have that. Give me a minute to get my toolbox, then I'll come right over."

She held up a hand to stop him. "That's okay. I was going to call Deke."

"And have him come out on this cold night when I'm right here?"

Her stomach flipped at the thought of Roan in her house. Then again, she was a responsible mom now, right? Her misplaced attraction came second to her children's well-being. "Are you sure? I don't want to bother you on the holiday."

"It's no bother."

"What about the girls? Don't you need to be with them?"

Emmie, Roan's youngest, and John were in the same kindergarten class. Kaylie attended middle school. Faith had waved in greeting the few mornings they were all leaving for school at the same time, the extent of their interaction since she'd moved in.

Trouble was, anytime she was within a few feet of Roan, her tongue slipped. He'd kept to himself when he'd first arrived in Golden, but Faith had taken notice. Immediately. Long work hours, family commitments and everyday life circumstances had kept them both from learning more about each other. Still, she was tired of seeming foolish in front of the man who made her insides do the happy dance whenever he was around.

Roan's deep voice made her realize she'd zoned out.

"They're at Gene and Laurel's house. I worked the day shift so the chief could stay home with his family."

It was on the tip of her tongue to ask why *he* didn't want to spend the day with *his* family, but she didn't want to intrude. Or judge. She'd had enough criticism heaped on her to last a lifetime and had worked hard to overcome the consequences of past choices. Besides, Lacey was burrowing her cold nose into Faith's neck, so it was time to move inside.

"I'll take you up on that offer to look at the furnace."

"Good."

He smiled at her and she froze. What was wrong with her? Had Lyle so messed up her confidence that she couldn't even carry on a regular conversation with her hero neighbor?

Another gust of wind attacked her neck. She shook, now more than ever desiring the comfort of a warm house. "The kids are getting cold, so we'll meet you next door." She took two steps then swung around. "Do you prefer hot tea or coffee?"

"Tea is fine," Roan called, already heading to the side garage door.

Making sure John was beside her, Faith hurried her small family toward their house.

"Mama, do you think it'll snow?" John asked.

"I don't know, although it feels possible right now." If they were lucky, they might get a couple of inches or so in the winter. This year had been unseasonably cold already, so the odds were on their side. "Maybe, if we hope real hard."

"For Christmas." A big smile crossed her

son's lips as he skipped toward the porch, as sure of his prediction as any child making wishes for the holiday.

Christmas. Just a month away. Would she be ready in time? She wanted this year to be special. The last two had been spent at her mother's house, since they'd all been living there. Faith had finally saved up enough money to move into this rental and wanted a family celebration in her own home, establishing her own traditions.

She wanted to create an atmosphere that her children would remember all their lives. Special times they would pass on to their own kids. The question was, where did she start? And how did she do it in a way that established her own family, separate from her ex?

Lacey struggled to be let down, and Faith realized a good place to start these traditions would be in a warm home. With a functioning furnace.

John looked up at her, excitement shining in his eyes. "Don't worry about anything, Mama. I'll send a letter to Santa. He'll make sure we have a warm house and lots of snow on Christmas Day." He started to walk away, then spun around. "Oh, and a puppy!"

To have the faith of a child. She'd run out years ago. Yes, most of the trouble she'd brought on herself, but Faith wanted to believe. Oh, how she wanted to believe.

"You write that letter. I'll make sure it gets delivered."

"Deal," John shouted as he ran up the steps and into the chilly house.

She envied his confidence. Postdivorce, she'd spent too many long nights figuring out finances, which had kept her grounded in reality. Raising two children alone made her doubt herself daily. Still, Christmas was around the corner, a time of wonder, of hope. If her son could see the possibilities, so could she.

His boots clomping up the basement stairs, Roan entered the kitchen to find Faith at the table, scribbling on a piece of paper. Expectation swept over her face when she looked up.

"Success?"

"Looks like faulty wiring," Roan said, closing the door behind him and setting his toolbox on the floor. A hint of cinnamon, from the sticks added to the tea, spiced the room. "That unit is pretty old."

"I heard it kick on so that's a good sign, right?"

She rose from the table to pour steaming water from a kettle into a mug and pushed it across the counter in his direction. Roan couldn't help but notice how pretty she looked tonight, her cheeks still pink from being out in the cold. Her ruffled tawny hair and bright hazel eyes grabbed his attention. She did look tired, though, and he wondered if she had as much help with her kids as he did with his own. Seemed rather personal to ask, so he didn't.

"I'm not sure how long that will last."

"I'll call Mrs. Masterson tomorrow."

"No need. I got in touch with her while I was in the basement. She promised a brand-new furnace would be delivered just as soon as Louis down at the appliance store can install one."

Her hand froze as she reached for her mug. "Why would you do that?"

"Since I was in a better position to explain what was going on, I figured I'd call her." He frowned. "Is there a problem?"

"No. I, ah…" She waved her hand, a frown wrinkling her forehead. "I could've handled it."

"I'm sure you could, but it was easier for me to talk to her."

"Right." She met his gaze, then looked away. "Thanks."

Even though the furnace rumbled steadily

and warm air streamed from the ducts, Faith
ran her hands up and down her arms.

He nodded at her. "Nice sweatshirt."

Faith looked down and rolled her eyes.
"Not my idea. Mama saw these turkey shirts
and got one for each of us to wear today." She
pulled the fabric out at the waist to view the
brown turkey with colorful feathers of orange,
red, maroon and black on a beige background.
"Mama made her shirt look grandmotherly
by bedazzling the feathers. Grace jazzed hers
up with pretty jewelry, black slacks and great
boots. I'm lucky I managed to get jeans and
shoes on."

"Hey, don't knock it. You look festive."

Faith seemed less than convinced.

"You didn't have to wear it, but you did to
make your mom feel good."

She chuckled. "More like John hounded
me all morning to put it on. I didn't have the
heart to argue."

"Kids have a way of making us do things
we'd rather forgo."

"Isn't that the truth," she said, before taking a sip from her mug.

Silence fell over the room. She picked at the
sleeve of her sweatshirt, not meeting his gaze.

"Am I making you uncomfortable?"

Her eyes went wide for a split second. "I'm a little more scattered than usual."

"The holidays?" he asked, before picking up his mug of the hot tea.

"Partly." She held up a finger and tiptoed to the opening between the living room and kitchen. She craned her neck, then after a few moments returned. "Just wanted to check on the kids. I bundled them in blankets and they both curled up on the couch to watch a movie. Thankfully they got warm pretty quickly and fell right to sleep."

"Big day."

"Between the excitement of going to Mama's house and seeing relatives, plus all the food and the football game in the yard, they're worn-out."

He couldn't deny his curiosity. "What about you?"

She shrugged. "With school and the kids' activities, taking night classes and working full-time, I don't get enough downtime to center myself. Not that I'm complaining. This is my life right now."

He liked that about her. She put her family first and didn't apologize.

"I get it. Although, I haven't had the girls home as much as I'd like. Working nights put a real kink in our schedule."

"That's why I haven't seen you much?"

"Yes."

Which was a shame. Something about Faith appealed to him. Maybe because she made her children her top priority? Or the fact that she drew men's attention and wasn't aware of her allure? Whenever he spied her around town, something he'd begun looking forward to more and more lately, he couldn't deny the spark of attraction he hadn't felt in forever.

He pushed up the sleeves of his uniform shirt as the room warmed. "Being the last hire means the worst work schedule. But Pete will be retiring December 1 and Brady Davis will be the new chief. We've hired two more officers, so I'll pass the night shift to one of them and get my days back."

It had been a rough year. When he'd gotten the job offer, his in-laws, Laurel and Gene Jessup, had stepped up, otherwise he wouldn't have been able to accept the position. Working for Roy Harper at the rental cabins by the lake been good at first, keeping Roan away from people while he got his head together, but he'd needed a steady gig. He was both mom and dad to his children now. Grieving had to move to a far second place.

When he'd heard about the opening in the

Golden Police Department, he'd jumped at the chance. Thankfully Pete had been impressed with his résumé, and before he knew it, he was wearing the uniform and protecting the town that had become home.

And then this pretty woman had moved in next door. Funny how life worked.

He jerked when Faith let out a soft laugh.

"What's so funny?"

"Brady. The police chief." She grinned. "We went to high school together. Attended quite a few parties together. But it's not surprising— he always was on the straight and narrow."

Roan shifted. Why did the thought of Faith and Brady hanging out bother him? Brady was a good guy. Single. Would Faith be interested in him? And why did it matter? He certainly couldn't wrap his mind around starting a relationship.

Faith leaned the small of her back against the counter and cradled the mug in her hands. "The girls must be happy you'll be around more."

He lifted a shoulder. "You'd think."

She raised an eyebrow.

"Kaylie is ready to spend more time at home, but Emmie will miss her grandparents."

"How old is Kaylie?"

"Eleven." He paused. "It's been the two of us for a long time."

"That's right—Emmie lived with your in-laws when you first moved here." She tilted her head. "We thought you only had one child for the longest time."

His neck grew warm. When he'd first come to Golden, he'd still been mourning Catrina and could barely take care of Kaylie, let alone another child too young to understand what had happened. "I never meant to mislead anyone. At the time, letting Emmie stay with my in-laws worked for us."

"I understand. I lived with my mother for a year and a half."

"And that's a bad thing?"

She sent him a rueful glance. "Would you want to move back in with your parents until you got your financial act together?"

Never. Roan would die before he'd see his parents again, let alone allow his children near them. He knew she spoke humorously, but no. Roan's parents had no idea where he resided, and they never would.

"Now we have a chance to be a family," he said. To convince Faith or himself?

"It is all-consuming, being a single parent."

"Your ex doesn't help?"

She shot him a suspicious look.

"Small-town gossip."

"Which I've never been able to outrun." She blew out a breath, the puff lifting a strand of hair that had fallen over her forehead. The highlights in her hair mesmerized him. He reminded himself to stop staring.

"But yes. Lyle is less than reliable."

So he'd heard. Faith's uncle had asked Roan to keep a lookout for Faith when she'd moved in next door.

"I'm sorry about your wife," Faith said in a quiet voice.

"Thanks. It's been a little over two years now."

Two long years of dealing with the anger and pain.

Mostly the anger.

"How are the girls adjusting?"

He shook off the dark cloud that seemed to always hang over him. "Kaylie remembers Catrina. Misses her. Emmie only has a vague memory but knows her mommy isn't around."

Faith placed her mug on the counter. "So, police work. How did you get into that?"

"I worked security for the Western Extreme Sports Tour."

"I remember Catrina from when we were growing up. Didn't really know her well. We ran in different crowds."

"Then you know Catrina's reputation as a world-class snowboarder. The highlight of the tour."

"That must have been exciting."

When he'd first met Catrina, everything had been exciting. Until it wasn't.

"We managed the traveling pretty well with Kaylie. Once Emmie came along, things changed."

"I imagine. It would be hard taking two children on the road."

"That, and Emmie suffered with constant ear infections as an infant. When she got a bit older, the doctor put tubes in her ears and the infections stopped."

But in the process, it had caused a major upset in the status quo. They could have worked around that, but Catrina's schedule, and her unwillingness to deviate from it or put the family first, had been the problem in their marriage.

"My time with the tour helped me get the job in Golden, so I can't complain."

She regarded him for a long moment, as if sizing him up. He bristled under her steady gaze.

Time to change the direction of this conversation. "How about you?"

"I manage Put Your Feet Up, our family business. The office is located on Main Street."

"That's right. You book, what? Vacations?"

"More like vacation adventures. We coordinate with local businesses who offer river tubing, horseback riding, zip-lining, all those excursions people like to take while up here. Instead of tourists trying to figure out who to call, I schedule the day trips for them. We also offer camping trips, which my brother, Nathan, runs. Now that Uncle Roy is semi-retired, I take the reservations for Gold Cabins out by the lake. Mostly, we're busy from March to mid-November. Now that the holidays are here, I get to catch my breath."

"I'll admit, with the vacation season winding down, things won't be as hectic as usual. Taking life down a notch for a few months will be nice."

"Now that Emmie will be around, maybe we can arrange some playdates. John would enjoy going to the park with someone his own age."

"We'll have to plan a day."

"Oh, and you'll get to be a part of the Christmas festivities at the school."

"Yay."

Faith's merry laugh filled the room. "Don't sound so excited."

"Christmas is just another day at our house."

Her hand flew over her heart. "Are you kidding?"

"No. I mean, we'll celebrate, but keep it low-key."

Sympathy simmered in her eyes. The expression irked him.

"The girls will be fine," he assured her.

Was that doubt he read on her face?

"Well, we're doing it up big in this house. A tree, lights, the whole nine yards."

"Going all out, huh?"

She took two steps to the kitchen table and picked up the piece of paper she'd been writing on. "While you were working on the furnace, I started making a list of activities the kids would enjoy. There's the annual town Christmas tree lighting, the Golden candlelight stroll, meeting Santa, of course. Caroling and baking." She stopped and frowned. "I'm sure there are other things I've left out."

"Sounds pretty ambitious."

Her smile said she didn't mind. "Since this is our first Christmas in this house, I want to make sure the kids have a memorable holiday. I also hope I get more time off to spend with them."

"You work with your sister, don't you?"

"Used to. Grace has focused entirely on her law office now. Mama and I keep Put Your Feet Up running."

"It must be nice, working with your mom and siblings."

She nearly choked on the tea she'd just swallowed. "*Nice* isn't exactly the word I'd use."

He chuckled. "Then what word would you use?"

"*Stressful, overwhelming, loud…* I could go on."

"That was more than one word."

"I work with more than one family member."

"It can't be that bad."

"When I first started, there were issues. We've all settled into our roles now." She radiated a determined air he understood. He'd had to establish a hard line or two in his life. "Once I finish my business classes, I hope Mama will take more days off."

"So you have big plans?"

"I did. Once. But you know what happens when kids come along."

Yes, he did. Plans changed. Responsibilities shifted. Having the girls home with him full-time would be a major adjustment, but one he looked forward to.

Thinking about all he had to do tomorrow, he said, "I should probably be going." He picked up his toolbox. As he did, her eyes narrowed.

"Did my uncle ask you to watch out for us?"

Surprise stopped him in his tracks. "Why would you ask that?"

"Because I know Uncle Roy. The fact that you have skills and you live next door—I wouldn't put it past him to have you on speed dial."

Seemed his pretty neighbor was determined to be self-sufficient. "If he did, I haven't done a very good job. This is the first time we've spent any significant time together."

She didn't look mollified, but he wouldn't sell out the man who'd given him a job when he needed it.

"I would have handled it."

Hmm. Sore spot?

"Never said you couldn't. I'm glad I could help."

She wasn't persuaded, if the twitch of her eye was any indication. "Right. Thank you. It's so much warmer in here now."

Faith dropped the paper and walked him to the front door. As they passed the couch, she tucked the blanket around Lacey's shoulders. Brushed a lock of hair from her son's forehead. The gesture zinged around his chest. He'd get a chance to do the same thing once his girls were home for good.

When they arrived at the door she said, "Maybe I can repay you by having you and the girls over for chili night."

Getting tangled up with Faith and her family was not on his agenda right now. He had to focus on the girls, and honestly, he didn't want the emotional upheaval of a rushed relationship.

"No need."

He could kick himself for his quick refusal when he spied the hurt in her eyes. Maybe they could just be good neighbors for now. "But we'll take you up on that offer."

She smiled and his chest squeezed.

When she opened the door, the wind swirled in, bringing with it dead leaves and a blast of cold. The air held a damp scent he always associated with winter.

He stepped onto the porch and tugged his collar closer around his neck.

"So we'll touch base about getting together. I mean having kids together." She cleared her throat. Red stained her cheeks. "Having the kids get together."

He bit back a grin. "They'd love it."

He really should get going but made no attempt to move. Until Faith wrapped her arms around herself as the cold air breached the house.

"Thanks again," she said.

He nodded, jogged down the steps and trekked across the stiff grass to his dark house. All the way he felt Faith's gaze on his back. When he finally reached the driveway, he turned, but she'd gone back inside. The outside light flicked off.

His breath escaped with a whoosh, misting the air before him. Looked like having Faith Harper for a neighbor was going to be more than he bargained for.

CHAPTER TWO

GAYLE ANN MASTERSON viewed her friends gathered in her living room—all members of the Golden Matchmakers Club. The group was her brainchild and the activity that made her feel necessary as she grew older. She also loved this special time of year, which was why she'd invited the club members over while she and Alveda trimmed the tree.

Standing beside a tall blue spruce, she smoothed her white hair into place and straightened the skirt of her navy power suit, ready to convene the meeting.

"How's our strategy coming along?" she asked Wanda Sue Harper, whose daughter, Faith, was the current recipient of the club's attention.

"So far so good. The fact that you had a rental available next to Roan's house moved the time frame along."

Gayle Ann waved a hand. "It wasn't chance. The couple living there was introduced to the perfect house. They jumped at the chance to purchase it. I let them out of their lease early so Faith could move in."

"Introduced?" Alveda Richards snorted as she lifted wiry arms to place an ornament on the half-dressed spruce. The outdoor scent permeated the warm room.

"Don't take that tone with me, Alveda. They were dragging their feet so I gave them incentive by showing them one of the houses I had on the market."

"Now, ladies," Judge Harrison Carmichael inserted as the two bickered. His silver hair gleamed in the midafternoon light. "Focus."

Gayle Ann grinned at her cohort, earning a wink in return. She and Alveda were old friends, having met when Gayle Ann hired Alveda as the cook at Masterson House. They were loyal to each other, more like sisters now that they were in their later years. When they'd plotted to match Gayle Ann's grandson to the love of his life, the club had been born.

"Well, I appreciate it," Wanda Sue said, placing her empty dessert plate on the coffee table. Alveda always made extra pumpkin pies during the holidays to share with friends.

Gayle Ann added an ornament onto one of the thick branches. "What better time to bring two deserving people together than at Christmas?"

"I'm not so sure Faith will go for it." An air of gravity settled over Wanda Sue. "She's had a chip on her shoulder since she was a kid. Now that Lyle is out of the picture and she's picking up the pieces, she's determined to prove she's changed."

Bunny Wright patted Wanda Sue's arm. "These young'uns of ours don't make it easy."

Wanda Sue nodded, but the worry on her face remained. "We have Grace and Deke's wedding coming up, which is exciting, but I don't want Faith to get lost in the shuffle."

Grace, Faith's older sister, had returned to Golden a few years earlier, finding love with Deke Matthews, who had originally come to town on an undercover mission. The wedding, scheduled for mid-December, was going to be a small, festive celebration.

"Which is why they need—" Gayle Ann paused to come up with the right description "—a tender hand steering them in the direction of love."

When Alveda huffed, Gayle Ann frowned at her from the other side of the tree.

"Why Roan?" the judge asked.

Leave it to Harry to ask a practical question.

"Many in town don't know it, but Roan volunteers his time to talk to young people, to encourage them, their pursuits, and to discourage them from getting into serious trouble," Gayle Ann informed them. "He suggests they check out programs designed to keep their attention focused on positive things, like not giving in to peer pressure. Since I donate funds to some of these programs, I've been able to talk to him at length. Roan is very protective. Of his children, the town, people he allows into his life. Yet, he's closed off, which means he needs a woman who will love him for his strengths and weaknesses. In many ways he and Faith would make a good match because they both love deeply, even if the years haven't been kind. I believe the similar trajectory their lives have taken will be the foundation to a deep commitment between the two of them and their families."

Gayle Ann walked to a nearby end table to pick up her Golden Matchmakers notebook. Looking over the group of friends who had joined her in pairing the stubborn young people of Golden with their perfect mates, she realized her sense of purpose. Getting older didn't mean you had to sit before the fire drinking tea and eating crumpets. No, Gayle Ann had plenty of life in her, as did her friends, and they vowed to use it wisely.

"If Golden is going to become a premier

vacation destination, we need families who are rooted and grounded in our beloved mountain town. Couples who want to see this town prosper."

"So," Alveda said, leaning down to pick up another heirloom ornament from a box. "Faith and Roan."

Wanda Sue's green eyes held concern. "That Roan Donovan is easy on the eyes, but like you said, he's pretty shut off. Not sure if Faith has it in her to breach his defenses."

Gayle Ann flipped a page in her notebook. "Roan's wife died in a tragic snowboard accident on the slopes. From what her mother told me, it seemed Catrina was practicing after a fresh snowfall and ventured into an area that was deemed unsafe. She misjudged the trail and lost control, falling into a rocky ravine."

Alveda shivered, pulling the cuffs of her cardigan over her hands. "Laurel and Gene were devastated. Their only daughter, gone to a sport that always made them uneasy."

"I remember her running around with my nephews." Bunny weighed in. "A free spirit, that one. They would all go off in the mountains, on a quest for one adventure after another. Seems the boys are still up for adventure, which partly explains why they're single." She pouted. "More reason to get them matched up with their soul mates as soon as possible."

Gayle Ann returned to her notes. "Roan moved here with the children to be close to the Jessups." She looked up. "Does anyone know about his family?"

"Roy said he doesn't talk about them," Wanda Sue answered. "Some bad blood, he thinks."

Nodding, Alveda said, "He's allowed the Jessups to have plenty of time with the girls, but now that he's moving to the day shift, he'll have them home. Laurel's worried about how they're all going to adjust."

"Which is why having Faith and her family right next door fits perfectly," Gayle Ann said. "They can support each other rearing children as single parents. Nothing brings people closer than having a common goal."

"But that isn't enough," the judge pointed out.

"True, but this is Golden at Christmastime. There are more than enough family activities to keep them in each other's company. I've written down the events we can steer them to." She picked up papers from the coffee table and passed them around. "This is the Golden Christmas calendar. I realize, with the age of their younger children, they can't do everything, so when they're at home, we make sure the two are still thrown together. Tree decorating. Making cookies. Stringing lights on the house. The things families do during the holidays."

"Are you sure this isn't a little much?" Wanda Sue asked as she perused the list. "Faith's got a loaded schedule right now, and if she doesn't get some downtime, it never works out good for her."

"This is just a guideline," Gayle Ann assured her friend.

Gayle Ann knew that Wanda Sue understood all about single parenting. After her husband, Earl, had been arrested many years ago on drug charges, she'd been on her own. Of the three children, Grace had stepped up to help take care of the family while Wanda Sue dealt with the shock and loss. Faith had acted out, making questionable decisions, and Nathan had almost followed in his father's footsteps. So the woman had room to fret.

"We all know Faith didn't make the best choices," Wanda Sue continued, "but my grandbabies are the best thing to ever happen to her. Now I want her with someone who will love her and make her happy." Her expression turned sad. "I owe Faith for getting lost in my grief and not guiding her better, not that she'd ever say so."

"Don't think such a thing," Bunny scolded. "You did the best you could."

"No, I wasn't a good mom for a while, and she suffered for it."

"Her daddy's the one who let her down," Bunny fumed. "Getting arrested and sent away."

"I retreated," Wanda Sue admitted. "As a result she went off the rails. I have the opportunity to help her more now than I did when she was a teenager, and I'm taking it seriously."

"We're going to make this happen," Bunny assured her. "That's why we're here—to do our best for our loved ones."

"Which is well within our scope as matchmakers to do," Gayle Ann offered.

"You make it sound like we went to school, took a course and now have a license to interfere in young people's lives," Alveda countered.

"We have life experience, which is more powerful than any piece of paper." Gayle Ann glanced around the group. "Do we all agree that we move forward?"

Wanda Sue and Bunny exchanged glances like they always did when pushed on a decision. Alveda shook her head with a cat-ate-the-canary grin. Harry regarded her with watchful eyes.

"Is there a problem?" Gayle Ann asked, sensing a shift in the atmosphere.

"I just don't want you to be disappointed," Wanda Sue said. "Faith could get prickly and ruin our plans before we even get started."

"Not to worry," Harry said. "Our fearless leader is fast on her feet. She can readjust with a snap of her fingers."

Gayle Ann beamed. "Why, Harry, thank you for the compliment."

"My pleasure."

His kind words made her glow. Glow! Good grief, she was as bad as the young women they'd been steering toward love.

She shook off the odd sensation and said, "Faith and the kids have already moved next door to Roan—step one. Now we'll move on to step two—gathering at the tree lighting in the town park."

Wanda Sue scanned the group. "I can't thank y'all enough."

"Don't thank us until Faith and Roan fall in love," Alveda said, then tapped a finger against her chin. "You know, that should be a rule so we don't get cocky. No thanks until the match is a success." She pointed at Gayle

Ann. "Write that down in your list of bylaws for the club."

"Excellent call," Gayle Ann said as she scribbled her friend's suggestion in her notebook.

"We don't want to get ahead of ourselves," Alveda continued, "but I agree, Faith and Roan will be good together."

"I second that," said the judge.

"I'm in," Bunny added her allegiance.

Beaming from ear to ear, Wanda Sue met each gaze, then said, "Let the Christmas magic begin."

THANKFUL THAT HER mother had agreed to man the office, Faith and her children arrived at Gold Dust Park just over a week after Thanksgiving to meet Roan and his girls. To say her nerves had gotten the best of her was an understatement. She'd made sure to apply makeup and had tamed her hair, then wondered why she was in such a tizzy. This was a simple Saturday morning playdate.

In the week following Thanksgiving, she'd run into Roan at school when they'd dropped off John and Emmie. Taking a chance, because she hadn't really been sure if Roan was just being nice when she mentioned getting the kids together or if he really wanted a playdate, she'd brought it up again. Her stomach had tensed as she waited for his answer, her mind telling her she'd been foolish to say anything. Relief flooded her when he said yes. Out of excitement for the kids, she assured herself. Over and over again.

A high-pitched beep-beep-beep grabbed her attention. Town workers backed a huge Douglas fir lying on a flatbed truck to the area where the tree would eventually stand. A pickup truck parked nearby. Two guys got out, one retrieving a tall ladder from the back, the other reaching into the truck bed to remove a fat roll of lights. The tree-lighting celebration was always held on the first weekend in December. The high school band would play, the mayor would make a speech and, once it got dark, the night sky would light up in multicolor while children, young and old, oohed and aahed. The official start of Christmas in Golden.

The wind had calmed and was nearly nonexistent today, but the lingering frigid air allowed her to see her breath. Armed with gloves, hats and scarves, she and the kids were ready for anything.

John pointed to the activity. "Mama, what's going on?"

On the way to the playground, Faith explained, "The workers are getting the tree ready for tonight. Remember I told you they're going to light it up?"

"Tree. Lights," Lacey shouted as she danced in place.

"Can we go?" John asked, his eyes alight with wonder.

"Of course. We wouldn't miss it."

If she were totally transparent, she'd admit that she wanted a dose of that holiday wonder right now. She turned and, like a gift, Roan strode into view. His thick black hair and broad shoulders caught the eyes of women passing by. His steady gait said he could take on the world and still have energy left over.

Faith's chest went tight, and she took a calming breath. *He's just a neighbor*, she reminded herself. She couldn't let herself hope that he might be different, that he wanted home and hearth and happiness. She'd learned long ago that those things were out of reach for her, but she couldn't bring herself to settle for anything less.

As she watched the family approach, a warning bell gonged in her head, taking the edge off the rosy glow that had blossomed over her. Roan wore a frown, Kaylie was busy chatting, her hands gesturing, and Emmie trailed behind, her arms tightly wrapped around her middle. She recognized the mutinous look on the little girl's face.

"Roan. Hi." She waved, shifting her ever-present mom bag over her shoulder.

He schooled his expression. *Smooth*. She'd already guessed that family day hadn't started out well for the Donovan clan.

Kaylie stopped short, giving Faith the once-over. Emmie lingered behind Roan, even when John went in for a fist bump from the tall man.

"Sorry we're late," Roan said in greeting.

Faith merely smiled, drinking him in. Up close, she could see that his cheeks were red, his hair mussed. He'd donned a heavy jacket with worn jeans and boots, but his head and hands were bare. She wondered if he'd had as much of a hassle getting two kids dressed to protect them from the elements as she'd had and forgot his own hat and gloves.

Curly blond hair escaped Emmie's hat, so bright against the intensity of her gloomy expression. Kaylie's eyes sparkled as she tugged her hat down over her ears. The sun, hidden behind the clouds today, popped out once in a while to tease those who had decided to spend the day outdoors.

"Look at the tree," John nearly shouted, pointing at the truck. The men were untying the straps around the bulky evergreen, ready to stand it in place.

"What are they doing with it?" Kaylie asked, her blue eyes a mirror of her father's.

"The whole town gathers tonight for the lighting." Faith stuffed her hands in her pockets. "It's a tradition going way back."

Kaylie looked at her father. "Why didn't you mention it?"

"With my schedule, I wasn't sure if we could make it."

"Or you didn't want to," Kaylie muttered, taking a few steps away from Roan to watch the men wrangling with the massive tree.

Hmm. Seemed like there was more going on below the surface with the Donovan family.

"We were headed to the swings," Faith said, taking Lacey by the hand. "Join us."

"Swings are dumb," Emmie said around an impressive pout.

"We can make it a game, like at school," John said, always the peacemaker. Faith's heart squeezed with so much love for her son.

"Whatever." Emmie shrugged.

Oh, that one had attitude.

The children ran to the play area, Lacey yanking her hand from Faith's. Since they were all close by, Faith let go, watching the toddler try to keep up with the bigger kids.

Faith met Roan's eyes to see the resignation there.

"So, your first week on day shift is going well?"

"Let's just say there have been some hiccups."

"Such as?"

He sent her a withering gaze. "You don't want to know."

"Sure I do. It'll make my morning feel like a breeze."

He chuckled. "Not that there's anything wrong with it, but the Donovan girls are strong-willed."

"And they get that from whom?"

"Me." He paused. "And their mother."

Faith nodded. She wasn't about to tread those waters uninvited.

"While I'm accused of being overprotective, my late wife was one to challenge the world. Needless to say, the girls and I butt heads quite a bit."

"I suppose that's part of growing up. Testing boundaries."

"I have to say, I'm not a fan."

John climbed the steps behind the slide, ready to slip down from the top, but Emmie started climbing up from the front, her hands gripping the sides, her boots slipping on the hard plastic.

Roan shook his head. "Case in point. Most kids go up the steps and then slide down. Mine go about it in the opposite direction."

"Makes them unique."

He placed a hand over his chest. "And gives me heartburn."

Faith laughed.

More people started arriving at the park— folks out for a stroll or to watch the progress of the tree delivery along with children glad to be out of the house, running around to burn off excess energy. A group of girls around Kaylie's age waved her over. She chewed her lower lip before asking, "Dad, can I go hang out with friends from school?"

Roan hadn't missed the exchange. "They're from your class?"

"Yes. You know Diandra." She tucked a strand of her shoulder-length, light brown hair behind her ear. "The others are pretty nice."

Pretty nice. Faith remembered that as code for a tough crowd to fit into and recognized Kaylie's nerves.

"Just stay where I can see you."

Kaylie rolled her eyes. "Thanks, Dad."

As his daughter joined the group of girls,

Roan puffed out a breath. "She's getting closer to being a teenager every day. Not sure I'm going to handle it well."

"She seems quite grounded."

"Which works in her favor. But once she turns thirteen or fourteen…"

"You listen to her. About anything."

He turned to study her, like he was privy to her thoughts. "Is this advice coming from experience?"

She lifted a shoulder. "Pretty much."

"You're going to tell me this and not elaborate?"

Surprised, she asked, "Do you want me to?"

"I asked."

She pointed to a bench not far from where the children were playing. They sat, the cold from the wood seeping into the seat of her jeans.

"You were saying?" he coached.

There was real interest in those blue eyes. Faith found herself wanting to share, in hopes it might help a fellow parent, even if she hated going down this particular road.

"It's kind of embarrassing now, but I got into trouble a lot during high school." She looked up at the gray sky and squinted. "No, back up. It started in middle school."

Roan rubbed his hands together against the cold. "Wouldn't have guessed."

"Hold on." She searched her mom bag and came up with a pair of pink gloves with fuzzy pompoms attached at the wrist, handing them to Roan. He stared at them like she was offering him hissing snakes.

"I always have extra on hand," she explained.

"You're kidding, right?"

"Too proud?"

He took one and tried to yank on the knitted cotton. The material stretched enough to cover most of his big hand. He took the other and pulled it on. "Looks like one size fits all."

She smirked at him. "Moms always know."

"So I've heard."

He stuffed his hands into his jacket pockets. To hide the gloves? More than likely it was the pompoms.

She tugged her hat lower on her head, reminding herself what they'd been talking about. *Right, trouble.* She couldn't help questioning the wisdom of sharing this information. Then she glimpsed Kaylie and the other girls. "I've changed. Had to when John and Lacey came along."

"Sure."

"Anyway, Daddy got in trouble and went

to prison. Mama lost her way, which left my older sister in charge. Grace tried to steer me in the right direction, but I was angry at her, at the world, really, and wouldn't listen."

"Why were you angry with her?"

Trust the law enforcement official to pick up on that point.

"She didn't do it on purpose, but Grace was the reason my dad got caught."

"I see."

He probably did. Every day.

"If my sister said to go right, I'd go left. If she told me not to go to a party, I'd sneak out of the house. She warned me about not marrying Lyle, but I did it anyway."

His eyes lit up. "I see a pattern."

"Exactly. Maybe if someone had taken the time to talk to me and confront my real feelings about our family struggles, I might have made better choices." She shrugged. "Or I may have done the same exact thing. Who knows?"

Roan hunched his shoulders, moving his jacket collar closer to his ears. "I appreciate the honesty."

"It's mostly common knowledge around here."

Did that still bother her? She brushed it off, acted like it was no big deal, but measuring up to those you loved was a gargantuan feat sometimes.

She shifted on the cold bench. "Your turn."

"I get a turn? Fun."

"Let me guess. You're the strong and silent type?"

He chuckled. "That has been brought to my attention a time or two."

"I get it. We really don't know each other. I probably gave you too much information as it is."

"Actually, your candor is a nice change."

A compliment? She'd take it.

"You'll be glad to know your new neighbor is doing everything in her power to make a happier life for her children. I think you have to own your past in order to make a better future."

Roan leaned over and their shoulders brushed. "Can't ask for more than that."

This close, his woodsy cologne mingled with the fresh air. Faith tried to control the galloping in her tummy, then thought, *Why not enjoy it?*

"So," he said, unaware of her inner turmoil—brought on by him, thank-you-very-much. "Did the new furnace get installed?"

When he moved away, she placed her hands over her topsy-turvy stomach. "It did.

Mrs. Masterson even came over to supervise the installation herself."

"Is she always that involved with her properties?"

"As long as I've known her. The Mastersons own most of the real estate in town, but she's very down-to-earth in dealing with her tenants. That's why everyone in town adores her."

"I've talked to her at a few meetings in town. She's certainly got a take-charge personality."

"We had a nice chat when she stopped by. She's—"

Shouting came from the direction of the playground, causing Faith to stop midsentence. Emmie was yelling at John. John had his hands out as if trying to stop her. From what? Emmie closed the space between them, shoving John hard. His hands flew up and he fell to his backside on the cold ground. Lacey started crying, and suddenly Emmie turned and ran in the opposite direction.

Roan was up like a shot, sprinting after his daughter. Faith jumped and ran to take Lacey in her arms. Holding her daughter tight she knelt beside John, helping him to his feet.

"John, what on earth happened?"

"I don't know, Mama." Tears shimmered

in his brown eyes. "We were talking about school and Christmas, and then I said Daddy was going to put up lights at our house, and she said her daddy was mean and she ran off."

Faith reran the run-on sentence in her head and tackled one topic before the other. "Daddy said he's hanging lights at our house?"

John sniffled and wiped his nose. "He told me last time I saw him."

Seems she'd missed that memo, classic Lyle, but they'd deal with it later.

Lacey squirmed in Faith's arms to get down, moving closer to her brother now that the situation seemed to have righted itself.

With trepidation, Faith asked the question that bothered her most. "Emmie said her daddy is mean?"

Okay, Roan had said things were tense at his house. But what did Emmie's words suggest? That she didn't get her way, or that he was…not a good person? She hoped that was not the case.

"I guess she wanted to go to see Santa today and he said no. Her grandparents said they'd take her instead, but her daddy said no. When he told her they were coming to the park, she said no."

There was an awful lot of no going on here. After John's explanation, relief swept through her that her worst suspicion hadn't been correct. Bottom line? Emmie just hadn't gotten her way. After dealing with similar issues without a spouse to support her, she knew it would be a tough road for the seemingly together man, but Roan would handle it. Wouldn't she, for that matter?

Looking over her shoulder, she scanned the park, but he was gone.

CHAPTER THREE

BY THE TIME Roan reached Emmie, she'd dashed onto Main Street. A car stopped short of hitting her, brakes squealing in the process. Heart pounding, he reached out, wrapped his arm around her tiny waist and lifted her out of harm's way. The driver honked the horn, yelled something Roan wouldn't repeat in polite company and moved on. Shaking, he brought them back to the sidewalk, trying desperately to corral his equal parts fear and anger.

"Emmeline Donovan, what were you thinking?"

"I want to go to Grandma Laurel's," she huffed, her cheeks beet red, her hat hanging haphazardly from her head.

He reined in his frustration. This had been a familiar refrain all week long.

"We talked about this. You won't be spending as much time at Grandma's house."

She crossed her arms over her chest. "I like it better there."

He tried to ignore the stab at his heart.

Calmer now, he said, "C'mon, let's find your sister and go home."

"No." Emmie stomped her foot.

He ran a hand through his hair. "We can't fix this here, sweetie."

Emmie glanced around, for the first time noticing a crowd drawing around them. She forgot all about being mad and ran to his side.

Wrapping his arms around his precious daughter nestled against him, Roan drank in the smell of her bubble gum–scented shampoo. He rested his chin against her fine, blond curls. He loved her beyond reason, but worried that she was headstrong and oblivious to danger, just like her mother. Would he survive her recklessness? Would she?

"What were you thinking?" he asked again.

Emmie lifted her head, regret swimming in her eyes. As fast as she could lose her temper, she'd be sorry for what she'd done.

"I was mad at John."

"Why? You were playing just fine."

"He said his daddy is putting lights on their house, and you won't do it. Grandpa Gene already decorated their house. I want to live there."

That was a lot to unpack.

"You live with me and Kaylie."

"Not always. You work a lot."

"But that's going to change. I told you I have new hours so we can be together more."

Her next words took on a challenging tone. "Are you going to cook spaghetti the way Grandma does?"

"Probably not, but we can do it together and you can show me the right way."

"Are you gonna tell me stories before bed like Grandma does?"

"Of course. I do that now."

"But you don't do the voices," she added with criticism.

Roan inwardly cringed. "I'll remember to do voices."

"You promise?"

He wanted to smack his forehead with his palm. Instead, he lifted his hand to stroke her hair, remembering the fuzzy gloves too late. Emmie noticed and let out a delightful laugh he hadn't heard from her in a long time.

"I promise."

"Then I'll go home with you."

He hugged her tightly, then righted her hat before taking her small hand in his. As they navigated the sidewalk, he said, "Before that, you're going to apologize to John."

"Why? Because his daddy likes Christmas?"

"No, because you pushed him. I told you, you never put your hands on anyone in anger."

She deflated. "Sorry, Daddy."

"I accept your apology, but you still owe one to John."

She nodded, but didn't look happy about it.

They made their way under the stone arch covered in festive holly and red bows that led from the main sidewalk to the park proper. Kaylie came running over, her expression filled with alarm.

"Are you guys okay?"

"Emmie had a little meltdown."

"It wasn't a meltdown," his youngest said with attitude. "I was mad at you."

"Same thing."

Emmie dropped his hand and stomped beside him as they headed toward Faith and her kids. Talk about an awkward moment.

Kaylie glanced up at him, worry shining in her eyes. "Really, is she okay?"

He sighed. "She will be."

"What are you going to do?"

"Deal with this at home."

Kaylie looked over at her friends. "Now?"

"Emmie needs to do something first." He nodded toward the girls. "Go on over and I'll call you when we're ready to leave."

"Okay." She hesitated, then made her way across the park.

As they got closer to Faith, his gut clenched. Emmie had been a handful in the past year, but she'd never intentionally hurt anyone. The change in his work schedule couldn't have come at a better time. He needed to be with his daughter daily, even though she was clearly going to miss her grandparents.

He met Faith's gaze and nodded. Then he put his hand on Emmie's shoulder.

"John, Emmie has something to say to you."

She dug the toe of her boot into the grass. "Sorry," she said at a barely there volume.

"We didn't hear you," Roan said.

She glared up at him. "I said sorry."

Louder, but still not acceptable.

"Tell John, not me."

"Sorry," she shouted, this time making him wince at the volume. To Roan's surprise, John walked over for a quick hug.

"That's okay," John said. "I get mad sometimes, but Mama says to use my words, not my hands."

Emmie nodded at his wisdom.

"We can still play if you want," he offered.

Emmie glanced at Roan. "Can I?"

"For a minute. I want to talk to Faith."

The two joined hands and ran back to the playground like nothing had happened. Lacey toddled behind, trying to keep up.

He blew out a long breath. "I am so sorry."

She held her hands out at her sides and said with a shrug, "Kids argue. At least they made up. Maybe learned a lesson."

Air lodged in his chest. "How can you be so calm?"

"I grew up with passionate siblings. We fought a lot."

He shook his head, still in shock over what his daughter had done, in spite of all his lessons. "I taught her better than that."

"She's six. Emotions run high. Children often act before thinking."

He ran his hand through his hair again. Pulled it away and stared at the pinkness of the gloves. "I'm going to go bald at this rate."

Faith laughed. The cheery sound grounded him, which came as a pleasant surprise.

"I'm afraid her attitude is my fault," he admitted.

"How do you figure that?"

"This isn't the first squabble she's gotten into."

Interest crossed Faith's face. "Really?"

"I had to sit down with her teacher."

Faith looked around them as if gauging

the people scattered about, then leaned in and said in a hushed tone, "Been there. Mrs. Walker is kind of scary."

"You think so too?"

"Big-time." She moved away, and her lips angled downward. "I'm sorry you had to meet with her."

"All the time Emmie's spent with Laurel and Gene is good, helpful to me. But now she's rebelling about coming home."

Faith hopped from side to side, blowing on her gloved hands. "Probably because she's still young enough that she equates safety with her grandparents. They've been there for her."

"I know, and I appreciate everything they've done, but she's my daughter."

She tilted her head. "Are they giving you a hard time?"

"Not exactly. They realize she should be with me, but when I make a decision, sometimes they overrule it and go their own way."

"So when she comes home—"

"She doesn't like me."

Faith looked over at the kids, then back to him. "The word *mean* was thrown around."

He met her gaze and read the questions there. His disappointment shot from one to ten in lightning speed. "I'm a loving parent and a decent person, who's trying to do his best for his kids."

She nodded, offering a sympathetic smile. "I'd already figured out it was a tantrum, nothing more."

"Thanks."

She touched his arm, and the gesture sent a sense of peace over him. "I'm sure you realize that when kids are unhappy and don't know how to express it, they act out."

"I do. But when she takes off like that… It scares me."

Roan searched for the kids, now happily playing as if nothing had happened. Emmie helped Lacey make her way up the steps of the slide while John ran around to the front to catch his sister when she slid down.

He found himself speaking before he had time to rethink the wisdom of it. "My wife was an adrenaline junkie. She'd hit the slopes, even if the conditions were bad. At first, it didn't bother me. It was part of her appeal. She had an innate confidence, sure of her world. But after the kids came along she got more—" he paused for the right word "—reckless. I couldn't keep her safe, so I doubled down on the girls. Catrina didn't like being told what to do, or me being overprotective of my family. I guess because her folks had always gone along with her free-spirited nature. But I couldn't be that cavalier. Bad things can happen and I…"

His words lodged in his throat. Memories long buried bombarded him. He shook them off and continued.

"No one knows this, but Catrina and I split before the accident. I blame myself for her going out after the storm."

"Doesn't sound like you could have stopped her."

"Maybe not, but if I'd been with her, perhaps it would have slowed her down. Sometimes I think she took chances just to prove to me that she could."

Faith moved close, hooking her hand around his arm, her body heat warm against his side. Her light floral scent, feminine and alluring, overtook his defenses.

"And you're afraid Emmie is like her?"

He nodded. "The Jessups are great, but they cave at her demands. I can't do that."

She shook her head. "No, I can't see you looking the other way."

"I want my girls to grow up respectful of others. I don't want Emmie throwing a fit because she doesn't get her way."

"It is a fine line." Faith nodded her head toward the playground. "Look at her helping Lacey. Emmie's really kind."

"I need to build on that."

She removed her hand and stepped away. He missed the warmth between them. "It's a good thing we're neighbors. Looks like we can help each other out when it comes to the kids. Or my house falling apart."

"Are you still mad that your uncle asked me to watch out for you?"

She jumped back and pointed at him. "I knew it!"

He laughed. "Yeah. I just didn't want to give him up the other night."

She grinned. "My family frustrates me sometimes, but I love them."

"As much as I need to spend more quality time with the girls, I appreciate the Jessups' help. I'm sure we can come to a happy medium."

"There you go, being all optimistic."

"With your prodding."

She averted her gaze.

He wanted to reach out, place a finger under her chin and tilt her head toward him so he could read her face, but she beat him to it, meeting his eyes again.

"You could have been outraged over what Emmie did to John," he said. "Instead you've been understanding."

Faith nodded toward the children. "They're okay now. Calamity averted."

"Thanks, Faith. I mean it."

She smiled just as the sun poked out of the clouds for a long moment. Her hair shone, her eyes sparkled and he was walloped right on the spot.

Clearing his throat, he said, "I need to get the girls home. We have some talking to do."

"My gang is probably hungry."

Together they walked to the children, who had climbed the jungle gym to watch the tree being lifted into its final resting position.

"Let's go," Faith called out as they drew closer.

John elbowed Emmie. "Later we get to watch the lights come on."

Emmie turned to Roan. "Daddy, can we go too?"

"How about we decide later."

Her excitement dropped. "That means no."

He bit back his own frustration, but still heard strains of it in his voice. "I didn't say that."

She turned her back on him.

Faith sent him a look of commiseration.

Before long the kids were rounded up and Kaylie joined them. Faith lifted Lacey into her arms. "We'll see you tonight?"

"I can't make any promises," he said.

She nodded. "I understand. Just…"

He lifted his chin. "What?"

Hesitating, she finally said, "Remember, they're only kids once."

As if he'd forgotten. "Point taken."

Along with a healthy dose of guilt.

"DAD, WE NEED to talk."

Kaylie sounded way too grown-up with that tone. In fact, she sounded just like Catrina before she launched into an argument.

"What's up?" he asked as they walked into the house. The furnace kicked on, emitting a gust of warmth from the vent. The lingering scent of bacon from their hearty breakfast still hung in the air. Emmie ran to her room, leaving them behind for what Roan was sure would be an uncomfortable discussion.

His daughter removed her heavy coat and tossed it on the couch. Her knitted hat followed. She fluffed out her thick brown hair and paced back and forth across the living room.

The oversize room with the soaring vaulted ceiling, which led to an open concept kitchen, was overly tidy for a family of three. The result of a housekeeper who worked once a week. No dust, no toys on the floor, no boots in the foyer, nothing out of place. Homey enough, but it didn't really feel lived-in. The house was devoid of emotion, a reflection of Roan's state of mind. Had he actually thought the girls were okay living in a home with no genuine warmth?

Slowly, Roan shrugged out of his jacket, stuffed the pink gloves in the pockets with a shake of his head and hung it on a hook by the front door. He pushed up the sleeves of his sweater and waited for Kaylie's bomb to drop.

"Are we going to decorate for Christmas?"

Not what he'd thought she'd say, but not unexpected either. The topic had come up lately, no matter how many times he evaded the questions. "I'll admit, I had been putting it off."

"We didn't do anything last year," his daughter said in her accusatory tone. "I get it. Mom wasn't there."

"I didn't think it was appropriate."

"None of us were in the mood. But this year is different. We want to remember all the things Mom used to do."

Catrina had always gone overboard during the Christmas season. He hadn't grown up in a household that made a big deal about the holidays, so he'd never seen the appeal, but he'd embraced his wife's zeal for all things festive. The tree went up on Thanksgiving night. The next day, lights went on the house. December included cookie making, parties, Secret Santa gifts and the big blowout on Christmas morning. The girls had loved every minute, and while Roan hadn't been opposed to all of Catrina's traditions, he didn't think he could replicate the happy years.

This year, the Donovan household felt cold.

"What about now?" Kaylie pushed.

If he had his way they'd tone down the holiday even more.

When he didn't respond, Kaylie continued, "Emmie just wanted to go see Santa today."

"We already had plans."

"Grandma could have taken her."

He reined in his irritation. As much as he'd been grateful for the Jessups' help, in the past six months they'd overreached. He supposed it was his own fault, but it still rankled. "I know, but I can take her."

"When?"

Sheesh. When had she grown so persistent? "When he comes to town?"

Kaylie rolled her eyes.

So much for levity. There was no way his daughter would let him escape this topic.

"I don't even know where the decorations are," Kaylie complained.

He hooked his thumb to point to the far wall. "There's a box in the garage."

"One box." She shook her head. "Okay. That's a start. But what about going to the tree lot? Can we even have a tree this year?"

A tree meant a mess and a mess meant life was returning to normal. Like the pins and needles prickling after a limb fell asleep. Uncomfortable and painful.

"There's plenty of time We can—"

"What about the Elf on the Shelf?"

He cocked his head. "The what?"

"You know. The little elf that you move around every day."

He went blank.

Kaylie placed one hand on her hip, the other moved in the air as she explained, "The elf is a special scout supposedly sent from the North Pole," she told him, as if reciting it from memory. "He's Santa's helper who watches the children every day and night, and then returns to the North Pole with a report." She speared him with pleading eyes. "Emmie believes the elf is real. And that the Santa we go visit at the mall is the real deal. And what about a letter to Santa? It has to go in the mail soon."

He started to run a hand though his hair, then stopped himself. "Your mom did all that?"

"And more. We went caroling and brought presents to needy kids. Made cookies for Emmie's class party and took socks to the nursing home."

"Socks?"

"Mom said the older people needed special socks in the winter."

He didn't understand, and was so far out of the Christmas loop, he was closing in on Easter. How had he gotten to thirty-four years without a Christmas clue?

"Kaylie, sit down."

She looked wary, but did as he asked. They both sank into the stiff cushions.

"What about you?"

Her eyes went wide. "Me?"

"I get that you want to make Christmas special for your sister, and we'll figure it out, but what about you? You remember all the things Mom did more so than Emmie. Is this bothering you?"

She brought her thumb to her mouth and started biting the nail. A sure sign of stress. "I can't do it alone."

"No one said you had to."

"But you're not doing anything."

Nor did he plan to. Still, her accusation hung in the air.

"It's not your job to fill in where you think I'm falling down on the job."

Her gaze moved all around the room when she said, "You never want to talk about Mom."

The breakup had left him raw, her death ramping up regret. He'd pushed it down deep, hoping if he didn't dwell on it, it wouldn't hurt. He was wrong.

"It's been hard for me," he truthfully told his daughter. This was the first time they'd really attempted this difficult conversation.

"Me too," she said. "Grandma says grief comes in stages. I don't really know what that means."

"It means we all process loss differently. I don't talk about it, which doesn't help you."

She swallowed and said, "I try to pretend the accident never happened. That Mom is still in Colorado and we just don't get to see her."

He reached over and tucked her close, his arm tight around her. "I guess neither of us has been doing a good job of moving on."

"Grandma says it takes time," came her muffled voice against his chest.

"She's right."

"She also said we have to make Christmas special for Emmie."

He pulled back. "Is that why Emmie's been so mad at me?"

"Some. She likes sleeping at Grandma's house."

He wasn't going to lie—that admission stung. "What's wrong with this house?"

Kaylie shrugged.

Seemed he'd need to sit down with his younger daughter soon.

He inhaled, then said, "How about we make a pact?"

"About what?"

"We agree that whenever we're missing Mom or that we're sad or even if we want to talk about happy times, we let each other know. The only choice for us to get through this is as a family."

"I guess. As long as you promise to be honest."

His daughter saw too much. "I'm not honest?"

"I know things weren't good between you and Mom."

He went still. His daughter had become so grown-up.

She sent him a pensive look and continued, "You guys used to fight a lot."

No use denying it. "I'm sorry you had to hear that."

She lifted her shoulder like it was no big deal, but Roan knew otherwise. "Plus, Grandma says Mom called her to talk about you all the time."

Great. He hated others knowing his personal business, more so when he hadn't been aware that his in-laws had insight into their marital problems.

"Kaylie, look, I promise to always be honest with you. And right now, I can tell you that I still have a hard time with the things that happened between your mom and me. But I love you and Emmie more than anything in the world. I will always take care of you and talk about serious topics, even if I'd rather have a tooth pulled."

Kaylie giggled. "You're weird."

The eleven-year-old was back.

She might think he was being humorous, but he never wanted his daughter to live through the same heartache he'd experienced. Unreasonable, yeah, but he hoped she never had her spirit broken.

"Back to Christmas," Kaylie reminded him.

He muffled a groan.

"Grandma said we were going to do all the traditions Mom did, only at her house."

"And I threw a wrench in the works."

"That's what Emmie thinks."

"What do you think?"

She didn't back down an inch, meeting his gaze head-on. "That I want you to make this Christmas merry."

Tall order for a man who felt more like the Grinch than Kris Kringle.

He closed his eyes for long seconds, then opened them to find Kaylie carefully watching him.

"Is that your Christmas wish?"

She nodded.

"Then it looks like I have some work to do."

She threw her arms around his neck. He squeezed her tight and held her for longer than necessary. He didn't want to disappoint her.

Could he deliver the Christmas his girls wanted when he didn't have a clue? He worried that reviving Catrina's Christmas traditions would only keep the girls' grief fresh. Could they be happy with only a tree? Nothing else? He didn't know if he had it in him to do much more.

He knew he'd just promised to be honest, but honestly, his heart wasn't in the season.

The phone rang, and Kaylie jumped up, running to the kitchen.

Rising slowly, Roan walked to the front window and stared outside. The sun had only made a brief showing today. The sky remained gray, the grass brown. It was downright depressing and kept him from buying into the "most wonderful time of the year" sentimentality.

A black SUV with a spray of dried dirt on the fenders drove by, slowing down before pulling into the driveway next door. From his angle he watched Faith hop out of the car, a smile curving her lips. Her cheery disposition loosened the tightness in his chest. Was it longing maybe? Had he ever been that happy?

John ran around the hood, animatedly talking the entire time. Once Lacey was out of her car seat and on the ground, she took a few steps, tottered, but kept herself from falling. Faith clapped with enthusiasm, then moved to the back of the vehicle to open the hatch and remove a huge evergreen wreath twined with red-and-white-striped ribbon and a big bow. When John jumped up and down with outstretched arms, she handed it to him. He tried to carry it, but the wreath was almost as big as him. Before Roan could see what happened next, they moved out of his line of vision.

The night he'd fixed Faith's furnace, she'd been making a list. Had probably checked it twice since then. She had more of the merry spirit in her little finger than he had in his entire body. Why couldn't he get out of his own head? Or forget the pain? What did that mean for his kids?

"Hey, Dad," Kaylie called to him.

He turned, rubbing his temples against the mounting ache. "Yes?"

"Grandma wants to know if you're taking us to the tree lighting tonight. If not, she and Grandpa will take us."

His in-laws meant well. It would be so easy to let them take over… "I'll take you and Emmie."

Kaylie grinned and returned to the call.

Shaking his head, Roan rubbed a hand down his face. Right now, he had to stay focused on his daughters. He couldn't risk taking his eyes off them, not for any reason. Not only did he want to keep Christmas at bay, which would be a huge feat after Kaylie's request, but he also needed to keep his beautiful neighbor, who embodied the Christmas spirit, at arm's length.

CHAPTER FOUR

"MAMA, HOW DO the Christmas tree lights turn on?"

Faith navigated her SUV down Main Street, inspired by the flickering lights hung around the shop windows and outlining the buildings. The seasonal decorations brightened the night sky, along with the general joy this time of year ushered in.

"There must be some kind of switch, John. The mayor will flip it on when the time is right."

"When the tree lights up, Santa will know where our town is," her son informed her in a very knowledgeable tone.

"Who told you that?"

"Emmie. She knows everything about Christmas."

Faith laughed. Roan must love that.

"Hurry up," John said for the tenth time, pulling against the booster seat straps. "We don't want to miss anything."

"Honey, we're early," Faith said as she

glanced at him in the rearview mirror. "Once I get to the end of the block, I'll park behind Put Your Feet Up."

Lacey clapped. "Yay."

Yay, indeed.

As she wove through the traffic, a car horn blared. Faith waved. Neighbors were out in droves for the annual tradition in Golden. Though Faith had found the small mountain town suffocating as a teen, she couldn't imagine raising her children anywhere else. Folks here looked out for one another, even if you didn't ask for their concern. Experience had taught her that she'd missed out on the wisdom of others who had sincerely tried to help. Hopefully she wouldn't ignore that same wisdom when it came to raising her children.

Families hurried down the sidewalks toward the park, making Faith smile. There was an excitement in the air only palpable this time of year. Faith couldn't deny the cheer. Even she looked forward to seeing the dark tree light up in bright colors. And best of all, she had her children to share all this with.

Golden at Christmastime. Her favorite.

Thick garlands wrapped around lampposts, red bows tied on top. In between every couple of stores, a theme-decorated tree sat on the sidewalk, brimming with shiny ornaments to make the holiday special. Over the doors of City Hall hung an oversize wreath, festively wrapped in glossy ribbon, with pine cones found in the local forest as an added touch.

A line had formed outside Sit A Spell Coffee Shop as folks opted for a beverage to warm them against the cold December night. Frieda's Bakery did a swift business, with people dropping in for a sugary treat before heading to the park.

Faith finally parked behind the family business. Before she had the engine turned off, John started unbuckling his booster seat.

"Whoa, mister. Wait for me."

"Mama! We need to find Grammie."

She grabbed her oversize bag, then opened the door to remove Lacey from the car seat. Once she had her daughter in her arms, she rounded the car and met John as he jumped out from his side.

"Ready?" Faith asked, her breath misting as she spoke.

"Let's roll."

Chuckling, she took John's hand as they safely crossed Main Street, then joined the folks streaming into the park. John skipped as they went, chattering about the lighting ceremony, Santa's upcoming visit and the presents he hoped to find under the tree on Christmas morning. Once they passed under the festively decorated stone arch into the park proper, Faith lowered Lacey, searching for her mother and sister. Her mother had texted to say they'd found a spot close to the tree, so Faith moved forward, keeping an eye out. She'd only taken a few steps when John cried out, "Daddy!"

Faith cringed as John took off. Lacey followed, but Faith lifted her before they reached her ex. She hugged her daughter tight as John launched himself into Lyle's arms. In return, Lyle twirled a delighted John in the air before setting the little boy back on his feet.

"Daddy. You made it."

"I told you I would."

Faith held back a snort. How many times had he made promises to John only to break them? And why hadn't he mentioned he was in town? The man always did whatever he wanted with no regard for anyone else.

Lyle glanced over John's head. "Faith."

Before she could get a word out, John grabbed his father's hand. "Come with us."

He shot Faith a questioning glance. She shrugged in response. No way would she ruin John's night, even if Lyle put a damper on hers.

With Faith in the lead, they wended their way through the crowd. She couldn't help it—

she found herself searching for a tall man with broad shoulders and windswept black hair. Would Roan change his mind and bring the girls tonight? If so, would he seek her out so the kids could experience the magic of the lighting ceremony together?

Get real. You want to know if he would seek you out because he's interested in you, not the kids enjoying the lights.

A long shot for sure, but hey, a woman could dream. Every time she looked into his blue eyes, her breath quickened. She wanted to know more about the man who held his emotions so close to the vest.

Her grumbling ex broke into her thoughts, complaining that there were too many people jammed into the park. John reached over and tugged at her hand. She looked down to see concern cross his precious face. On second thought, maybe Roan not being here tonight would be a good thing. All of them together would be awkward. Still, she couldn't block a flash of what-if.

What is wrong with you? Hadn't Faith learned her lesson from the man walking behind her? Instead of letting his son enjoy the festivities, Lyle crabbed about one thing or another. Memories of too many times Lyle had made promises and let them all down washed over her. Like when he'd take off for days at a time, finally returning home like his desertion was normal. She wasn't all that great at picking stable relationships.

Could Roan be different?

With his residual issues over his wife and her passing, a relationship with him would probably be foolhardy. Or out of the realm of possibility altogether.

She glanced over her shoulder at Lyle.

"You shoulda seen that tree," he said, in the process of telling John that in his travels, he'd seen the tallest Christmas tree in the world. "Too bad you hadn't been with me to get a look at it since it was a lot bigger than the Golden town tree. Not that you can go on the road with me, but trust me, it was better."

John looked confused, then glanced at her, his eyes bright with tears. Oh, how Faith wished she could stop Lyle. Did he ever think before he spoke? Consider his children's feelings?

Finally her mother's frantic waving caught Faith's attention, and she tucked all thoughts of men who were bad bets away. Tonight was family night. No wishing on a sparkling Christmas star for things that could never be.

Grateful they'd reached their destination, Faith let out a tiny breath. His smile return-

ing, John zipped around her to hug his grandmother, then his aunt, Grace, and her fiancé,
Deke. Faith bit back a smile when Lyle stiff-
ened at the sight of Deke. Yeah, Lyle could
sniff out law enforcement from a mile away.
Although Deke had resigned from the Georgia Bureau of Investigation to move closer to
Grace and work for Put Your Feet Up, Lyle
had run into the upstanding man before. Faith
had to admit, her ex had an innate instinct to
make himself scarce when cops were around.

When they'd first separated, Faith and the
kids had moved into one of her uncle's cabins
with her sister, located on the shore of Golden
Lake. Lyle had stopped by one afternoon to
take John for the day, but Deke questioned if
Lyle had an approved car seat for his son and
if his tricked-out truck was the legal frame
height. She hadn't been there, but Grace had
told her how Deke, ever sincere and straight-
forward, put Lyle in his place. Faith had loved
Deke ever since.

"Didn't know your entire family would
be here," he muttered under his breath as he
moved alongside her.

"Don't know why you'd think differently,"
she replied sweetly.

Faith passed Lacey off to Grace, knowing Lyle wasn't particularly interested in his

daughter. When Deke moved closer, Faith knew Lyle would bolt without making a scene, for which she was grateful.

When the family stared at Lyle, he seemed to do his level best not to cringe, but his distaste for them leaked through his facade.

"Evening, Wanda Sue. Grace." Lyle wouldn't meet Deke's eyes. "Deke."

Wanda Sue nodded. "What a surprise."

"I was nearby and decided to stop by." He turned to Faith. "If you have a minute, I really need to talk to you."

"Tonight?"

"Not sure when I'll be in these parts again."

Same old song and dance. Lyle had a wanderer's spirit, which had drawn Faith to him in the beginning. Also, her family didn't particularly like him, which had been a giant shove in his direction. Their big plan to travel the country had ended when Faith discovered she was pregnant with John. Well, it had ended for her anyway. Lyle had managed to fulfill the dream in the ensuing years, while she took care of the kids. Why had she stayed with him as long as she had? Pride? Stubbornness? She had no clue but didn't regret her decision to move on with her life, minus Lyle.

As John regaled his Grammie with Christmas stories, Faith turned to Grace. "Mind watching the kids?"

Grace scowled, her perceptive gaze moving between Faith and Lyle. "Are you sure?"

"Yes. This shouldn't take long."

Lyle reached over to rub John's head, a clear goodbye gesture if Faith ever saw one. John, distracted, waved at Lyle before they moved toward the back of the park. Heads turned, speculation in many eyes, but she ignored them. The sooner she found out why Lyle had come here tonight, the sooner she could get back to the festivities.

She found a relatively empty area and stopped. "What's so important you couldn't call me?"

"Hey, I don't need an excuse to see my kids."

"Like you even try."

"Don't start with me, Faith. I didn't have to come by and talk to you in person, but I did."

At the serious light in his eyes, she paid attention. He might be her ex, but she didn't wish anything bad on him. "Is everything okay?"

"Not bad, actually."

"What's going on?"

"I got a new job."

She blinked. Lyle drove a semitrailer on cross-country hauls. He loved it.

"There's a small outfit in North Carolina that needs a logistics manager. With my experience, I landed the position."

"I didn't realize you were looking for a change."

"It sorta fell in my lap."

"Congratulations."

"Thanks. Now I won't be on the road as much and I can get the child support to you quicker."

Which she would dearly appreciate.

"There's more." He took a breath and grinned. "I'm getting married."

"I… Ah…" Shock left her wordless. Rambler Lyle was settling down?

"I know, can you believe it?"

"Not really."

He frowned at her slightly sarcastic tone. "Don't get all jealous."

"Jealous?" She sputtered out a laugh.

"Whatever. Look, Cheryl's a great gal. This will work out."

Was he trying to convince himself? She almost felt sorry for the mystery woman.

"How did you two meet?"

"I had a layover and met her when I went out dancing."

It had been ages since Faith had gone dancing.

"Anyway, we clicked. Actually, she got me the job."

"She works there too?"

"Her daddy owns the business."

Oh, boy, that was a recipe for disaster. But she didn't have a say in his life any longer, so she kept her mouth closed.

"Anyway, I wanted to tell you in person. Soften the blow and all."

"The…blow?"

"Look, I've moved on. You haven't."

Her face heated. "Because I'm raising our children."

"Which I appreciate."

She opened her mouth to blast his fake sentiment, but he spoke over her.

"I don't start the new job until after the first of the year. I still have to make a few runs this way before Christmas. I want to stop by to see the kids, if that's okay."

She gritted her teeth and said, "Yes."

He shot her the charming grin that had been her undoing in high school. "And maybe you can tell John the good news?"

She closed her eyes and counted to ten.

"You should do the honors," she told him. "I think he'll take it better from you."

Coward.

Anger bubbled up in her. "John and Lacey are going to have to meet this woman at some point, Lyle."

"Now isn't a great time."

She tilted her head, reading the guilt flashing across his face. "You haven't told her you have children, have you?"

"It hasn't come up."

Exasperation washed over her. "Lyle, you're going to marry this woman. You have to tell her."

A mutinous pout formed on his lips. "I'm working on it."

"You haven't changed at all," Faith accused.

"Look, I'm not getting into my personal life here. Not in front of these people. What I do is my business, no one else's."

Translation: he was going to mess up yet another relationship.

Instead of getting in deeper, where nothing she said would change a thing, she pasted a weak smile on her face. "Thanks for the heads-up, Lyle."

His chest puffed out.

She mentally rolled her eyes. "And I'm happy for you. Really."

"Good. Great." He looked over his shoulder. "Look, I gotta run."

Of course he did.

"Tell John and Lacey I'll see them soon. Got a special surprise lined up to make their Christmas the best ever."

"I'll tell them."

Before she could walk away, he closed the distance and pulled her into an awkward hug. She went stiff. Her arms dangled at her sides. If she'd been able to glance in a mirror, she was sure she'd read shock in her expression. What was Lyle thinking?

He clumsily patted her back, as if consoling her. When she finally got her wits about her, she pushed him away with both hands against his chest. Right when Roan and his daughters walked into the park, along with Mrs. M. and Alveda.

Like a radar, Roan's gaze zoomed to hers. She took a wide step back from her ex, shocked by Roan's presence. He'd changed his mind and brought the girls after all. Her delight faded when he spoke to Kaylie, then headed in her direction, an impressive glare crossing his face when he singled out Lyle.

ROAN DIDN'T LIKE the expression on Faith's face. Or her stiff body language, which radiated discomfort. Who was that guy manhandling her? He intended to find out.

He met Faith's troubled gaze. "Everything okay here?"

Faith shot a quick look at the guy, then back to Roan. "Yes."

He didn't much like her clipped reply either.

The guy turned around, got a glimpse of Roan and groaned. "Not another one," he muttered.

Faith stepped forward. "Roan, this is my ex-husband, Lyle. Who was just leaving."

"Yeah. I'll… Ahh… See you soon," he stuttered, then took off like his feet were on fire.

The glare remained until Lyle disappeared, then Roan's expression gentled when he turned back to her. "You're okay?"

She waved her hand between them, stirring up a current of cold air. "Just ex stuff."

"Daddy," came Emmie's plaintive voice. "The tree."

Faith shook her head and shot him a strained smile. "You came."

"The girls wanted to be here."

"Right." She rubbed her gloved hands together. "Then let's move to a better spot. My family got here early to claim a prime piece of Christmas tree lighting real estate."

She swept past him, marching over to the girls and greeting the older women. "Mama found a place up front. I'll take you there." She claimed a hand of each of his girls and started through the crowd, leaving him with at least a dozen questions, as well as his brain telling him to mind his own business.

His gut rejected the idea.

Before long, they joined the Harpers and Deke. John pointed out the workers bustling about on the stage to a captivated Emmie. Kaylie picked up Lacey to give her a better view. Wanda Sue, Mrs. M. and Alveda greeted one another. Deke nodded at him. While all this was taking place, he kept an eye on Faith, noticing she'd gone quiet in the midst of the holiday enthusiasm.

The fir tree took up much of the platform. This close, he sniffed the pine scent he associated with presents and cookies.

A tall man moved front and center, holding a microphone. The mayor. He tapped on the end, then cleared his throat and said, "Welcome to the Golden Christmas Tree Lighting."

Cheers and claps filled the air.

"As master of ceremonies, I want to thank you all for coming out on this cold night."

"Get on with it," someone yelled, followed by laughter.

"First, thanks to Masterson Enterprises for making the lighting possible this year. Also, to all the local businesses that keep the Christmas spirit alive during this season. One day, Golden will be *the* vacation destination in these mountains, but for now, may our small-town spirit shine."

Again, the crowd responded with whoops and hollers.

"Now, let the festivities begin."

The children screeched in anticipation as the surrounding lights in the park were extinguished. Deke took Lacey from Kaylie, lifting the little girl higher so she could see over the bodies in front of them. Faith lifted John. Following suit, Roan scooped up Emmie while Kaylie moved close to his side, a huge smile on her face. If the tightness in his chest was any indication, his children's joy had become his own.

The mayor switched on a flashlight and angled it at his face. "Everyone, count down together. Five... Four..."

In the din, Roan heard Kaylie and Emmie count along. "Three... Two... One!"

There was a slight pause and all at once the multicolored lights illuminated the shiny green needles on the limbs of the tree Roan and his girls had seen delivered to the park earlier in the day. Seconds passed before the school band started to play holiday music. Then, the lights flashed with the rhythm. Emmie bounced in his arms, pointing.

"Look, Daddy. The lights are moving."

"So they are."

She took his face in her small hands, forced him to look at her and exclaimed, "This is the best night ever!"

His throat grew tight, but he was saved from responding when Emmie insisted he put her down so she could talk to John. As he rose, his line of vision fell on Faith. She was staring at the tree, a pensive expression lining her lovely face. Why wasn't she smiling and joining in on the celebration like everyone else? Did this have something to do with her ex? Something personal between them? They were no longer married. But there could still be an emotional minefield left behind.

Like your experience? came a taunting voice in his head.

Before he could sink deeper into those thoughts, he was jostled when folks moved closer to take pictures in front of the tree. Minutes passed and soon the crowd began to disperse. Kaylie grabbed his arm.

"Can we get a picture, Dad?"

"Right now?"

She frowned at him and mouthed, *You promised.* So he had. He extracted his phone from his jacket pocket and held it out to Deke. "Mind doing the honors?"

"My pleasure," Deke said as he took the phone. Kaylie led him and Emmie to the tree.

"Smile," Kaylie instructed softly.

He complied. Before he knew it, the Harpers joined in. After shuffling around, flashes of light captured the kids, mugging for the camera. Then Deke and Grace, beaming at the camera. Wanda Sue, Mrs. M. and Alveda posed, as well.

Mrs. M. pushed him forward. "One more," she said, somehow with his phone in her hands. Wanda Sue nudged Faith over and Mrs. M. cried out, "Smile."

He and Faith exchanged a glance before facing forward. A hint of her floral perfume hung in the air. Her arm brushed against his, and he had to hold his breath for a few seconds in order not to react to her closeness. Or—rephrase that—in order for no one else to notice his reaction to her standing by his side. Her laugh charmed him, and when John ran forward to take Faith's hand, he had to contain his regret.

"There's hot cocoa, Mama."

Faith inched away from him. Roan had to admit, the impromptu photo session had been fun. But then, he was learning that Faith made everything fun. Maybe no harm would come from Kaylie's request that he make Christmas merry after all.

"Daddy, can we have cocoa too?" Emmie asked, bouncing up and down on her tiptoes. After a healthy dose of chocolate, he pictured her bounding around the house for hours when they got home.

"Only one small cup," he warned, but she'd already turned to take John's hand.

"Sit A Spell always has a cocoa station set up on the sidewalk after the lighting," Mrs. M. told him, patting his arm. "The whole group is going."

He watched as the kids followed Deke and Grace, trailed by Wanda Sue and Alveda. Faith was still behind, gathering up the kids' lost gloves and scarves.

"I'll be there in a minute," he said.

"Not to worry," Mrs. M. assured him. "We'll limit Emmie's cocoa intake."

"Much obliged."

The older woman hurried off, leaving him with Faith and a few other stragglers taking pictures or just enjoying the scene before them.

"Got everything?" he asked.

"I think so, thanks." She shook her head as she slung the mom bag over her shoulder, her tawny hair visible from under her hat, swirling over her shoulders. "How do my children end up losing half the outerwear we leave the house with?"

"It must be like the 'losing a sock in the dryer' phenomenon."

She chuckled.

He stuffed his hands in his pockets to remove the puffy gloves she'd loaned him. "Wanted to return these."

She took them in her hand and held them up. "Sure you want to give them up? They make quite a fashion statement."

"More than sure."

She shoved them in the bag. "Your loss."

He pulled out another pair. Black leather. "I came prepared."

She lifted a shoulder. "I still think you look good in pink."

Now it was his turn to chuckle.

They slowly brought up the rear as their group disappeared under the park arch. He might not have much time with her alone, so he launched right in.

"Listen, I want to apologize if I came off pushy about your ex earlier."

"It was a little…intense."

"In my defense, you looked kinda rattled. That tends to bring out my protective streak. It's gotten me into hot water more than a few times."

"I appreciate you looking out for me, but it was nothing nefarious." She bit her lip, then said, "Lyle had just shared some news. What you saw was his bungling attempt to reassure me."

"Are you reassured?"

"Yes, well, no."

"Clear answer."

She held her hands out at her sides. "It's complicated."

He nodded. He and Catrina might not have gotten as far as divorce, but things had still been uncomfortable between them in the months leading up to the accident. He imagined Faith's vagueness stemmed from being in the same category.

"Want to talk about it?" he offered, not sure where his largesse came from. Normally he didn't pry unless it came with his job. But in the short time since Faith had moved in next door, Roan found himself overly interested in his newest neighbor.

"It's not exactly a Christmassy topic," she said.

"Sorry, didn't mean to push." A breeze gusted by. He shivered. "Again."

"No, I…" She tilted her head. "Sure you won't mind?"

"The kids are in good hands for a few minutes."

She stopped some steps from the lingering crowd and lowered her bag to the chilled ground, rubbed her hands up and down her arms.

When he noticed her discomfort, he realized he could have brought this up when they were in a warmer location. Seems Faith had him turned all around. He wasn't sure what to make of that fact.

"You're cold. We could head to Main Street."

"No." She glanced around them. The park was thinning out. They took a spot beside a glowing lamppost nearby. "To be honest, I don't want anyone to overhear."

He clasped his hands behind his back and waited.

After a long pause, she said, "Lyle wanted to tell me he's getting remarried."

He rocked back on his bootheels. "Oh. Okay."

"Yeah, it came as a surprise."

Was she upset about Lyle remarrying? Did she still care about her ex? Another reminder that this was none of his business.

Not exactly sure about the protocol in this situation, he asked, "Do you have a problem with his news?"

"No," she rushed to say. "It's not that."

"I noticed you weren't exactly present during the tree lighting." He dug a little deeper. "Are you upset?"

"Good grief, no."

Relief, swift and profound, struck him after her emphatic reply. He brushed his reaction aside, not ready to evaluate the undeniable response.

She seemed to be gathering some inner strength, then said, "He wants me to tell John the news."

"Coward." The word came out so fast, he didn't have time to edit his quick retort.

"I know, right?" She blew errant strands of hair from her face. "I don't know why I give in to him."

"Because it's about your children."

She met his gaze, surprise and pleasure in her eyes. "Thank you."

"I've seen how you look out for them."

He could have sworn her eyes grew shiny as she quickly turned away. When she faced him again, her features were more composed.

"I'm not sure what John will make of this. Even now, he doesn't understand why Lyle is out of the picture."

"It's tricky. Emmie knows her mother is never coming back, but it still doesn't make things easier."

Her heartfelt puff of breath misted before her. "One more hurdle in this single parent life."

"Don't worry. You aren't alone trying to keep things on an even keel."

Now she looked curious. "Fallout from Emmie's meltdown today?"

"In a way, but probably not what you'd expect."

She tilted her head. "Try me."

Guess he owed her an explanation after goading her to reveal the situation with her ex. "Kaylie made me promise to make Christmas merry for Emmie."

Faith's eyes went wide. "Because you aren't already merry?"

"I sorta fell off the happy holiday train. Many years ago."

"Yikes."

"So I have some making up to do."

"Is that why you're here tonight?"

"Yes. I tried talking them into staying home to make popcorn and watch a movie, but it didn't work."

"Well, of course not." She shook her head. "Don't you remember the anticipation of Christmas from when you were a kid?"

His shoulders went rigid, like they always did when he thought of the past. "Christmas wasn't a priority at my house."

Faith blinked. "Sorry."

"You didn't know."

She paused a moment, then asked, "Are you going to carry through?"

"Yep. Just like you're going to be the one to tell John about his father. Someone has to do the heavy lifting."

The corners of Faith's mouth drooped. "I was afraid you'd say that."

"Look on the bright side."

She shot him a disgruntled look. "There's a bright side?"

"We're both figuring out this single parent-hood thing together."

"There is that."

"Unless you don't want your ex moving on."

She held up a hand, palm out. "Trust me, that's not an issue."

After releasing a breath he hadn't realized he was holding, he raised a questioning brow.

"First of all, I don't want to be married to Lyle. Any feelings for him were extinguished a long time ago."

Strangely relieved by her answer, he asked, "So what's the real problem?"

"It's silly."

"Hey, secrets remain secrets between us single parents."

The reluctance in her tone told him she was debating what to say. "I have this weird feeling of being…stuck. He's moving on and I'm…in the same place I've been for years now."

That's how he'd felt, and why he'd brought the kids to Golden. If he were honest, some days it still didn't feel like he'd made much progress.

"But you aren't, really," he said, as much to encourage himself as Faith. "You have the kids. A house you just moved into."

"I agree, I just…" She waved her hand in an impatient motion. "It isn't important."

He sensed it was, but it seemed that Faith hadn't quite put a finger on what was bothering her.

"I guess with so much going on, I'm wondering who I am in all this." She scanned the park as if the cold night air held all the answers. "I didn't listen when I was in high school, then all too soon I became a wife and mother. Now I'm a student and run a business." She turned to him. "That should be enough, right?"

"Not necessarily. We all like to know who we are deep down inside."

Her expression turned pensive, but she shook off her mood with a rueful grin. Her pretty face glowed under the lamplight, a picture he wouldn't forget anytime soon.

"No one needs to get all introspective at Christmastime. There are too many other things that are more important."

"Like?"

"Focusing on the kids and the holiday," she said, hoisting her bag over her shoulder. "Everything else can wait."

"Easy for you to say. I have to be jolly and I haven't got a clue."

She chuckled as they resumed their walk. "How can a seasoned father not have a clue?"

"My wife took care of all the festivities."

"Ah."

Unbidden, his defenses went up. "I hear condemnation in that ah."

"Not condemnation. More like resignation." They circled a family before she continued. "Lyle didn't help me much during the holidays when we were together."

"So you're saying we have to work harder?"

"Yes, sir." She laughed as she patted his arm. The casual gesture sent a shot straight to his tight chest. "How about we go get some of that cocoa and toast to being single parents at Christmastime."

"Too bad we couldn't find something a little stronger," he muttered.

"I'm driving, Officer, so no."

Great, she'd heard him. "Ditto."

They exited the park. When some kids ran by, Faith was jostled closer. He put his hand to the small of her back to keep her from toppling over, his touch lingering seconds longer than was necessary.

"Thanks," came her breathless reply. Her cheeks were pink. From the cold or from being so close? She brushed her hair from her pretty eyes, a flare of heat dancing there. One he refused to decipher when his face heated in return.

As they drew closer to their families, Emmie's laughter reached his ears. He turned his head at the sound. He found her immediately, the center of attention, as the adults listened to a big story she told with lots of gesturing. He owed Emmie the joys only childhood could bring, and he owed it to Kaylie to keep his promise. The idea of making Christmas special for his girls was so daunting, he slowed his steps. Faith looked up at him with a questioning gaze.

"So if I had holiday-related questions, could I give you a call?" he asked, hoping she didn't hear the desperation in his voice.

"Absolutely. And if I need, I don't know, appliance assistance, can I count on you?"

He puffed out his chest. "Anytime, day or night."

A grin curved her lips. "I'll take you up on that."

"I hope you do."

They stared at each other, the moment in time stilling until it was just the two of them. His pulse pumped harder with every second that passed. He found it terrifying and exhilarating all at once.

Her children rushed over to Faith, so they moved apart. She hugged them, then shot him a glance he couldn't interpret. Could she be as confused as he was?

As he joined the others, Roan smiled at the scene, purposely not trying to figure out his strong reaction to his neighbor. He may not be looking for a romantic entanglement, but to his surprise, he meant every word about them working together to make the children's dreams come true.

CHAPTER FIVE

"I'LL BE THE first to admit," Gayle Ann said to the group of matchmakers gathered around her kitchen table the following Monday morning. "The tree lighting ceremony didn't go exactly as planned. Roan and Faith didn't spend nearly enough time alone together."

The dueling scents of coffee and freshly baked cinnamon streusel filled the warm room. The day had started off gloomy, the typical winter weather matching the long faces on everyone in attendance.

"I'm afraid Lyle twisted a knot in the chain," Wanda Sue said. "His showing up put Faith in a mood."

"What did he want?" Alveda asked.

"She wouldn't say, but she's been real quiet ever since." Wanda Sue pressed her lips together. "Usually doesn't bode well."

"Maybe she's got a lot going on, juggling Christmas with the kids and all," Bunny said, always the cheerleader.

"I don't know." Wanda Sue shook her head.

"It reminds me of the summer she and Lyle separated."

Gayle Ann tapped her spoon against a place mat. "Please don't tell us she's not over Lyle."

Wanda Sue sat up straight. "Heavens, no, it's not Lyle. Not directly anyway."

The room went quiet until Judge Harry Carmichael spoke up.

"If I recall from a previous meeting, it was mentioned that Faith doesn't do well when overwhelmed."

"True," Wanda Sue confirmed. "She's been like that since she was a kid. Pushed into a corner, she'd make the worst decisions imaginable."

"Perhaps she has too much on her plate," Gayle Ann suggested.

"I have to say, since she decided to get her life together, she's been working real hard. Those business classes she's been taking have boosted her confidence. Grace has also noticed a big difference."

"So let me get this straight," Harry said. "She's taking classes, working full-time and tending to her children solo?"

"She is. Even though the semester break is coming up, the classes are important." Wanda Sue grimaced. "Maybe more than romance?"

Gayle Ann cleared her throat. "Let's go back to the mission at hand, to show Faith and Roan that they can depend on each other and then fall in love."

"Doesn't seem like Roan's any less busy." Alveda moved the spoon in her cup around in circles. "Laurel told me he doesn't drop the girls off at their house much since his shift changed. Got her all in an uproar."

"Sounds like Roan's trying to make it all work," Bunny said as she took a bite of the crumbly cake.

"But I know Laurel. This entire plan could turn around and go south if we aren't careful," Alveda added with heat in her tone.

"At some point," Gayle Ann told the group, "Roan was going to want to keep his family with him, whether Laurel likes it or not."

Alveda's eyes went squinty. "Yeah, but that woman can hold a grudge and cause trouble."

"We won't let her," Gayle Ann replied firmly.

To which Alveda harrumphed.

"You made your position known," Gayle Ann told Alveda before turning to Wanda Sue.

"The point," Wanda Sue cut in, "is that those two have important responsibilities. Their families and jobs come first. I know we think we're helping them, but maybe we're pushing them together too soon."

Gayle Ann frowned. "I see your point, but I still think being together will benefit them in the long run. All the things you mentioned are important, yes, but they're doing it alone. Together, they'd have each other to lean on. Talk to. Weather the changing climate of life as the years go by." On a roll, her voice rose. "These hurdles notwithstanding, they deserve a chance. We need to maneuver those two to the same place at the same time. Any suggestions?"

Wanda Sue thought about it for a moment. "Faith made this list of Christmas activities to do. She wants to get a tree for the living room but hasn't gotten to the lot just yet."

"I love Kemps' Christmas Trees," Bunny said, her eyes sparkling. "Larry has added so many fun things for families to do when they stop by. The idea of keeping hayrides going after the autumn season ended was pure genius."

"Larry always was a shrewd businessman." Alveda added her two cents.

Wanda Sue cut the chitchat. "Ideas, people."

"I spoke to Roan today," Gayle Ann said.

"He mentioned that he's not the least bit ready for the holiday. He also needs a tree."

"So what are you thinking?" Bunny pressed.

"If Wanda Sue keeps nagging Faith, we can get a heads-up when Faith goes to the lot. We'll come up with a police matter that'll encourage Roan to be at the lot, as well."

Alveda sent Gayle Ann a puzzled frown. "What possible police matter could you have at a Christmas tree lot?"

Gayle Ann rubbed her chin in thought, then snapped her fingers. "That the police officers in Golden get a free tree at Kemps' lot."

Everyone went silent for a drawn-out moment.

Bunny spoke first. "Who's going to pay for it?"

"I will, of course," Gayle Ann answered.

"You do realize," Harry drawled, "that you will be required to pay for all the officers' trees."

"That's not a problem." Gayle Ann waved a hand. "It's something we should do anyway. The officers are important in Golden, so it'll actually be my pleasure."

"What about the timing?" Bunny asked.

Gayle Ann grinned. "I'll tell Roan about the free offer and recommend he make it a special outing by inviting his neighbors. When Wanda Sue finds out when Faith is going to the tree lot, we'll all show up."

Alveda rolled her eyes.

"Do you have a better idea?" Gayle Ann pressed her friend.

"Seems convoluted if you ask me," Alveda said, crossing her thin arms over her chest.

"Actually," Wanda Sue said with a grin, "Emmie and John are in the same class at school. If Roan doesn't say anything to the neighbors, John is certain to tell Emmie when they're going."

"Who will then beg Roan to take them to the lot," Bunny finished.

"Either way, this just might work," Harry told Gayle Ann, admiration in his tone.

Gayle Ann lifted her coffee cup and said over the rim, "As if you had any doubt."

Harry's eyes crinkled at the corners. "None whatsoever."

TAKING A BREAK from what seemed like endless paperwork, Roan pulled up the pictures taken at the tree lighting on his phone. He grinned at Kaylie and Emmie, their cheeks red, smiles wide and eyes bright. Then he scrolled through, stopping on the snap of him and Faith. While he looked resigned to all the hoopla, Faith came off as amused. Yeah, she had his number. So why did he keep going back to this picture?

"I need that report before you leave," Brady said from behind him.

The noise of the squad room slowly filtered into Roan's consciousness. He quickly set down his phone, but not fast enough. Brady's smile told him that the new chief of police had caught him in the act of thinking about Faith Harper.

Thankfully Kelly Montgomery and Evan Stiles, the new hires, joined them.

"Did you guys see the tree at Sit A Spell sponsored by Operation Share?" Kelly asked.

"Remind me again," Roan said, who'd been out on a call when she pitched the concept to their boss.

"It's a charitable program to give Christmas gifts to children, especially those who may not be getting other presents."

She'd been instrumental in getting the program off the ground when she first arrived in Golden.

"We do all the work—from finding a drop-off for the gifts to wrapping them and making sure they are properly labeled with an appropriate age to be certain each gift gets into the right kid's hands. We make sure to have extra gifts, that way no one goes without."

"Is that what you were doing?" Evan asked. "When you were busy making paper ornaments with a kid's age along with gift suggestions?"

She nodded. "The ornaments are on the tree and folks are stopping by to pick out a child to sponsor. If you want to help, you'd better think about getting there before they're all gone."

"I'll bring Kaylie and Emmie after school. Let them each pick out a child to sponsor." He paused, thinking this was a new tradition he could be on board with. "I'm always looking for ways to get them to think of others. Giving to those in need is something I want them to value as they grow up."

"Excellent." Kelly beamed. Then her eyes turned shifty. "So that means I can sign you up to volunteer at the party?"

Brady's eyebrows angled. "What party?"

"We gather all the children in town for a big blowout. Santa is the guest of honor. And Mrs. Arnold agreed we can store the gifts at the community center and then have the open house party after the town parade on Christmas Eve morning. It's for a good cause."

Not only was she smart, she was one per-suasive woman.

Everyone exchanged glances.

"I'm in," Evan said.

"The girls and I will be there," Roan added.

Brady shook his head. "One of us has to be on duty."

"Do I hear you volunteering?" Roan quipped.

"Looks that way. Now, back to work."

Kelly and Evan took off while Roan glanced at Brady. "Sure you don't mind work-ing on Christmas Eve? You've been putting in a lot of long hours."

"Comes with the new title. Even though I've worked for GPD for a long time, this pro-motion has a learning curve." He shrugged. "Besides, I don't have a family at home, so it's all good."

"Thanks."

Brady leaned a hip against the desk and crossed his arms. "So, thinking of asking your neighbor to join you in the festivities?"

Roan tried to pull off a blank face.

"I saw that picture with you and Faith."

"Ever heard of privacy?"

Brady laughed. "For what it's worth, Faith is good people."

Forcing himself not to shift in his chair, Roan nodded. "It's the kids. They all get along."

"Right."

With an amused grin, Brady sauntered off. Roan itched to pick up the phone and gaze at the pictures again, but instead he grabbed a pen and worked on the report Brady needed by end of day.

FAITH SAT AT her kitchen table on a windy Wednesday evening, chewing on the end of her pencil as she read the last question on her accounting exam. The final test of the semester was taking her much too long to complete. Thankfully the kids were quiet, watching a Christmas program on television while she tried to finish her task before dinner.

"One more answer and the holiday is yours," she said to herself.

Shaking out her shoulders, she reread the question, but had trouble coming up with an answer. She hadn't slept well since Lyle had blown through town last weekend. Plus, Christmas events were ramping up at school and around Golden. She didn't have a tree yet, which—according to the list she'd stuck on the refrigerator—should have been up and decorated last Sunday.

On the plus side, Put Your Feet Up kept

abbreviated hours this time of year, so she'd been able to get a pot of homemade soup started earlier this afternoon. She glanced out the window over the sink. Evening shadows of purple and navy descended over the barren trees in the backyard.

"C'mon, Faith. Focus."

Blowing out a disgusted breath, she tossed the pencil on top of papers scattered around the table. Why couldn't she concentrate on one last question? Closing her eyes, she used a technique she'd found on the internet when she'd searched for ways to manage stress. Breathing deeply was the first step. She filled her lungs and exhaled slowly. So far so good.

Next, she repeated a mantra she'd adopted once she'd become a single mom. "You are a strong, capable woman. You are a present mom. You can finish what you start."

Right after she said the words, doubts rushed at her. Could she finish her education? Get a degree? Why had she even started taking classes? Maybe she should have stayed with Lyle. A little bit of help was better than no help at all.

She put her head in her hands and leaned onto the table. No. Lyle was not the answer. He'd never been, no matter how much she'd wanted him to be once upon a time.

I'm getting married.

And there was the problem. Lyle was moving on while she carried all the responsibilities of parenthood. Lately she didn't have a clue about who she was or who she wanted to be. Could this doubt stem from the fact that she was a tiny bit jealous of Lyle? Probably. She had no romantic prospects in sight and didn't see that changing anytime soon.

A picture of Roan flashed in her mind, standing in her kitchen on that chilly night after fixing her furnace. Thick black hair. Dreamy blue eyes. A man trying hard to do the best for his daughters. But after hearing about the state of his marriage before his wife died, it was apparent the man's heart was off-limits.

With a shake of her head, she glanced at the computer screen, then out the window again. She couldn't go for a walk right now, her other go-to approach to free her mind. It was cold outside and too close to dinner. Plus, she didn't want to disturb John and Lacey when they were quiet. Instead, she got up, stretched her arms over her head and bent side to side at the waist. Feeling better, she sat down, picked up her pencil and read the question again. This time she was able to scribble out the mathematics on a clean sheet of paper before typing in the answer. She was so close. One last check and…

"Mama?"

She jerked her head up at the sound. John stood beside her, his hand on her arm. How long had he been there?

"I've been calling you, but you didn't answer."

"Sorry, baby." She pulled him into her arms. Drank in his little boy scent. "I was trying to get my test finished."

"I didn't mean to make you stop."

"I'm almost finished." She pushed her hair back. "What can I do for you?"

"I need an envelope."

"An envelope? For what?"

"To send a letter."

"Who do you…" Then it dawned on her. "John, you already sent your letter to Santa."

"I did, but I have a friend who has to send one now, or it won't get to the North Pole on time."

"A friend at school?"

He shot a glance toward the living room. "Sorta."

What was her son up to? She drew out the word when she said, "John?"

His face contorted. He wasn't the least bit sneaky. "Okay, it's for Emmie."

"Can't Emmie's dad mail her letter?"

"He's not into Christmas," John replied in a sad tone.

After her conversation with Roan on Saturday, she already knew this. But hadn't he said he was going to work harder at making his daughters' Christmas special this year?

"I think she should talk to her dad about this."

"Oh, Mama, please? We were just going to…"

"We?"

His eyes went wide.

Busted.

Faith rose and walked into the living room to find Emmie sitting on the floor beside the coffee table, drawing a picture with Lacey.

"Emmie. I didn't know you were here," Faith said, keeping her tone casual.

The young girl's head popped up. "John said we had to be quiet until you finish school."

Apparently they'd been extra quiet because Faith had never heard the front door open or the kids talking.

"Does your father know you're here?"

Guilt flashed across Emmie's face. "He was busy so I walked over."

"Oh, boy." How long had Emmie been at the house? Did Roan know she was here?

Turning on her heel to retrieve her phone from the kitchen table, she realized she didn't have Roan's number. She carried the phone into the living room and asked, "Emmie, do you know your daddy's phone number?"

The little girl rattled off the memorized contact. Faith quickly tapped out a text message telling Roan his daughter was here.

Emmie's fingers fiddled with the crayons. "My daddy is busy. You can't disturb him."

Faith walked to Emmie and lowered herself to the girl's height. "Honey, he's probably worried about you."

"No, he and Kaylie have important Christmas business to do. He told me."

"That may be so, but you can't leave your house without telling an adult."

Emmie held on to Faith's arm with two hands in a death grip. "Please don't tell him. I'll sneak back into the house and he'll never know I was gone."

The doorbell rang.

"Uh-oh," John gulped.

Faith removed Emmie's hands and squeezed the little girl's shoulder as she stood. "It'll be okay," she said, not entirely sure the situation warranted that kind of assurance, but she couldn't ignore the fear on the little girl's face. Emmie knew she was in trouble. In Faith's experience, that should be enough to have her shaking in her tiny boots.

She left the living room, readying herself for the encounter. Roan would not be happy.

She opened the door and there he stood, his face a thundercloud. Dressed in a sweater and jeans, no coat, he must have run out of the house and straight over to hers. She pushed open the screen and held up a hand to stop him before he ran in. "First of all, Emmie is fine."

"I just got your text," he said, pushing a hand through his already windblown hair. He came in and Faith closed the door as the cold air seeped through. She shivered due to the elements and one unhappy father.

"Daddy," Emmie said and rushed to his side as he entered the room. "I couldn't tell you I was coming to see John."

Roan's voice was tight when he asked, "And why not?"

"Because you said you had to talk to Kaylie about Christmas stuff. I want Christmas to come to our house, so I left without bothering you." Tears filled her eyes. "I'm sorry."

Faith watched as Roan's anger fled his face and his shoulders slumped.

"I'm sorry, Mr. Emmie's Dad," John said, sidling up beside his friend. "Emmie had to, um…do a Christmas chore and she needed my help."

Roan got down on one to knee to face the children. He seemed to have a hard time deciding how to handle the situation, so Faith hurried over.

"Kids, let's give Mr. Donovan a minute, okay?"

They nodded, regret shimmering in both pairs of eyes. Roan scrubbed a hand down his face and rose. Faith took his arm and tugged him into the kitchen. "I know this looks bad," she said.

"Ya think?"

"No one is hurt. The best judgment wasn't used here, but they meant well."

"You'll have to excuse me if I'm not ready to have a rational discussion. Emmie scared me half to death. Again."

Faith thought about the day in the park when she'd run off. Clearly this was a pattern.

He pulled out his phone and typed a text, then paced the length of the room. "One minute I thought she was playing in her bedroom, the next I found it empty."

Not sure what to say, she let Roan dial down his fear. He stopped directly in front of Faith. His gaze pierced hers. "Why didn't you call me?"

"I didn't know she was here." She swallowed hard. "As soon as I realized Emmie had left without telling you, I got your number from her to inform you she was at our house."

Both eyebrows rose nearly to his hairline.

"In my defense, I was taking an online test, and the kids were so quiet, I didn't know any mischief was going on."

Roan rubbed the heel off his palm over his chest. "She's going to be the death of me."

"I hope not," Faith said, knowing he was being overly dramatic. Still, she wanted Roan in her life. Weird time for that thought to crystallize.

Roan blew out a breath.

The doorbell rang again.

"That's Kaylie. I texted her to let her know Emmie was safe."

By the time she got to the door, Emmie and John had beat her to it. Kaylie had her little sister in a tight embrace. John hovered, Lacey came over to check out the action and seconds later, Faith felt Roan's breath on the back of her neck.

She fought off a full-body tremor. He was

so close, so warm, his cologne enveloping her. Faith had to admit, she was overwhelmed by his presence. Why were these reactions growing more intense rather than simmering down? She needed to get her emotions in check.

Kaylie's gaze met her father's in an unspoken exchange. Faith felt him move a fraction before Kaylie untangled herself and wrangled the children back into the living room. Roan stood at the entrance to the room, watching his daughters. When Faith joined him, he crossed his arms over his impressive chest, his expression softer than when he'd first arrived.

"She's just a kid," Faith started before he sent her a sideways glare. *Okay, no more free advice.*

Not sure what the rest of the evening would entail, Faith went to the kitchen to fill the kettle and turn on the stovetop. Once Roan calmed down, he might want a beverage. Moments later he joined her, his face still communicating he was at a loss.

"Tea?" she asked.

"No, thanks."

"Then how about we discuss this."

He sighed. Ran a hand over his attractively mussed hair. "This is all the elf's fault."

BLINKING AT HIM, Faith's expression revealed her confusion. "An elf?"

He tried to avert his gaze, but she deserved an explanation. "I don't know how an Elf on the Shelf works, so Kaylie and I were having a secret meeting. We told Emmie we were doing important Christmas stuff so she wouldn't listen in on our conversation. I guess she took it seriously."

"She did mention something about not bothering you."

"This is why this time of year makes me so crazy."

Faith pressed her lips together. *Trying not to laugh?* Probably. Other than Emmie giving him a permanent case of heartburn, this whole thing was absurd.

"How did the tutorial go?"

Roan shook his head in disbelief. "Did you know kids can't touch the elf, so I have to move it around every day?"

She coughed. "Yes. I had heard something along those lines."

"You can stop laughing."

"I would, but this is too rich."

Now that the fear had subsided, he managed a tiny smile. "Emmie's not all wrong in this. We did make a big deal about talking privately." He placed his palms on the counter behind him and leaned back. Crossed his ankles. "At least she didn't walk to my in-laws. The idea of her hiking through town will give me nightmares."

"I think she and John had their own secret Christmas meeting."

He went alert. "Meaning?"

"John asked for an envelope so I'm assuming a letter to Santa."

"Emmie's been after me to take her to visit Santa so she can give him her list. Unlike you, I've fallen down on the job."

"Me?"

"The night I fixed the furnace you were making a list highlighting your family events."

She glanced over at the refrigerator. "A list I have yet to tackle."

He turned his attention to the table, taking in the laptop and papers. "Did we take you away from something? You mentioned an online test."

"Final exam."

"Single mom and student. I'm impressed." He pushed away from the counter. "We should let you get back to it."

She clicked the mouse a few times, then closed the computer. "I'm almost finished. Besides, it's not due until Friday. I like to get a head start."

"That's right, you're working toward…?"

"A business degree," she said as she tidied up her work space. "When I started at Put Your Feet Up, I realized I could be of more help if I understood how the business ran. I took a pretty basic accounting class so I knew how the computer software worked, and I'll admit, I was interested. I mentioned it to Grace and she encouraged me to go back to school."

"How much longer until you graduate?"

"A year. I'm not taking a full semester class load. It would be too much with the kids, work and life."

He nodded. "When I got on the Golden PD, I had to take some refresher courses. With kids, time management is critical."

"Exactly, I—"

Her phone dinged. She lifted it to read the screen and quickly scowled.

"Trouble?"

"No. My mother checking in to see if I got a tree yet."

"Ah. The list that hasn't been entirely fulfilled."

She pointed to the paper on the refrigerator. "One item checked off. The tree lighting. Otherwise, zip. And in the middle of all the activities, my sister is getting married. Who gets married in December?"

"People with no kids?"

Laughter spilled into the cozy kitchen from the other room. Roan walked to the opening to check on the children. "Looks like they're enjoying a movie."

After cleaning off the table and moving her school supplies, Faith removed the top of a large pot on the stove. Immediately the tangy scent of spices reached Roan's nose.

"We should probably take off."

As she stirred, Faith said, "I have more than enough. Do you and the girls want to stay?"

He hadn't thought about dinner plans yet, so the timing of the offer was perfect. "You wouldn't mind?"

"No. I stopped at the store for freshly baked bread before we came home, so there's plenty."

"Then, yes, we'll stay."

Her phone dinged again. She placed the lid on the pot and grabbed the device. This time she rolled her eyes. "Mama. She's texted me every night this week. She's positive all the trees will be gone from the lot if we don't go soon."

Before Roan had a chance to really think out a plan, he said, "You know, Mrs. M. told me that trees for the officers were paid for this year. I need to swing by and pick ours up."

An idea formulated in his head thanks to Mrs. M. having suggested that the two families go to the lot together. Before he thought better of it, he added, "Why don't we all go after dinner?" He grinned. "With your mom pushing you, she's kinda pushing me too."

"I… That would be great." She picked up her phone to text her mother.

He'd already made a commitment to be merry, starting with the whole Elf on the Shelf thing, so why not a fresh tree? They didn't have to go overboard, like his neighbor with her list. As he watched Faith telling the kids they were staying for dinner, and the children responding with a cheer, he realized that Christmas was happening whether he wanted it or not, so he should get on board.

He glanced at Faith again, her cheeks pink from the heat of the stove, her eyes sparkling with Christmas cheer. She embodied the spirit of the season.

He swallowed hard. Forced a smile when she glanced his way. Yet again, without even trying, she'd managed to help him make this Christmas happy for his girls.

So much for his resolve to keep her at arm's length.

CHAPTER SIX

"I DIDN'T EXPECT your mother's posse to show up too."

Faith chuckled at Roan's remark, which seemed to be half exasperation, half awe at the rapid circulation of small town gossip.

She watched her mother lead the children between a row of freshly cut trees, the Pied Piper of Christmas. Bunny, Alveda and Mrs. M. brought up the rear. The kids were in high spirits. Thankfully she and Roan had waited until after dinner to tell them the plan, otherwise the meal would have been overly raucous with the kids asking when they'd be leaving. With their tummies full, and dressed in warm clothing, they were free to expend their pent-up energy, giving Faith a few minutes to unwind.

She shouldn't have been surprised her mom had shown up after Faith told her they'd be here. Mama had been after her to get a tree for a week, and had hinted that she wanted to be part of the family outing. Plus, the owner included a hayride for the children, a big hit. To top it off, John and Lacey were happy their Grammie was here. And to be honest, Faith liked sharing these memories with her mother, especially after settling down since her wild years. There had been too much turmoil, blame and bad blood in the Harper family, particularly after her father went to prison. They were finally making strides in the right direction, and Faith didn't want to rock that boat.

She looked up, seeing that Roan waited patiently for her to lead. She inhaled his masculine scent mingling with woodsmoke and evergreen, still stunned by his suggestion they all go to the tree lot.

"Mr. Kemp and our family go way back," she explained. "When we were growing up, it was always a big deal to come here and pick out a tree. Oh, the arguments we had." A reminiscent smile curved her lips. Grace had wanted a perfectly symmetrical tree. Nathan had wanted it tall and full. And Faith? No one had really listened to her request, so she'd stopped offering her opinion, preferring to hurry off and hang out with her friends. If they had asked, what would she have wanted?

"I'll admit, I haven't been here in quite

a few years," she said as memories floated about her.

"Because you don't like real trees?"

"No." Her face heated. "I was dating Scott Kemp and kind of dumped him for Lyle. Afterward it was too awkward to come around."

"I get it." Experience laced Roan's tone. "Certain places hold memories we'd rather not revisit."

"Is that why you left Colorado?"

He shrugged inside his heavy jacket. "Partly. Our family needed a change, for sure. But moving closer to the Jessups meant I had family to help with the girls."

"What about your family?"

"I cut ties with them a long time ago," he answered in a clipped tone.

Okay, there was some baggage here. Since it was obvious Roan didn't want to elaborate, she returned to the original topic.

"Do you miss Colorado?"

"Some. The terrain is different here, but the people of Golden have been welcoming. Very accepting of a single father trying to raise two daughters without any drama."

Faith laughed. "How's the no drama part working out for you?"

He sent her a sidelong glance and his lips curved a fraction, sending a quiver that had nothing to do with the cold night through her. "You, better than anyone, know how it's working out."

"Daddy," Emmie cried out, dancing in place as she waved Roan to her side.

"Must be a winner," Faith said.

They stopped before a tree that had to be twelve feet tall.

"Uh, Emmie, this tree is too big. It won't fit in the house."

"But I like it."

"It's very pretty. Maybe we can find another one shaped like this, only shorter."

"Okay."

"Kaylie," he said, turning on his heel. "Where'd she go?"

Faith pointed out a group of girls standing by a table where teens milled about. "Looks like her friends from school are here."

Roan's forehead creased, but before Faith could ask why, Emmie tugged his sleeve. "What about this one?"

This time she picked out an eight-foot tree. Much more likely to fit in the living room. "Good job, sweetie." He turned and called over to Kaylie. She shot him an embarrassed look Faith remembered so well.

Kaylie hurried over and huffed, "Dad."

"What?"

"You didn't have to yell."

"I didn't." He exchanged a questioning look with Faith. She pressed her lips together to smother her amusement. Then he nodded to the tree and asked his daughter, "What do you think?"

"It's fine. Whatever."

Roan focused on his daughter. "What's wrong?"

"Nothing. Can I go back to my friends?"

"Sure."

As Kaylie ran off, he asked, "What was that all about?"

Faith leaned in. "Nothing worse than having a parent yell for you when you're with friends."

"I didn't yell." He glanced at her, eyebrows angled together in confusion. "Besides, who cares how I get her attention?"

"A nearly teenage girl, that's who."

"Seriously?"

"Seriously."

"But she's the one who wants me to go along with all this tradition."

"Welcome to the mysteries of the teenage mind."

He muttered something under his breath that Faith couldn't hear.

"Mama," John called out. Faith followed

the sound of his voice around the corner to the next row. Her mother had pulled out a tree and the two stood examining it.

"So?" Faith asked. "Do we have a winner?"

"Winner," Lacey repeated, then tugged on a low branch. Needles fell to the dirt-packed ground.

"Next," Faith suggested, already envisioning the mess.

Her mother returned it and pulled out a backup. This time when Lacey tugged, the needles stayed attached to the branch.

"This one will work," Faith said, striding to her mother to handle the tree.

"Faith, do you mind if I take the kids on the hayride?"

"No. You guys have fun. While you're gone, I'll pay for the tree."

Mama wrangled up the three youngest and joined her friends to line up for the next ride.

Half dragging, half carrying the tree, Faith nearly collided with Roan as he brought his selected tree to the checkout.

"Looks like tonight is a success."

He reached out to grab hold of the tree, but she pulled it away. "I can carry it."

"Really? Because it looks like a wrestling match and the tree is winning."

"Funny." She moved her hands around for a better grip. "I can do this."

Roan watched her for a moment, eyes hooded, then nodded. She finally made it to the front of the lot, blowing out a puff of air as she set the tree against the table Mr. Kemp worked from.

"Good to see you, Faith," the older man said.

"Same. And I'm happy to finally have a tree for the kids."

"That's one thing about young'uns, they sure make life more interstin'."

"They do," she said, pulling a few twenties from her jeans pocket to pay the man.

Mr. Kemp made change while carrying on the conversation.

"You should see Scott now. He's a big-time attorney down in Atlanta. He's got some political aspirations too."

"Nice to hear."

"Got him a terrific wife and a baby on the way."

Was Mr. Kemp rubbing Scott's success in her face?

"Lemme get some twine so we can secure the tree to your car."

Faith stepped to the side, bumping into Roan. "I'm so sorry."

Roan chuckled. "Am I that invisible?"

Invisible? Far from it. He was tall, broad shouldered, extremely gorgeous and...nice. To her anyway. More and more, the man took up residence in her head.

He moved around her and pulled out a few bills.

"Nope," Mr. Kemp said. "It's already been taken care of. Your money is no good here."

Even though Mrs. M. had told him in advance that the cost of the tree was covered, he still wanted to pay. "Are you sure?"

"You betcha."

Before long, Roan had the trees secured to both of their vehicles' roofs.

"Now what?" he asked, rubbing his bare hands together.

She went to her SUV to retrieve an extra pair of purple gloves and handed them to Roan.

He stared down at them. "Does everything you own have to be so bright?"

"Don't complain. Your hands are turning red."

This time he didn't question the gloves any further and slipped them on, seemingly grateful for the immediate warmth.

"Care for some hot cocoa?" he asked.

She followed his gaze to a stand set up by the local high school band.

"Why not? The kids aren't back yet."

He ordered two cups, and when she tried to pay, he stopped her. "I've got this."

"You don't have to."

"Hey, you fed us tonight. It's the least I can do."

She accepted. The cup was toasty in her hands. The steam rose, bringing with it the sweet aroma of chocolate. She took a sip and went right to her happy place.

"This is so good."

"I don't have much of a sweet tooth, but this is tasty," Roan agreed.

They wandered away from the stand, close to the edge of the lot, where the wagon would deposit the children once it returned.

"Thanks again," she said, taking another sip, enjoying the burst of flavor. "We'd better drink this before the little ones return and want a cup."

"Huh?"

Noticing his distraction, Faith followed his gaze.

"You've had your eye on Kaylie since she started hanging out with her friends. What's up?"

"One of the girls she's been spending time

with named Diandra is suspected of shoplifting at Kelloggs' Five and Dime."

"Oh, no."

"I haven't mentioned it to Kaylie. She's been having a hard time fitting in, and I'm not sure how she'll feel about her dad, the cop, accusing one of her friends."

"I remember how important being in the right crowd feels at that age, but she should be aware."

"I know." He rubbed his bristly chin with a gloved hand. "I don't want to come down heavy-handed, but at the same time, I don't want her getting into trouble."

"Kaylie seems like a levelheaded girl."

"Most of the time she is. But she's still only eleven." He tossed his still-full cup in a nearby trash can. "It's been a tricky balance since their mom died. Kaylie was struggling in Colorado before we left. I hate to see it still going on here."

"If it helps any, I grew up with Diandra's mother. She's a good kid."

"But the others?"

Faith shrugged. "No clue."

Faith could read the conflict on Roan's face, of how much he wanted to protect his daughter while giving her space. She imagined he balanced being the tuned-in dad, while at the same time, realizing Kaylie needed some space.

"I remember what it's like making the wrong choices in order to be part of the popular crowd. How spectacularly things can blow up in your face."

His gaze met hers and blazed for a moment. "Part of your past?"

"Yeah." She hated that she had this kind of experience to share, but maybe Kaylie could benefit from a cautionary tale.

"Trying to fit in is so hard," Faith said, averting her gaze as she spoke. "When I was growing up, I was the typical middle child. Grace was the oldest and an overachiever. Nathan was the youngest and a boy, Daddy's favorite. When Daddy went away, we all retreated to our separate corners. I soon found out that any attention, even bad, was better than nothing. Made it much too easy to get mixed up with the wrong crowd."

She found the strength to face him after her dismal admission. "You have a lot going on, Roan. Maybe Kaylie feels left out? It's amazing how far just being included goes toward bolstering one's self-confidence."

He considered her for a drawn-out moment. She tried not to let the intensity of his gaze make her fidget. "Do you think I'm intentionally avoiding her?"

"No. I think you're a single dad, trying to figure daughters out," she answered. "It's got to be tough for you to stand on the sidelines."

"What I really want is to keep them in a bubble," he said, his expression fierce.

"Not possible."

"And now her mom's not here to guide her."

"There are others who can fill in."

"Like you?"

"Roan, I would never overstep."

"I didn't think you would." He ran a hand over his hair, mussing it even more. "But you could listen."

"*If* she wanted to confide in me. That's a big if."

He seemed to be struggling, then said, "This is hard for me, but if she did approach you, I'd be okay with it."

"Are you sure?"

"Yes. Unless you advise her to go out and get attention any way possible."

She held her hand up. "Been there, done that, wore the T-shirt. I would never send her down that path."

"I know." He met her gaze. The serious gleam in his eyes reflected his trust in her. She was surprised by how much that meant to her. "But if you learn anything I should know, you need to tell me."

"Of course. I would never hold back anything about your daughter."

He nodded, but Faith could sense he had a hard time easing up on even the smallest bit of protection. How would her life have been different if she'd had a dad like him? Roan's girls didn't know how lucky they were.

The wagon came around the bend and soon the tired group headed to their cars. The night temperature had dipped at least five more degrees and the kids were starting to shudder. Lacey fell asleep before they made it home. John's eyes were at half-mast when she pulled into the driveway.

"Thanks, Mama," John said.

"We had fun, didn't we?"

"Yes. Can we decorate tonight?"

"No, baby. You guys need to rest so you can give your full attention to hanging the special ornaments I bought on the tree."

"Okay," he said.

Her chest squeezed with love for her little boy.

As she got out of the car and went around to get Lacey, Roan appeared. She stopped just short of barging into him.

"Roan. Is something wrong?"

"No. Kaylie took Emmie inside. I want to make sure you get the tree in the house in one piece."

She couldn't control a grin. "Because I'm not a wrestler?"

His gaze locked with hers. She couldn't deny the heat reflected there. "Something like that."

John came around the side of the SUV. "Mama, let's go inside."

"I'll be right there, John."

She opened the door to get Lacey, warmth racing up her neck. Was Roan's gaze really that intense or had she just imagined it?

After getting Lacey upstairs, changed and into bed, she found Roan and John downstairs, tightening the screws in the tree stand. They'd turned a lamp on beside the couch— otherwise the room was cast in shadows.

"All done, buddy," Roan said, holding out his fist to bump with John's when they both rose from the floor.

John scooted by to run upstairs.

"Brush your teeth," Faith said.

"Aw," came her son's reply.

"You're all set," Roan said. He didn't seem to be in a hurry to leave.

"Thank you," she said, her voice more raspy than normal. With just the two of them in the muted light of the living room, the air grew taut between them.

"My pleasure." He held out the gloves she'd loaned him. "I need to get home and make sure the girls are ready for bed."

When she moved closer to take the gloves, their fingers tangled, sending a rush over her skin. Their breath mingled in the scant space between them. Faith grew jittery, not from the temperature, but from the hope that Roan might lower his head to brush his lips against hers. She wouldn't stop him if he took the chance. In fact, she swayed toward him, letting him know she wanted his full attention. Wanted his embrace. Wanted to be wrapped up in his strength and warmth. He blinked, then slowly leaned down. Inches now...

John's yell broke their haze.

"Mom, I can't find my pj's!"

Faith jumped.

Roan eased back, his eyes dark and fiery.

It took a few tries to get her voice to work. "Sounds like I'm needed."

Roan nodded and walked to the door. "Good night."

Was he going to say anything about the near kiss? Apparently not, because he opened the door and stepped onto the porch.

She followed him. "Good night," she barely

got out, her chest tight as she watched him jog down the steps, leaving her alone with a million questions racing through her head.

WHAT HAD HE been thinking?

Only that Faith looked lovely in the soft lighting. That he wanted to kiss her in that moment more than he'd wanted anything in a long time. He would have too, if John hadn't chosen the right second to break the spell.

"Stupid," he muttered as he untied the tree from the car and headed indoors.

Thankfully he'd left the heat on in the house before they left earlier. Roan tugged the tree into the living room to find that Kaylie had already put the tree stand on the floor.

"Emmie went right to bed," she informed him.

"Thanks for seeing to her."

She pointed to the box sitting on the coffee table. "This is all the Christmas stuff from Colorado?"

"I think so."

"There's barely anything in there."

"Are you sure?"

She sent him a disgusted look that was so much Catrina.

"Mom had more than one box of decorations. Where'd they go?"

He shrugged out of his jacket. "Honestly, I thought it all got loaded up when we moved."

Kaylie leaned over to pull out the contents. "All that's here is a lame stuffed reindeer, a plastic Santa and a bunch of sparkle garland that looks old."

Could the other boxes have gotten misplaced in the move? It had been a hectic time. Back then, Christmas decorations hadn't been on his list of items that had to make the trip to Georgia.

"We can't hang this on the tree." She'd plucked up the sad-looking garland and was holding it up as if it were evidence.

"I'm sorry, Kaylie. I truly don't know what happened." Roan saw a trip to the store in his future. "We can get new ornaments and lights for the tree after school and work."

His daughter's shoulders slumped. "It's okay. Going through Mom's stuff would have been depressing anyway."

Roan's chest ached at the sight of his dejected daughter. "I'll check with your grandparents to see if the boxes somehow ended up at their house."

"Okay." She picked up her coat and headed toward her bedroom.

"Kaylie, wait."

She swung around.

"I wanted to talk to you about your friends."

As if a switch was flipped, Kaylie's defenses went up.

"What about my friends?"

"You've been spending a lot of time with these girls, and I don't know them."

"I told you, they're in my class at school."

"Okay. I thought I could give their parents a call—"

"Dad!" Horror crossed her face.

"I just want to know more about them."

"And you can't take my word that they're okay?"

"I know that there have been some issues."

Her face went tight. "Every kid has issues."

"But I don't want you mixed up in anything."

"Dad, I can't talk about this."

She turned on her heel and rushed to her room, closing her door loudly behind her.

As he stood there debating what to do, the phone rang. He went to the kitchen to pull the handheld from the cradle.

"Roan Donovan."

"Roan, it's Laurel."

He closed his eyes. He really didn't want to hear from his mother-in-law on the heels of his conversation with Kaylie.

"What can I do for you?"

"I'm calling to set up a time to pick out a tree for the children."

He stemmed his annoyance. "We already picked one up."

Silence.

"Laurel?"

"I thought we agreed to go as a family."

He hadn't agreed. "Sorry. It was a spur-of-the-moment decision."

"Fine. Then when will you trim the tree?"

"I need to go to the store first." He paused, hating to ask. "Did some of our boxes end up at your place?"

"What boxes?"

"The containers with the Christmas tree items."

Censure heightened her tone. "Don't tell me you misplaced them."

"Never mind. I'll search around here again tomorrow."

"Catrina would never have lost her Christmas collection."

There wasn't much he could say to counter that claim, because it was true, but he didn't want to get into it tonight.

"Don't worry about it, Laurel. We'll make do."

"Why don't you let me take the girls to the store. I'm sure we can—"

"I appreciate the offer, but I'll take them."

"When will your work schedule allow it?"

"Now that I have a day shift, I have more time. We'll figure it out."

"You don't have to. Gene and I are more than happy to fill in."

"I know. But I've been absent for too long. I don't need you guys to fill in as much as before. I'll take them."

Laurel's voice went tight. "If you insist."

"I do. I'll have the girls call you with our schedule in a few days."

"Fine," Laurel said, ending the call.

With a shake of his head, Roan made his way down the hallway to the bedrooms. Kaylie's door was shut tight. No light streamed out from underneath. Either she was already in bed or she'd turned off her light so he wouldn't disturb her. Most likely she had her tablet out, reading a book.

He crossed the hall to enter Emmie's room. A cheery night-light cast streaks of light over her face. He knelt beside the bed, brushing her curly hair from her forehead. Emmie stirred, but didn't awaken.

He loved the girls. More than Laurel could ever imagine. Yeah, rhythms had been off when they'd first moved here, but now that he had a regular schedule, he needed to be present more, needed to let the girls know he was there for them. Like tonight. Going to the tree lot with Faith and her kids had felt… Good. And while he did appreciate his in-laws' help, he was going to have to make a stand. Even if the Jessups might not like it.

After running a finger over his daughter's forehead, he rose and went to the living room to place the tree in the stand. The activity immediately made him think of Faith. He'd been so ready to kiss her, and if he didn't miss his guess, she'd been just as interested.

Again he asked himself, what was he thinking? This was no time to get involved with his neighbor. He'd bet Faith would agree. But the idea of his lips on hers…

He shook off the image and turned off the lights. Tonight and all the nights following would be the same as they had for the past two and a half years.

Lonely.

CHAPTER SEVEN

WITH THE CHRISTMAS countdown on, a large volume of shoppers had crowded the big box store. Roan had expected this to be the case, but couldn't persuade the girls otherwise when the search for the Christmas boxes came up empty, and both his daughters were adamant that they get everything they needed today. No way would they let the tree remain bare another night.

First, they visited the toy department so his girls could pick out gifts for the Operation Share program. To his great pleasure, they'd been thrilled to participate. Put real thought into the toys they selected. He couldn't have been more proud.

"Daddy, should we get sparkly lights or ones that stay lit?" Emmie asked, staring at the multiple types stacked on the shelves.

"Which do you like?"

Emmie considered both, then said, "Sparkly."

"Sparkly it is." He estimated how many

strands they'd need, grabbed a handful of boxes and tossed them in the cart.

"What about a topper?" Kaylie asked.

"Why don't you pick it out," Roan suggested. In return, he got a wan smile from his oldest daughter.

The outing hadn't started out as one of the Donovan family's finest. Kaylie was still upset with him after their conversation two nights before. He hoped letting her lead the decoration hunt would make things better between them.

"I kinda like this star," she said, pulling it from the shelf.

Roan remained silent. The star looked similar to the one Catrina had gotten the first year they were married. Right from the beginning, she'd been better at all this Christmas hoopla than him.

"I think your taste rocks, so go for it," he said, giving Kaylie a quick hug. She rolled her eyes, but he could tell she was pleased.

"Daddy, look." Excitement filled Emmie's voice. She was standing before a display of a Victorian village set up at the end of the aisle, her face filled with wonder. "Can we do this at home?"

Roan took in all the houses and stores, tiny people and trees, fake snow, even a miniature train and knew there was no way Emmie was going to let up on her request.

"That's quite a project."

"We could set it up under the tree. Just think how pretty it would be."

For the first time in months, Emmie wasn't trying to guilt him into getting her what she wanted. His daughter was truly mesmerized by the tiny town. Her wide eyes and captivated expression had his heart aching.

"If I say yes, are you going to make sure all the pieces stay in one place?"

Emmie had a tendency to scatter her dollhouse collection all over the house.

"Daddy, it has to stay in one place, otherwise the magic goes away."

"Magic, huh?"

She turned and giggled. "Sure, silly."

Now it was his turn to be captivated.

"How about you pick out a few of the things you like best and we'll make sure to place it under the tree once we finish with the lights and ornaments."

Her eyes went wide. "Really?"

"I think you're old enough to have a project all your own."

Emmie jumped up and down, then hurried over to decide what her village would look like. "She's going to be a mayor someday," Roan muttered under his breath.

Kaylie sidled up beside him. "Do I get to have a project?"

"Sure. What did you have in mind?"

"I saw craft kits to make stockings. Can I give it a try?"

"We do need stockings, so if you think you can get it done before Christmas Eve, go ahead."

Her genuine smile had him grinning.

After a moment she said, "Thanks, Dad."

"For what?"

"Coming through with your promise."

"You didn't think I would?"

She shrugged and offered a weak smile.

Pain lanced through him. He had a lot to make up for to regain his daughter's faith in him.

A raucous holiday tune blared on the store speaker system. Roan rubbed his temples, wishing they were already home and he was on the sofa with his feet up.

While the girls were distracted, Roan roamed down the ornament row. He selected four boxes of shiny glass balls with different designs and several separate pieces—including a reindeer, Santa and other cheery holiday favorites the girls would like.

Kaylie had seemed defeated when they couldn't find their old decorations, and he couldn't blame her. Catrina had always gone the distance to create magical memories for the girls. He suddenly wished he had found the holiday items Catrina had collected so the girls had that connection to their mom. He stared at the ornaments in his hand. Maybe Catrina's over-the-top Christmas traditions weren't so bad after all.

He'd just dumped it all in the cart when he heard a familiar voice.

"We got the gifts for the toy drive. Why do we need to stop in the Christmas department today? We already put our Christmas swag out yesterday."

He turned to find Faith following her mother, who was pushing a shopping cart with Lacey perched in the seat. John gazed about the store with wide eyes.

"In the house. What about outside?" her mother responded.

"Lyle told John he was going to string the lights, but I haven't heard from him."

Roan walked to the main aisle, his gaze tangling with Faith's. He thought her cheeks heated and guessed she was thinking about their near kiss. He knew he was.

"Why, Roan, whatever are you doing here?" Wanda Sue asked in a sweet tone.

Faith shook her head.

"Getting stuff for the tree," he replied. "We've gotten behind."

"Then it's a good thing we happened along." Wanda Sue pushed Faith in his direction. "Clearly the man needs help."

"Roan is more than capable."

Wanda Sue shot her daughter a scowl.

"Thanks, but we're nearly finished."

John spied Emmie and took off in her direction.

"John, wait," Faith said, following after him.

Roan pushed the cart in her direction when suddenly Mrs. M. stopped before him. He hadn't even noticed the older woman's presence.

"Roan. What a surprise."

"That I'm shopping with my children?"

Mrs. M. chuckled. "No, that you have a cart full of memories."

Is that how she saw it? Made sense, he supposed.

"What brings you here?" he asked.

"With so many good things happening in my family this year, I wanted to find specialty ornaments to give to my grandsons. Logan is getting married next year. Reid and Heidi are finally a couple, so I want to find them just the right gift."

"That's…nice."

Mrs. M. patted his arm. "Wait until your daughters grow up. You'll be glad you made the holidays memorable. And sharing the excitement with your neighbors? What fun."

It hadn't started out that way. He'd have been happy to mount a wreath on the door and call it a day, but Kaylie had convinced him otherwise. Plus, he wanted to show Faith he wasn't so rigid. She had many of the same struggles as he did, yet she hadn't thrown in the towel. She accepted what life had thrown at her and adjusted accordingly. Maybe he could do the same for his girls.

Kaylie chose that moment to return to the cart, placing her crafting items inside.

"Just the young lady I needed to see."

Kaylie glanced around her before saying, "Me?"

"You seem like an ornament connoisseur."

His daughter glanced at him, confusion written on her face.

"Mrs. M. is on a mission."

The older woman walked to Kaylie and hooked her arm through the younger girl's. "Care to help me?"

"Sure," Kaylie shrugged and went along with Mrs. M.

"What was that all about?" Faith asked when she headed back to his side.

"Mrs. M. including Kaylie in her ornament hunt."

Faith grinned. "I'm not surprised. When we were kids, Mrs. M. had a big ornament-decorating event at the community center. I guess it was her method of connecting with the kids in town. To spread the joy. I went every year until I got into my teens."

"Do you still have your creations?"

She squinted her eyes. "You know, I have no idea. Maybe Mama still has them tucked away."

"I have to hand it to her, Mrs. M. loves Golden."

"She does. And to her, there's no better time of year. I think she'd keep the town decorated in a Christmas theme year-round if she could get away with it."

"Speaking of decorating," he said, Mrs. M.'s comment in his head. "Why don't you come over to my house after we check out and join in the fun."

She narrowed her eyes in accusation. "You don't want to do this alone."

"The more the merrier."

"You've finally gotten into the spirit?"

"How can I resist with everyone's help?"

Faith sneaked a sidelong glance at her mother. "Sorry about that. She's super motivated this year for some reason. Maybe because of the wedding."

He shrugged. "It happens."

She tilted her head, disbelief on her face. "You're okay with my mother interfering?"

"I wouldn't go that far. Besides, she means well."

"To which I respond, don't underestimate her. Where do you think I get all my Christmas determination from?"

Roan laughed. Faith showing up had brightened his mood. And if she agreed to bring her brood over, the evening would be so much better.

"So, what do you say?"

"John and Emmie will be thrilled."

He wanted to ask if she would be too, but wisely held his tongue.

Once everyone gathered again, Roan said, "Faith and her family are coming over to help us."

"Really?" Emmie said excitedly. "John and Lacey are helping?"

"They are. Let's go pay and head home." He noticed Wanda Sue and Mrs. M. standing to the side, and in an effort to be polite added, "You're welcome to come."

"Thank you for the invitation," Mrs. M. said, "but we're going to get a cup of coffee and catch up. You all go along."

It didn't take more than a few minutes to get through the line and out to the parking lot. Before the two families broke off to walk to their respective vehicles, Faith said, "I have the ingredients ready for chili. How about I make a batch while you all work."

"Sounds great." He paused. "Wait, you're not going to work?"

"Nope. I plan on sitting back and watching you make Christmas merry."

He frowned. "I should never have mentioned that."

"But you did, so now you have to show up."

He rubbed his chin. "You're tough."

She grinned and walked away.

He felt his own smile and to his surprise, found himself humming a carol under his breath. Then a whimsical thought occurred to him. Faith Harper was a Christmas whisperer.

TWO HOURS LATER, the Donovan tree was finally decorated. A fire crackled and snapped in the fireplace. The savory scent of slow-cooking chili filled the air, along with the buttery scent of the popcorn Faith had made for a snack. The lights on the tree winked in and out, creating a merry mood. Right now, John and Emmie were strategizing over how to set up the Victorian village, while Roan entertained Lacey with a puzzle.

Faith had to admit, when Roan had lifted Emmie up to place the star on the top of the tree, she'd found herself more attracted to him than she'd thought possible. He might be as gruff as a bear about all this, but didn't withhold his affection. It meant he put others before himself, and she was impressed.

For the briefest of seconds, she wondered what it would be like to join their families, enjoy the holidays and work together, like they had today. Her attraction to Roan didn't help her musings any. Especially, since they'd all rallied and had a good time in the process.

When Kaylie started the stocking craft, Faith joined her at the table.

"Thanks for letting your kids come over," Kaylie piped up, watching the others. "Dad is really helping."

"Is that a surprise?"

Kaylie nearly rolled her eyes. "Yeah."

Faith laughed. "I did get the impression that your father wasn't into this time of year."

"Mom took care of everything."

They fell into a companionable silence. Faith watched with amazement as Kaylie concentrated on her precise stitching.

"You're awfully good at this. I can manage a glue stick, but that's as far as my crafting abilities go."

"My mom and I always did Christmas crafts together."

"Your dad must be proud of you."

Kaylie shrugged, not the least bit nonchalant. "He doesn't know. My mom taught me how to sew."

"I imagine you miss her. Especially this time of year."

"Yeah. She always listened."

"And your dad doesn't?"

"Not like she did." Kaylie was quiet for a moment, stitching a bit more. "He usually does all the talking."

Not a far stretch, Faith thought. "Sometimes it's more comfortable talking to another girl." Faith leaned in and whispered, "He wouldn't know that."

"He tries, but he doesn't get how hard it is to fit in."

"School troubles?"

"Not with my classes. It's more with the other girls."

"The group you were with the other night?"

Kaylie nodded. "Diandra and I became good friends right away, but lately she's wanted to hang out with a different group."

"And you don't?"

Kaylie lifted a shoulder instead of answering.

"I remember what it was like trying to fit in at school. Unfortunately, I didn't pick the best friends."

Kaylie quickly glanced at her, then away. "These are the popular girls."

"Hmm." She paused for what she hoped was the right amount of time. "Let me just say, I hung with that group in high school. When I should have run in the opposite direction, I chose to follow. Turns out, they really weren't my friends, and when things went wrong—I was on my own."

That caught Kaylie's attention. "What did you do?"

"It's not what I did, it's what I didn't do."

Kaylie frowned.

"Instead of listening to that voice inside my head, I chose to hang out with people I knew were trouble."

"What happened?"

Faith could give the young girl a lengthy list,

but since Kaylie was only eleven, she streamlined the consequences of her wild days.

"I went places I wasn't supposed to. Ended up at the police station." She paused. "My suggestion is that you find true friends, not a group that looks good from the outside."

Kaylie continued stitching, but Faith knew she was taking it all in.

"In retrospect, the thing I regret the most was putting off college. Now I'm taking classes and trying to catch up."

"My mom didn't go to college. She started on the tour when she left high school and then got famous."

"College isn't for everyone."

Kaylie glanced at her. "But if you wanted to go?"

"Then good grades are a must. And getting involved in activities at school looks great on applications." Faith swallowed and said, "The main thing is that you listen to your inner voice. Do what is right, even if it's not what the popular crowd does."

Kaylie nodded, lost in thought.

Hoping she'd made her point, but not wanting to oversell, Faith changed the subject.

"What do you like to do? Any hobbies, besides sewing?"

"Um… I like to dance."

"Fun. Have you taken classes?"

"Yes. My mom signed me up when I was five. Until we moved here, I was always involved at the studio."

"What about here in Golden? There's a dance studio downtown."

"I don't know. Daddy's been busy and my grandmother didn't seem like she wanted me to get involved."

"But you'd like to?"

Kaylie's eyes brimmed with desire. "I'd love it."

Faith dropped her chin into her palm. Stared across the room at Roan. He and Lacey were still on the floor, working on another puzzle. Her blood zinged at the sight of him. They had bonded over single parenthood, and he was concerned about Kaylie's choice of friends. Maybe she could put her two cents in, just this once.

"Would you mind if I mentioned this to your dad?"

Kaylie gasped. "Would you?"

Faith blinked at the surprise and hope in Kaylie's tone. Had no one been a champion for this girl who clearly missed her mother and was having a hard time fitting into this world?

"Sure. I think we've been friends long enough that he'd listen to me."

"That would be awesome."

Faith tried hard not to blow on her fingertips and scratch her shoulder like this mission was no biggie.

Kaylie focused on her task with more enthusiasm than before. If only someone had tried to make a difference in Faith's life when their family had blown apart. In retrospect, Mrs. M. had tried, but Faith hadn't wanted to listen, too busy licking the wounds that came from their dysfunctional family. Mama had been lost in her grief. Grace and Nathan had their own issues to handle. True, Grace had stepped in when necessary, too little too late, but Faith had taken her sister's concern with resentment and refused to listen.

She was correct when she'd told Kaylie she was catching up. Nearly thirty and still not entirely sure who she was or wanted to be. Did that make her pathetic?

"Can I ask you something?"

Lost in thought, Faith quickly focused again. "Sure."

"Do you like my dad?"

Oh, dear. "Like? Sure, he's a nice guy."

"No, I mean, *like*, like."

If only Kaylie knew Faith was wrestling

with that very question. Truth be told, *like* was too tame a word to cover her feelings for Roan, and the idea scared her.

"Would you go on a date with him if he asked?" Kaylie pressed.

"I don't know."

"He talks to you more than any other person."

"We have things in common."

"Things that could make him your boyfriend?"

How on earth had she fallen into this conversation? Oh, yeah. She'd wanted to be that voice of wisdom. How that had turned on her.

"I don't think my mom would mind," Kaylie said, as if Faith had asked permission.

"How about we put this topic on the shelf for now and enjoy the holidays."

Kaylie grinned. "Daddy always does that. Changes the subject when he doesn't want to talk."

Smart man.

"I reserve the right to pick this conversation up at a later date," she said, trying to sound official.

Kaylie giggled.

Deciding she needed to escape this intelligent girl's grasp on the state of events, Faith went into the kitchen to check on the chili.

She lifted the lid and stirred the tangy mixture. Moments later, Roan appeared.

"How's dinner coming along?"

"Great. The kids?"

"Kaylie took over puzzle duty. She sent me in here."

Faith nearly choked.

"What's wrong?"

"Are you sure your daughter is only eleven?"

He bristled with protectiveness. "What did she say?"

"Nothing important." Not that crushing on Roan wasn't important, but Faith would figure that out on her own.

"Did you know Kaylie misses dance?"

He frowned. "She never mentioned it."

"I don't think she wanted to bother you."

"Huh." He scratched his chin. "I'm surprised Laurel didn't get her signed up."

"I don't think that was an option."

He looked surprised. "Why not?"

"Kaylie seemed to think her grandmother didn't want her to take classes."

Roan's eyes grew dark.

"But the good thing is, you can get her enrolled." She pulled her phone from her pocket and searched for the downtown studio. "Here we go. Divine Dance. Just off Main. I'll text you the number."

"Thanks." He leaned against the counter. "I should have remembered how much she thrived in dance class."

Faith put her phone away. "Well, now you know."

"Thanks. I really should…"

Why had he paused? "Should?"

"Thank you properly."

The heat in his eyes as he focused directly on her lips made Faith's pulse begin to pound. He leaned in, drawing ever closer…

The doorbell rang and seconds later Emmie shouted, "Grandma and Grandpa."

"Oh, no," Roan muttered.

"Problem?"

"I told Laurel I'd let her know when we were trimming the tree." He met her gaze with a look of dread. "She's not going to be happy."

Taking a breath, Roan walked into the living room, Faith following. When she saw Mrs. Jessup's face, she read trouble.

"What's all this, Roan? We were going to decorate. As a family."

"Sorry, Laurel. We ran into Faith and her kids at the store and invited them over."

Mrs. Jessup acknowledged Faith, displeasure written on her face.

"Hi, Mrs. Jessup."

Emmie had pulled her grandfather into the thick of the village setup, but Mrs. Jessup held her ground. Feeling uncomfortable, like she'd intentionally gone where she wasn't invited—an old feeling she hated—Faith said, "Roan, why don't I round up the kids so you can visit."

"You don't have to go."

Mrs. Jessup's cheeks turned red.

Yep. Unwanted.

"We had a great time, but we should head home." She crossed the living room to the foyer to collect the children's outerwear. "John. Lacey. Time to go."

"Aw, Mom," John whined. "Can't we stay longer?"

"Emmie needs to show her grandparents all her new decorations."

John dragged his feet, but did as asked. Lacey ambled over and held her arms out so Faith could tug on the sleeves of her jacket. As quickly as possible, she had the kids out the door. They'd just started to cross the lawn when Roan came dashing outside.

"Faith, what about dinner?"

She tried to keep her voice steady. "You enjoy it with your family."

"But what about you?"

"We'll cook hot dogs over the fire. How does that sound, John?"

Her son perked up. "With french fries?"

"Whatever you want." She reluctantly met Roan's gaze. Frustration, mixed with disappointment, shone there. "We'll be fine."

With that, she hustled the kids along, afraid Roan might see the doubt and resignation on her face. She'd looked forward to having dinner with the Donovans, but they weren't her family. She'd do well to remember that.

CHAPTER EIGHT

TYING HER BATHROBE the next morning, Faith yawned as she shuffled into the kitchen and switched on the coffee maker. Surprisingly, they'd all slept in. She stared out the window, the bright sunlight lifting her dreary mood. She'd tried not to dwell on the Jessups' arrival last night, deciding it had been a good thing they'd showed up. She and Roan might have this off-the-charts chemistry igniting between them, but she sensed there were probably too many roadblocks for them to have any kind of a future.

She'd tossed and turned the entire night, finally getting up at 1:00 a.m. for a glass of water, when she had a mini epiphany. Yes, she had a past she wasn't proud of. But she'd worked hard to make changes.

The day she'd made the decision to go back to college had cemented her future. Going to the local campus to sign up in the business program she'd researched online had taken every ounce of confidence in her. She'd been a nervous wreck, but once she'd eased into the classes and started to thrive, there was no going back.

No one could take her accomplishments away from her. In fact, she'd been her own harshest critic. But the days of wallowing in her mistakes were over, as was letting other people's opinions determine her self-worth. If she didn't believe, no one else would.

As she pulled a mug from the cabinet, a thumping at the front porch caught her attention. Curious, she crossed the living room to peer out the window. Roan stood in her front yard, eyeing her house.

"What on earth?"

Pulling her bathrobe tighter over her flannel pj's, she marched to the foyer and yanked open the front door.

As he stood in the morning light, his black hair gleamed and his sparkling eyes were so blue it took her breath away. He'd dressed in worn jeans and boots, a brown leather jacket over a cable-knit sweater. She glanced down at her attire and grimaced. Too late to do much about the state of her clothing.

"Roan, what are you doing?"

"You need outside lights on your house. I got mine up last night." He furrowed his brow. "Wasn't this on your list?"

"Yes, but how... Where did you get all these lights?"

"You have a secret Santa."

"Come again?"

"Found these on my doorstep this morning with a note to return the favor and string your lights."

Totally confused, she asked, "What favor?"

"I'm assuming you helping us decorate our tree yesterday."

"But you were going to decorate even if you hadn't asked us over."

"Someone thinks differently."

She made her way down the steps. The nippy air bit at her skin, but her curiosity kept the cold at bay. A large inflatable snow globe rested on the ground, waiting to have air pumped inside. Next to it, evergreen garland circled in a tight coil.

"Who left this?"

Roan shook out a string of lights. "I think you're missing the point of *secret*." He winked, then sauntered to a ladder she'd just noticed beside a window.

"You're doing this now?"

"I'm off today."

"Let me get dressed and then I'll come out and help."

Just then the door burst open and John ran out in his feet pajamas.

"Mama, we're having lights?"

"Looks like it, buddy."

"Did Daddy send them?"

"Good question."

As usual, Lyle had made promises, but he hadn't reached out since the tree lighting. It made Faith so angry that the feelings of his children meant so little to him. That had been his MO from the start. She shouldn't expect anything different. But then, who was she to talk? Look how long it had taken her to finally walk away from a man who put his own desires first. Being a mom had taught her she needed to put her children's needs first, and she wouldn't have it any other way.

She wondered if Lyle's new girlfriend had a clue about what her future looked like.

"I can help," John yelled, running straight for the ladder.

Faith caught him. "First we get dressed. And wake your sister."

"She's up," John informed her, sidetracked by the ladder.

Faith ran inside to find Lacey safely watching television. She placed a hand over her thudding heart. Hustling both children upstairs, she supervised John first, then let him join Roan. After dressing herself and Lacey, she went to the kitchen and filled two mugs with hot coffee, then ventured outside.

Roan had just climbed down the ladder. She handed him the mug.

"Thanks."

"It's the least I can do."

"For my being neighborly?" His lips quirked. "Besides, I still owe you for a dinner you made but didn't get to eat."

Yeah, she didn't want a rehash of last night.

"Thank you for doing this." She set her mug on the porch railing. "What can I do to help?"

"Probably just point out where the lights are sagging. John and I have it from there."

"I'm helping," John yelled, getting himself tangled up in a strand.

Faith scanned the yard. "Where are the girls?"

"They went home with Gene and Laurel last night."

She nodded.

"Sorry about how their stopping by turned our plans upside down."

"No need to apologize."

"I feel like I need to. You left so fast, I was worried."

Ah, the almost kiss. Was he thinking about it too?

She waved off his concern as if imagining what his lips would have felt like on hers hadn't kept her awake all night. "We had fun roasting hot dogs."

"If it's any consolation, your chili was delicious."

Hoping her grin hid her disappointment, she said, "I do make a mean chili."

He chuckled. Was that admiration in his eyes? Something more? She covered a shiver.

"I'm sorry you didn't stay."

"Maybe another time." She rubbed her hands together. "Now what?"

"We finish outlining the house." Roan handed her a bag of clothespins. "You can hand me a pin, then I'll connect the strand to the roof edge."

Roan untangled the lights around John before helping the little boy lay them on the ground in a straight row. Then he took the end and climbed the ladder while Faith waited below. He'd removed his jacket now that the sun had warmed the air, his back muscles flexing under the sweater with each movement. His tanned skin spoke to his enjoying the outdoors. Good grief, the man was more handsome every time she looked at him.

"Faith?"

She snapped out of her woolgathering to climb up a few steps to hand him a pin. Their fingers brushed, and a jolt of awareness shot up her arm. He must have felt it too, because he sent her a slow, devastating smile. If she wasn't careful, the man would steal her heart.

She stepped back, pretending Roan hadn't just rocked her world.

"Do you think we have enough lights?" John asked, oblivious to her reaction to their neighbor.

"I think so, buddy," Roan said, climbing down to retrieve another strand.

John beamed. Either he'd forgotten Lyle had promised to hang lights—unlikely— or he was going with the flow like he normally did. She couldn't have asked for a more sweet-natured kid.

Twenty minutes later, they stood back to admire their hard work.

"Something is missing." Faith tapped her chin. "Oh, the wreath I bought the other day."

She hurried to the back porch, where she'd stored the wreath outside to keep it fresh and forgotten about it. Then she detoured to the garage for a hammer and nail. When she returned, she handed the tool to Roan.

"Double duty?" he asked.

She shrugged. "I was once told, very sternly, that I had no place working with tools."

"That must be a story." He chuckled, taking the hammer. He quickly pounded the nail into the door and hung the wreath. Faith couldn't contain her grin. "Perfect."

"I agree."

She sent him a sidelong glance, surprised by the heated expression that flashed when his eyes met hers, then quickly disappeared. What had she missed? She cocked her head.

"It's a perfect day for working outdoors," he said.

Her stomach pitched. Had she been expecting a compliment? For him to say she was perfect? Her imagination was running away with her again.

"I don't see anything sparkly," John piped up as he stared at the house.

"We need to turn the lights on after the sun sets," Faith explained. "To get the full effect."

Lacey jumped up and down. "See the lights."

Faith swooped her up and kissed her cheek. "After dinner."

The four of them stood facing the house, John in between them. After a few moments, he wrapped his little arms around her and Roan's legs.

"John…"

"It's okay," Roan said.

They stared at each other over John's head. Suddenly there was so much to say. How she liked having Roan around. How his strength brought comfort. How he looked out for her and her family—something she wasn't used to but realized she profoundly wanted. How, when he stared at her this way, his eyes dark with secrets, with just enough flame to let her know he recognized her as a woman, she wanted to throw caution to the wind and lean over to brush her lips against his.

"Emmie's going to love this," John said, fracturing the magic swirling between them. Roan blinked and turned away.

Lacey cuddled closer against Faith.

"I have an idea," she said, turning to Roan. As much as she'd wanted the moment to last, it couldn't. But there were other methods to keep the good feelings going. "Why don't we have a special preview tonight? We flip the lights on at both houses after it gets dark."

"I like it. Since the girls were gone last night, I was going to surprise them anyway."

"Then it's settled," Faith said. "Around seven to make sure the sun is completely down?"

"That'll give me time to pick up the girls and—"

Roan's phone rang. He tugged it from his back pocket, his face going dark when he glanced at the screen.

"Golden PD," he told Faith as he swiped the screen to answer.

"Donovan."

His face paled and his troubled gaze met hers. "I'll be right there."

Dread filled her. "Roan?"

"That was Brady. Kaylie is at the police station."

ROAN STORMED INTO Golden PD, his eyes searching for his daughter. He found her in a chair next to Brady's desk, sipping from a paper cup. Her eyes went wide when she saw him. She set the cup aside and stood.

He strode to her, enveloping her in his arms. "Are you okay?"

"I'm not hurt. Well, except you're squeezing me too hard."

Roan let go. Barely.

He glanced at Brady, who pointed to the interrogation room located down the hallway from the duty station. As the three headed in that direction, Brady said, "It's not what you think."

"I have no idea what to think."

Brady nodded.

Once in the room, Brady closed the door behind them, while Roan and Kaylie each took a seat at the table.

"Actually, Kaylie came in on her own. Before the trouble started."

Roan glanced at his daughter, who was biting her thumbnail.

"She asked if she could sit here for a while. She was worried her friends were getting into mischief. Turns out she was right. Mr. Kellogg caught two girls leaving the store with pockets full of candy and makeup."

He sat back, speechless.

"I knew what they were planning," Kaylie offered, "so I left."

"Did they know you were coming here?" he asked, slipping into cop mode.

"No," she rushed to say, horror in her voice. "I didn't want them to think I told on them."

Roan was confused. "So you left and walked here?"

"I wasn't sure what to do. Then Brady drove by. I waved at him and he stopped to give me a ride. He gave me hot chocolate and called you."

"The call came in a few minutes later," Brady said.

"Am I in trouble?" Kaylie asked.

"No, honey. You did the right thing."

Brady hooked his thumb toward the door. "Kaylie, why don't you finish up that hot chocolate before it gets cold."

Kaylie hopped up, but before she left, turned and said, "Sorry, Dad."

"For what? You did the right thing."

She sent him a smile that did strange things to his composure.

Once she was gone, Roan said, "There's more?"

Brady crossed his arms over his chest. "It was only a matter of time. We knew some girls were swiping merchandise from local stores."

The shoplifting incidents had been on their radar since the beginning of the month.

"Evan caught the call," Brady continued. "When he got to the scene, the girls were trying to weasel their way out of the accusation, but Mr. Kellogg witnessed the entire exchange. Evan called their folks."

"So what's the problem?"

"They all blamed Kaylie. Said she took the first handful of candy, then ran away."

Roan tried not to see red.

"I know the truth, but there will probably be problems for Kaylie at school."

Roan thought it through. "Was Diandra with them?"

"Yes, but according to Evan she was in another part of the store when the others stuffed their pockets." He shook his head. "Mr. Kellogg installed cameras for instances just like this."

At least Kaylie's good friend wasn't directly involved.

"Thanks, Brady. I'll handle it from here."

"So," Brady asked, humor in his tone. "Enjoying small-town life yet?"

Roan wasn't sure how to interpret Brady's mysterious smile.

"Heard you got a little shopping in."

"For the love of—"

"Hey. We all have to fall sometime."

"Meaning?"

"You've got a thing for your neighbor. Don't deny it."

He couldn't if he tried.

"So sit back and enjoy."

If only it was that easy.

"I'll take that under advisement." He rose. "At least my daughter didn't fall victim to peer pressure."

Brady responded with a hearty pat on the back.

Roan returned to the office area and pointed

his chin at the door. Kaylie tossed her cup in the trash, waved to the people Roan worked with and followed him outside.

"Good job," Roan said.

She shrugged.

He had a million questions but went with the obvious. "What made you leave your friends?"

"Faith told me a little about when she was a kid. Said I should make good choices." She sent her dad a *duh* expression. "Even I know shoplifting is not a good idea."

Roan laughed.

They walked to the parking lot.

"How did you even end up with those girls? I told your grandparents that I'd be picking you and Emmie up sometime this morning."

Kaylie's face turned sheepish. "Diandra knew I was staying there. She and the other girls came over to see if I could go downtown with them, and Grandma said yes."

Roan ground his teeth.

She peered up at him as he opened the passenger door of the sedan for her to climb in. "Am I in trouble for leaving their house?"

"No." But Roan would have words with his in-laws later. "But I do have an idea."

"What?"

"We aren't far from the dance studio. What

do you say we drop in and check out the class schedules?"

Her face lit up. "Really?"

"Yes. It's time you get involved in that again."

"But… Why now?"

She'd asked for honesty, so he said, "That day you asked me to make Christmas merry for Emmie made me realize that since we moved here, you haven't gotten back to the things you enjoy."

"It's okay, Dad. I knew you were sad and didn't want to bother you."

How had he not seen what his daughter was going through? It was one thing to stick his head in the sand, but to not be aware of what Kaylie was missing?

He placed his hands on her shoulders and leaned down to peer directly into her eyes. "Kaylie, it's my job to make things good for you, not the other way around."

She pressed her lips together before saying, "I have missed dance, but I was afraid it might remind you of Mom."

Roan leaned back. "Mom did a lot for you girls, but now it's my turn. If you need something or just want to talk, you should come to me."

"Are you sure?"

Her uncertainty undid him.

"Positive." He paused for a moment and asked, "I'm not the big, bad bear, am I?"

"Sometimes." She grinned as she patted his chest. "But you're getting better."

"Then let's get over to the studio."

Kaylie threw her arms around him. "You're the best!"

Roan could argue that point, but he wasn't willing to burst this bubble of happiness right now. He'd let the girls down since Catrina died. He needed to do better for both of them.

Once they were in the car, worry crossed Kaylie's face. "Are you sure it's okay? Grandma didn't want me to take classes."

"She didn't?"

"I think it made her remember how Mom always gave her updates about my dance classes and recitals."

"What did Grandma say when you mentioned it?"

"That I could do it in the future." Kaylie bit her lip, then said, "She told me not to bother you about dance stuff."

Roan ran a hand over the back of his neck. Make that two things to talk to the Jessups about.

When they arrived at Divine Dance Studio, a class was just finishing. He and Kaylie were able to speak to the owner, Candy, and before long, signed up and had a schedule in hand. It would be tough juggling the girls' activities, but he vowed to make this work.

Far too soon they pulled up in the Jessups' driveway. He dreaded the confrontation, but it had to be done. He'd never shied away from tough situations before, and he wouldn't now, especially regarding his daughters.

Roan opened the door to the house for Kaylie, mentally preparing himself for the upcoming conversation. "Go get your sister's and your things."

Kaylie nodded and headed toward the other end of the house as Laurel came out of the kitchen.

Surprise crossed her face. "Roan. What are you doing here?"

"I told you I'd pick up the girls today."

She wiped her hands on a dish towel. "It wasn't necessary. Emmie is staying."

Roan quickly got a handle on his frustration and leveled his voice. "No. She's coming home with me."

"But it's been decided."

"Not by me."

Laurel frowned. "Well, Kaylie won't be home for a while, so you'll have to come back for her anyway."

"In fact, I brought Kaylie with me. She's getting their stuff together right now."

Guilt flashed in the older woman's eyes. "Then you know she went out for a little while. A girl that age should be socializing."

"Even when I specifically asked that she stay here?"

Laurel waved off her dismissal of his request with her hand, then turned on her heel to head into the kitchen. "She only wanted to visit with her friends."

Roan followed. "Even if those friends got into trouble?"

Laurel spun around. "Kaylie?"

"No. Not Kaylie."

"Thank goodness." Laurel blew out a breath.

"She used surprisingly good wisdom for an eleven-year-old, but she should never have been in that situation to begin with. If you'd listened to me, she wouldn't have been there."

Laurel's eyes went wide. "Are you blaming me?"

"I had a reason for asking you to keep her home. You went against my wishes."

"I think I know how to raise a girl," Laurel said, voice dripping with disdain. And also truth. This all went back to Catrina.

"Look, I appreciate all you and Gene have

done for me and the girls. When we came to Golden, I certainly needed—"

"Of course we would help," she said, her voice indignant. "They are our grandchildren."

"But now we're on a pretty good schedule. They're settling in at home."

"Meaning?"

"Perhaps they should stay here less frequently. Well, Emmie anyway."

"She needs us more than Kaylie does."

Roan took a deep breath and changed tack. "You knew Kaylie wanted to get back into dance."

Laurel looked away. Suddenly the landscape in the backyard grew more interesting than him. "She might have mentioned it."

"She told me she asked and you shot her down. You never said a word to me."

Laurel swung around. "For her own good, Roan. She can't get caught up in an activity to the exclusion of all else."

Like Catrina and snowboarding.

"I understand. I often want to control Kaylie's and Emmie's environments to keep them safe, but we both know that doesn't work. Kaylie wants to get back into dance, and I agree it's a good idea."

"You think you know what they want, but

you don't, Roan. You've been missing in their lives."

"Only since we came to Golden. But in Colorado, I was involved enough to know what they were doing." He paused. Accepted the consequences of where he was about to go. "I'm not entirely sure what Catrina told you."

"Enough to know that if you'd loved her more, she wouldn't have died."

And there it was.

"You also know as well as I do that Catrina did what she wanted, no matter that you or I might disagree."

A sheen of tears filled Laurel's eyes.

"And I'm sorry we'd hit a rough patch, but that doesn't mean I'm going to fall down on the job with my girls."

"Even if you've been hanging around Faith Harper? She's bad news, you know."

Surprise caught him off guard. Was some of Laurel's anger toward him because of Faith?

"She's my neighbor. John is in Emmie's class at school."

"That doesn't mean you have to spend time with her." Laurel's face slowly reddened. "I saw you two cozied up in the kitchen when we came over to decorate the tree."

"First of all, she made dinner. And secondly, my friendship with Faith is none of your business."

"It is if it affects my grandchildren. I won't stand for it."

"Actually, it was because of Faith that Kaylie stayed out of trouble." He searched her face, hoping he was making his point clear. "And really, they're my children. So, it's my decision."

It was clear she was about to blast him again when voices came from behind him.

"Daddy," Emmie said, flinging herself at him.

He caught her and pulled her close. "Say goodbye to Grandma so we can hit the road."

Emmie ran to her grandmother for a hug. "Bye. Thank you for buying me the new doll clothes."

"You're welcome, sweetie," Laurel said, still giving Roan the stink eye.

"Thanks, Grandma," Kaylie said, already moving to the front door.

"Let's go," he said, then met Laurel's gaze. "I'll be in touch about Christmas."

She opened her mouth, then thought better of whatever she was going to say and simply nodded. Roan assumed the wheels were turning in her head and she'd find another route to get the girls on her side.

On the drive home, Emmie chatted while Kaylie stared out the window, perhaps finally realizing what might come from her decision to walk away from trouble. He hoped she'd be okay, but he'd be there for her, no matter the fallout with her friends.

As for his lovely neighbor, he owed her. He didn't care what his mother-in-law, or the town, for that matter, thought about her. Faith loved her kids and was spending every hour to make a better life for them. Everyone had a past, and she was rising above hers. The fact that he admired her for working toward a better future was part of the attraction.

Only part.

His mind flashed back to the near kiss the night before. How badly he'd wanted to taste her lips, but timing had prevented him from that sweet reality. Things might be a little complicated for all of them, but he found himself wondering if the opportunity would arise again. If it did, no way was he missing out.

CHAPTER NINE

A FEW HOURS LATER, after they'd eaten dinner and the sun had set, Roan stood in front of his brightly lit house with the children. Woodsmoke tinted the air. The clouds obscuring the moon made the night inky dark, the lights shining brightly as a counterpoint.

Kaylie held Lacey as the little girl jabbered nonsensically. Emmie and John, totally enraptured by the colored lights hanging from the roof, were unusually speechless. It wasn't as cold as the previous nights, even though the temperature had dipped. There was a slight breeze—not enough to have a body quaking in response, but enough to make one thankful for gloves.

"You did good, Daddy," Emmie finally said as she gazed at the lights outlining their house.

"Thanks."

"What about John's house?" She pointed. "It's dark."

"Not for long."

He pulled out his phone and texted Faith. From inside her house, she flipped the switch and the house lit up.

John jumped up and down. "Look. My house too."

Faith came running outside, her eyes bright as she joined them at the border between houses.

"Good job, Mr. Donovan," she said, holding out her hand for a fist bump.

He brushed his knuckles against hers. "All in a day's work, Miss Harper."

They grinned at each other, his heart thudding a little harder than normal, and soon the kids were racing around them.

"If there was snow, this night would be perfect," she said on a sigh.

"You're right."

When the kids were out of hearing range, she said, "I didn't get a chance to talk to you since you took off earlier."

"Sorry. It's been a busy day."

He explained what had happened at the police station, then told her about taking Kaylie to check out the dance studio, picking up Emmie and his conversation with Laurel.

Her eyes were wide. "Wow. You weren't kidding."

"Thankfully, events with Kaylie turned

out okay." He paused. Weighed his words. "I understand I have you to thank for the outcome."

Surprise crossed her features. "Me?"

"Your talk with Kaylie made an impression."

"Really?"

"It couldn't have been easy, but thank you for whatever you said to make her think twice about throwing in with those girls."

Faith blinked. "I've never been a mentor before."

"There's a first time for everything."

Her puzzled countenance warmed him. She seemed stunned, yet pleased. With the lights flashing behind her as she considered the impact of his words, she was beyond beautiful.

"Hey, you okay?" he asked when she remained silent.

"It's just sinking in that I did something right."

He hated the doubt in her voice. "C'mon, don't be so hard on yourself. You have good advice to offer."

"Sure, because my past was a mess," she said with a wry grimace.

He chuckled. "Experience is the best teacher."

"Please. I'd rather forget all that, but you're

right, I have been making better choices for a while now." A slow smile blossomed. "It feels good."

His pulse raced as he moved closer. He snagged Faith's gaze. They stared at each other for a long moment before Emmie ran up to him. "Daddy, can we walk down the street and look at the other houses?"

He shook off the pleasant web Faith had ensnared him in. "Sounds like fun."

Emmie cheered and started to run.

"Wait," Roan called out.

Emmie stopped and turned. "Why?"

Apparently his daughter was still in the do-whatever-you-like phase. "We need the others to catch up."

Before long, the children were walking in front of them, enjoying the festively decorated houses, Emmie giving a running commentary. Faith was close enough that occasionally their arms brushed. Would it be too much to throw his arm over her shoulders? No, too soon, if that would ever even be an option.

"Your daughter certainly has no problem holding back," Faith commented.

He loved the humor in her voice, the fond way she regarded his daughters. "She does have an opinion about everything."

"It's sweet. John hangs on her every word."

He knew the feeling.

Faith smiled. "When I think about it, it must have taken Kaylie a lot to open up to you. I'm sure she doesn't want to disappoint you."

"Yeah. She's…"

"Stubborn?"

He chuckled.

"Like her father?" Faith finished her thought.

"Guilty. I've been told it's a family trait."

Faith tilted her head. "Who told you that?"

"My brother. A long time ago."

She stopped walking. "You have a brother?"

He paused with her. How to answer? He didn't generally talk about his family. No, strike that, he didn't talk about them at all. But he'd opened the door by mentioning Kerry.

"Yes, I have a younger brother. He lives up north."

"Well, that's helpful," she said, knocking her shoulder into his as they resumed their stroll.

Now that he'd started, he wasn't inclined to stop. Something about Faith, perhaps her sunny outlook despite what life had thrown at her, unlocked him. She brought down his walls and made him wonder what he was defending, and what he lost by keeping others out.

"It's been a long time since I've seen him."

She chuckled. "I can't imagine not seeing my family for more than a few days. We've always been in each other's way, like it or not."

His voice grew thick as memories bombarded him. "Not everyone has the perfect family."

Faith snorted. "The Harpers are far from perfect." She sent him a sideling glance. "I told you my daddy was in prison."

"I've heard." Small-town gossip at its worst.

"In my experience, the idea of a perfect family is unrealistic. People are messy. But as long as we love each other, we can overlook a lot."

Roan hadn't thought about that much until he'd had his own family. Sure, he and Catrina had grown apart at the end, but in the beginning, they'd been happy. If she hadn't died, would they have made their way back to each other? The thought haunted him. So he focused on his daughters, his job and the people of Golden. Plus Faith. He couldn't leave out Faith.

"Since I've met you," he said, "I don't see who you are because of your past. I see a strong woman who I really like."

Her mouth dropped open. "Oh."

"Is that all you're going to say?"

"Oh, my."

He pondered the strange ache in his chest. His words had stunned her. Had no one ever told her how amazing she was? Complimented her on being a great mom? Instead of asking, he relished the small grin on her lips. "That's better."

They kept walking in a comfortable silence, enjoying the night while watching the kids have a good time.

"So anyway," she went on. "Your family?"

"Let's just say there wasn't any love there. My father never held back with his brand of discipline, even when it hurt."

He clamped his mouth shut. He'd said too much already.

Faith placed her gloved hand on his thick jacket sleeve. Despite the layers of fabric, the touch made him aware of her nearness, as if she'd touched his skin.

"I didn't mean to pry."

"And I didn't mean to reveal as much as I did."

She shifted away, taking her warmth and floral scent with her.

"So, going forward with Kaylie?" she asked.

He sought out his daughter, pleased to see the smile on her face. He also appreciated Faith picking up that he preferred to switch topics.

"When we moved here, I thought giving her space was best for her. Seems what she really needed was for her dad to listen. So I did."

"And?"

"Signed her up for dance class while we were at the studio."

Faith's face lit up. "You took my advice."

"Yeah, I get things right once in a while." He glimpsed his daughter dancing down the street. "Emmie, on the other hand, needs a constant eye on her."

"I have to agree with you on that count."

"I'll do everything in my power to keep them safe," he vowed to himself and to the woman who was becoming much more important than he'd ever expected.

Before long, the temperature had dropped lower, turning the air frosty. Their breath misted as they spoke, and he couldn't help but stare at Faith's lips. His gaze moved to her eyes, and he didn't miss the longing there. Did she want him to kiss her as much as he wanted to kiss her right now? He leaned forward, measuring her reaction. She swayed.

He took his hands from his pockets, ready to pull her in.

Emmie's laugh broke the spell. Faith jumped back, lowering her gaze.

Frustrated, Roan stuffed his hands back in his jacket pockets. "I guess we should call it a night," he suggested.

They corralled the kids and headed back. Kaylie took Emmie by the hand to bring her into the house while Roan walked Faith and her children home. Once her kids were inside, Faith hovered by the door.

"Thanks for tonight. It was fun."

"Spending time with you is always fun," he said, voice husky.

Her eyes went wide and she leaned toward him. Taking a chance, he bent his head. She moved closer, and before long, his lips were against hers. When she didn't pull back, he circled his arms around her waist and pulled her close. Her hands landed on his chest while the kiss increased in intensity. Disconnected from the world, he was lost in the touch, the taste and presence of this amazing woman.

Lacey called for her mother, startling Faith. Roan reluctantly let go and stepped back.

She tucked a strand of hair behind her ear. Almost shyly, Faith said, "Thanks."

"For the kiss or the night?"

He swore she blushed under the porch lighting.

"Both."

He nodded, then backed down the stairs. When she closed the door behind her, he made his way home.

Crossing the yard, he jammed his hands in his jacket pockets again. Wind swooped through the trees, sending a chill over his neck. He shrugged into the collar to fight off the nip in the air.

On second thought, maybe the shivers came from the kiss he'd shared with Faith, not the elements.

FAITH STARED OUT the back window Sunday morning, watching the sun sparkle on the frosted dew sprinkling the grass. The coffee she sipped, hot and strong, gave her a much-needed kick.

Roan kissed me.

She still couldn't believe it. Had it been a dream? She groaned at her flight of fancy. She'd wanted him to take that initial step, but honestly didn't know who'd made the first move. It was like they'd inched closer at the same time, both on the same mission. She'd wanted to know what his lips would feel like against hers, and now that she knew, boy, she wanted him to kiss her again.

Stop getting ahead of yourself.

"Good advice," she muttered to the empty room.

Yes, the kiss had been… More than she'd ever expected. Old dreams she'd put aside after her divorce had resurfaced because of it. She didn't want to hope—she was living proof that so many things could go wrong—but how could she not? She had to keep reminding herself, it was one kiss. Maybe never to be repeated. Not enough to build a future on.

Her hopes came more from the fact that he'd opened up to her. Talked about his family, even if only a tiny bit. There had to be something below the surface if he trusted her with his secrets, right? Or had she worn him down?

"Stop." She put down her mug and rubbed her pounding temples. Not enough sleep and too many circular thoughts were giving her a headache.

Little voices came from the living room and Faith realized the kids were awake. On autopilot, she gathered bowls, cereal from the pantry and milk from the refrigerator. As the kids shuffled in, she poured them each a bowl.

"Weren't the lights awesome?" John gushed as she set Lacey on a booster chair.

"They were."

"Mr. Roan did a good job."

"He's very handy."

John munched for a moment, then said, "I like him."

So did Faith. Too much.

"Can we go to the park?" he asked, already moving on to a new topic.

"Sure. We'll change out of our pajamas and stop by Grammie's house to pick her up. We need to talk about Aunt Grace's wedding."

"Yay," Lacey said, managing to knock her spoon out of her hand, covering the table in milk.

Faith grabbed a dish towel just as the sound of a souped-up engine came from the driveway, announcing Lyle's arrival well before he rang the doorbell. She glanced at the stovetop clock. What was her ex doing here at nine o'clock on Sunday morning?

"Stay here," she ordered, then wiped her hands on a dry towel and hurried to the door. Unfortunately, John also heard the truck and followed her.

"Daddy's here. Daddy's here."

Blowing out a breath, she went back to take Lacey from her seat, and by the time she got to the foyer, made sure to temper her annoyance in front of John. She unlocked the door and it swung open just as she heard a tiny bark.

Oh, no.

The door fully open now, Lyle stood on the other side with a big smile on his face, holding in his arms the most adorable Golden retriever puppy, a red bow around its neck. John scooted past her and stared up at the dog, his mouth open wide with surprise and wonder.

"Merry Christmas," Lyle announced without looking directly at her.

She bit the inside of her cheek. They'd had many discussions about the timing of getting the kids a dog. Faith wanted a pet, eventually, but not in the midst of busy holiday schedules, the wedding and trying to keep the kids calm until Santa's visit. With everything on her plate, adding another living creature to her list of responsibilities was too much. How would she carve out time to train a puppy?

Lacey tugged on her pajama leg. Faith bent down to pick her up. When her daughter spied the puppy, she beamed. Love at first sight, along with John, who tentatively reached out to touch the puppy's fur.

It became crystal clear that Faith was not going to win this battle.

"Surprise," Lyle said, stepping into the foyer and setting the puppy down, where it immediately piddled on the floor.

Faith set Lacey down, sending a stern glance at her ex. "Keep them from stepping in that mess while I get paper towels."

After the initial excitement and taking care of the accident, the children lured the puppy into the living room, leaving her alone with Lyle.

"I have all kinds of supplies in the truck, including training pads. Let me run out and get them."

"You do that," Faith muttered. She tossed the soiled towels in the garbage, washed her hands and grabbed her mug for a quick swig, grimacing at the cool coffee. She dumped it in the sink, then peered into the living room. The puppy was running around sniffing surfaces, her delighted children in tow. John noticed her and stared up at her, joy reflected in his eyes.

"Mama, I can't believe my Christmas dream came true." He looked at the dancing puppy. "A dog. We actually have a dog!"

No way could she send the puppy home

with their father, otherwise she'd be getting coal in her stocking on Christmas morning.

She heard the door hit the wall as Lyle returned, balancing two overflowing bags to set on the kitchen table. More stuff for her to figure out where to store.

He held up a hand. "I know what you're going to say. We talked about a pet, but this opportunity kinda fell in my lap and I couldn't resist."

"Without asking me? Or at the very least, giving me a heads-up?"

"Look, you knew this was going to happen at some point. The kids wanted a puppy, and I gave them what they wanted."

Exasperated, she threw up her hands. "Which is exactly the problem. Just because they want something, especially a pet, doesn't mean you just give it to them."

"I'm not here to argue. I wanted to deliver this early Christmas present before I go away for the holidays. This will be my last chance to see the kids before I go."

Faith pressed her lips together to keep from blasting him. But honestly, why would it matter? The man always did what he wanted.

Lyle glanced over his shoulder, then back to her. "Did you tell John yet?"

"No, Lyle. I did not tell John your news."

"When are you going to do it?"

She placed fisted hands on her hips. "Since you put this on me, I'll decide when to sit down with him. I don't need any additional pressure from you, considering you should be the one to tell him about your future wedding."

Behind them a voice said, "Daddy's wedding?"

Faith closed her eyes as dread filled her. Centering herself, she got down on her knees to face her son. "Yes, John," she said with all her patience. "Your father is getting married."

John looked up at Lyle, confusion swimming in his eyes. "But what about Mama?"

Faith waited for Lyle to explain, but the man suddenly went mute.

With John's hands in hers, Faith said, "You know that Daddy and I aren't married anymore. Daddy found someone he wants to spend his life with, and we should be happy for him."

Tears surfaced in the little boy's eyes. "But I don't want a new mama."

"Oh, honey, I'll always be your mama, but now you get to have another person in your life to love you as much as your daddy and I do."

John scrunched up his face and stamped

his foot. "I don't want a new mama." He turned and ran from the room. Footsteps thudded up the stairs, and a moment later a door slammed.

"So much for making the transition easy," she said as Lyle stared at the wall. Before he could say anything, a barking came from the living room. Lacey squealed.

"Shoot." Faith glared at Lyle, who shrugged. "I forgot about the puppy." She hurried into the living room. The puppy sat before the fireplace, one of Faith's sneakers sitting on the rug before it, chewed up.

Lacey pointed. "Puppy."

Faith hung her head. Looks like they had chores ahead of them, including multiple types of training—dog and child. Plus a doggy door so the puppy didn't have any more accidents inside.

Lacey giggled as the puppy picked up the sneaker and Faith tried to wrestle it away. She finally won, holding a wet, ripped shoe in hand.

Ho. Ho. Ho.

"Listen," Lyle said as he walked into the room. "I gotta run."

"Now?"

"Yeah. I have to get ready for my trip."

"And leave John heartbroken?"

"He'll get over it."

It was all she could do not to fling the soggy sneaker at his head.

"I'll bring Cheryl over when we get back so she can meet the kids."

"If you bother to tell her."

"I will once we're at the mountain cabin. I'll start a fire, pour a glass of wine, snuggle under a blanket with her and break the news."

Faith gaped at him.

"What?"

"You're unbelievable!"

"Thanks. I knew the puppy would be a hit."

"No. You're…" She growled. Literally growled.

Lyle hightailed it for the door. "I'll be in touch," he said as he scurried outside. The truck started up with a grumble, and before she had a chance to even catch her breath or come up with her next thought, he was gone.

The puppy trotted over to lie on her foot with a whine. What did that mean? She glanced down and the big chocolate-colored eyes did her in. She bent over to scratch its head, then realized she didn't know if it was male or female. She wasn't a veterinarian, for Pete's sake.

Her phone dinged. She managed to ease away from the dog to find the device and read a text from Lyle telling her the puppy was a boy.

One question answered, five hundred more to go.

While she had the phone in her hand, she texted Roan. Funny how automatic it had become. What she wanted to ask him was if he knew ways to cure a little boy's broken heart. No, she'd have to figure that out on her own.

Instead, she sent, So, what do you know about dogs...?

CHAPTER TEN

With only a week and a half until Christmas, Faith found herself as tight as a ball of twine. Her sister's wedding was in just a few hours and she was far from ready, evidenced by her walk-run from the alteration shop off Main Street. The wind whistled and slapped her cheeks. Her dress, protected in a garment bag, bounced against her arm as she hurried to make it on time to get prepared for her sister's big night.

Grace had chosen the historic Sever House, a three-story Victorian mansion located on one end of Gold Dust Park, for the wedding venue. The wide, wraparound porch and black shutters brought an elegance to the building, which could be rented for special events. There was plenty of room in the open, first-floor area for the guests to mingle before and after the ceremony. Attendance was limited to family—Deke's had traveled from Florida—and close friends.

Faith burst through the door, catching her

mother's look of surprise. Mama was already dressed in her wedding finery—an evergreen-colored dress and matching shoes. She stood in the middle of the aisle between rows of white fabric-covered chairs that led to an arch outlined with tiny white sparkly lights on one side of the room. On the other side, a long table had been set up for a light buffet, and there was room for a DJ. Smaller round tables, covered in red and green cloths topped with Christmas centerpieces, were scattered about for guests to sit and eat.

"You were supposed to be here thirty minutes ago," Mama scolded.

"Sorry. Uncle Roy was a few minutes late picking up the kids, then I had to get my hair done and get my dress."

Mama tilted her head.

"It's a Wednesday night, for Pete's sake. People have jobs and responsibilities, besides showing up for a wedding."

"You know weekends were out. This was the only date they could reserve after they decided on getting married in December."

"And they leave tomorrow for the cruise they booked."

When Faith drooped, Mama walked her way, placing a warm hand on Faith's cheek.

"Deep breaths, baby. You have plenty of time to get ready."

Faith resisted looking at her watch. She could feel the minutes ticking down.

"Grace is in the bride's room," her mother said. "Go join her."

Faith hurried to a small room off the main area, finding her sister already decked out in a beautiful floor-length dress, lace covering satin, in a subdued shade of champagne. Her blond hair, normally cut in a blunt bob, had been pulled back with gold combs, a few tendrils curling around her face. Lace sleeves showed off her toned arms. The only accoutrements were a delicate gold bracelet Deke had given her and her engagement ring.

Faith stopped short. "You look amazing."

Grace spun around from the mirror where she was finishing her makeup.

"Not too plain?" she asked, worry in her green eyes.

"Are you kidding? You're perfect. Deke is going to lose his mind."

Grace grinned. "As was my intention all along."

Faith rushed across the room to hang the garment bag, missing the wall hook twice before securing it. "Sorry I'm late," she said as she zippered open the bag.

"Slow down. Everything is under control."

"Are you sure?"

"Positive. Mama and I went over the lists and checked them twice." She stopped to giggle at her Christmas reference. "I'm all ready, so we can focus on you."

"It should be the other way around," Faith said as she slipped out of her jeans and holiday-themed sweatshirt to don the gorgeous red bridesmaid dress her sister had picked out for the event. A similar cut to Grace's, this dress also featured lace sleeves, but the hem swirled around her knees. "I don't know how you've been doing the candlelight stroll *and* gotten ready for your wedding." Faith held up her hand. "Wait, you're Grace. You can do everything."

Grace chuckled. "Actually I can't. Deke and Mama have been a big help."

The candlelight stroll had been a side project of Put Your Feet Up for years. At Christmas, and again in the summer, Grace led a guided historical tour of downtown Golden while dressed in period clothing. Tourists loved it, so it was a staple of the town's vacation industry.

"Why haven't you called me?"

"With two children to focus on, along with running our family business?" Humor sparkled in her sister's eyes. "And a puppy, I hear."

Faith tried hard not to roll her eyes but failed. "Lyle strikes again."

"If it's too much, can't he take the puppy for a while?"

"And disappoint John? He's already upset that Lyle is getting remarried."

Grace's jaw dropped.

"I guess I forgot to tell you."

"You guess?"

"He told me at the tree lighting. Asked me to tell John for him."

Grace muttered something under her breath.

"Then, when he dropped off the puppy, he asked if I'd told John yet, and John overheard. He's confused and acting out. Yesterday I caught him scribbling Lyle out of family photos with a crayon. I've tried to keep a dialogue going, but he's clearly not dealing well."

"Oh, Faith, I'm sorry."

She blinked back tears for her son. She didn't know how to help John make sense of the upcoming changes. "It's always something."

"What can I do?"

Faith gaped at her. "You're getting married and going on your honeymoon. That's enough."

"But I can do more."

Faith shot her an *oh, really?* look.

"You're right. But I will be involved when I get back."

"Fine. Let's just be thankful there are no last-minute hiccups tonight."

Grace's face telegraphed concern. "Maybe I can find someone else to wind up the candlelight stroll this weekend so you don't have to."

Faith groaned. "We both know I'm the only one who can handle that nightmare."

"It'll be fun."

Faith shot her a skeptical frown.

Grace grinned. "I pass the itchy period piece dress on to you with love."

Faith turned her back to her sister so Grace could zip her up. Over her shoulder, she said, "You love interacting with tourists. It's your superpower."

"You mean being a top-notch attorney isn't enough?"

"Admit it, Grace. You love our town traditions."

"I do." She patted Faith's shoulder to signal she was done. "It's one of the reasons I moved back to Golden from Atlanta."

"Besides tall, dark and broody?"

Grace sent her a sappy smile. "Yes, because of Deke."

"Which is why we all love him." Faith hugged her sister, then pulled back to meet her gaze. "I'm so happy for you, sis."

"Thank you."

While their relationship had been difficult when they were teens, Faith was glad they'd had a do-over when Grace came back to Golden. Faith finally understood that Grace had done her best to redirect the out-of-control days because she loved Faith, not to paint her in a bad light. The first few months after Grace returned had been tough until Faith let her guard down and actually took her sister's advice. Over time, Grace had let Faith run the business she'd previously handled with an iron fist, without worrying that Faith would screw up. It was a major milestone for both of them—a celebration when Faith had succeeded and an affirmation she'd secretly treasured.

Grace grinned. "You'll find real love one day."

"Advice coming from a woman head over heels? Of course you see love everywhere."

Unbidden, a picture of Roan filled her mind. When Faith fell in love for real, she wanted to make sure the man was solid, a man who would be there for her and her children. Who would put her first. All the things she'd never had with Lyle.

"Right now, you're the center of attention. I'll be fine," Faith assured Grace.

"Are you sure?"

Faith slipped on the red satin pumps. "I'm too busy to worry about love right now."

"Sometimes it swoops in when you least expect it."

Faith could only hope.

"Speaking of busy…"

Faith glanced up, uneasy over the serious expression on Grace's face.

"I hate to pile on, but can you come into the office early tomorrow? Something has come up and I need to talk to you before I leave."

Her stomach dipped. "Did something happen?" She hadn't messed up, had she? Things had been going so well. Too well?

"No. A business opportunity." Grace waved her hand. "We'll talk tomorrow."

Faith had a million questions but kept her tongue. Grace had more important affairs to focus on, like a groom waiting for her. Still, what was going on?

Moving to the mirror to apply her makeup,

Faith pushed aside any trepidation that had arisen with Grace's words.

"I like your haircut," Grace said.

She bit her lower lip, then asked, "It's not too…different?"

"It's lovely."

Faith stared at her reflection. Her usually messy, shoulder-length hair had been trimmed and layered in a way that complemented her face. The stylist had talked her into highlights, which caught the overhead light, making her tawny-colored hair shimmer. She'd also splurged on a French manicure, the first time she'd done anything for herself in ages.

After adding gold earrings, the sisters stood before the mirror, arm in arm.

"The Harper women are looking good," Grace said as she squeezed Faith.

"As if there was any doubt," Faith countered, to which they broke into giggles.

A knock came from the door, then it opened as their brother, Nathan, popped his head into the room. The youngest sibling looked handsome in a black tux, his dark blond hair slicked back from his face. "Ready?"

Mama pushed in from behind him.

Soon, the Harper family stood together one last time before Grace said her vows.

"We don't do this enough," Mama said, wiping a tear from her eye.

"What, dress up?" Nathan teased.

Mama swatted at his arm. "Spend time together."

Grace held up her hand, folding fingers down as she counted. "Busy law practice for me. Children, job and school for Faith. Camping and…" She tilted her head and sent her brother a puzzled look. "What exactly do you do, Nathan?"

He chuckled. "She thinks that just because it's her wedding day she's a comedian."

"It was funny," Faith said, getting into the family spirit. Her mother was right, even though they all crossed paths at work, they didn't get together often enough.

"And you want me to give you away?" Nathan asked.

"Children, enough," Mama said. She looked each one in the eye before saying, "I'm proud of the lot of you. We've been through tough times, weathered unpleasant storms, but we're here, sharing a joyous occasion in our family. I love you all so much."

Returned *love you*s were murmured. The door opened. John ran in, wearing an adorable suit he was so proud of, with Lacey following in a red dress, white tights and black patent leather shoes—the ring bearer and flower girl. Uncle Roy brought up the rear, looking sharp in his tux.

"What's this?" he asked. "A family confab and I wasn't invited?"

Grace hurried over to hug the children then her uncle, and soon voices were bouncing off the walls as the minutes before the ceremony counted down.

Faith went to the side table to collect their flowers, and when she didn't see them, glanced around the room. "Grace, where are the bouquets?"

"What?"

Everyone searched, coming up empty. Grace went pale. "I saw the florist here earlier. Maybe they left them in the other room."

Mama patted Grace's arm. "Let me go check. Nothing to worry about."

She left the room with the children, Uncle Roy and Nathan in tow.

"So much for no hiccups," Faith said.

"I guess there had to be something."

"Which means your wedding will be spectacular."

"Says who?"

"Your sister, who predicts no more surprises and a beautiful night."

"You promise?" Grace whispered.

"I promise."

Happy now, Grace turned back to the mirror for a final check.

Faith's heart squeezed. Grace was so happy. A happiness Faith realized she hoped for too. She wanted a love for the ages. Roan's image flashed again in her mind, and she swiftly closed her eyes. He was becoming so dear to her, but could their relationship go anywhere? He was still struggling with his wife's death. What made her think she could be the one to make Roan see he could love again? She'd failed at a marriage with Lyle. Did she have what it took to be a good partner?

She wasn't sure, but she desperately wanted to find out.

SEATED AT HIS desk at the Golden PD, Roan had just finished writing up his final report for the day when his phone rang.

"Donovan."

"Oh, Roan. Thank goodness I caught you. This is Wanda Sue Harper."

He immediately thought of Faith and her children. "Is everything all right, Mrs. Harper?"

"No. Yes… Are you finished with your shift?"

"I'll be on my way out in a few minutes."

"Then you're just the man we need."

Curious, he asked, "What can I help you with?"

"You know Grace's wedding is tonight."

"Yes, ma'am." He hadn't talked to Faith in a few days since they'd both had so much on their respective plates.

"It seems the florist forgot the bouquets when they delivered the flowers. The shop is a few doors down from the station. Could you be a lifesaver and swing by to pick them up and then bring them to Sever House? Everyone is already here, and I don't want to make Grace nervous."

"Sure. I'll be there as soon as I can."

"I can't thank you enough."

He hung up and glanced at the clock. He was supposed to pick up Kaylie after dance. He wouldn't be able to do both. Emmie was already at Laurel and Gene's house, so he called his father-in-law.

"Gene. Something has come up. Can you pick up Kaylie at the dance studio in thirty minutes?"

"Of course." He paused. "Work emergency?"

"Wedding emergency."

"Come again?"

"Grace and Deke's wedding. Missing flowers."

"And they called you to investigate?"

Roan chuckled. Despite the difficult relationship with Laurel, he'd always enjoyed Gene's company.

"Something like that."

"You go on. We'll feed the girls dinner, if that's okay. Laurel and Emmie are in the middle of a big gingerbread project."

"That would be great."

"They should be finished by eight if you want to pick them up then."

Roan agreed and hung up. It was closing on six, the scheduled time for the wedding. He cleared his desk and stuck his head into Brady's office.

"I need to run. I'll finish up later."

Brady looked up from his own stack of reports. "What's the hurry?"

"Wanda Sue Harper called. Apparently the florist didn't deliver the bouquets for Grace's wedding. She asked if I'd pick them up and deliver them to the venue."

A slow grin curved his boss's lips. "So you're off to play knight in shining armor?"

"I don't think there is such a thing."

"Still, the gesture will make points with Faith."

"Who says I'm trying?"

Placing both hands behind his head, Brady

leaned back in his chair. "You're trying, my man, otherwise you wouldn't be running off."

Roan ignored his hypothesis. "See you tomorrow."

"With cake," Brady called after him as he strode to the door.

In record time, he went to the florist, picked up the bouquets and hightailed it to Sever House. To see Faith? No. Just doing his duty.

As he entered the venue, he scanned the seated guests, his gaze searching out Mrs. Harper. She noticed him and hurried over.

"Thank you, Roan. Grace wanted to forgo the flowers, but I told her she'd regret it later."

"It was no problem."

He was backing toward the door when she touched his arm.

"Why don't you stay? It's the least I can offer since you saved the day."

Stay for the wedding? Brady's knight comment echoed in his head.

"Unless you have other plans."

He didn't. The girls would be fine, busy with their grandparents. He could go home to an empty house or stay and see Faith. He'd been imagining her in her bridesmaid dress all day. What could it hurt?

Just then Faith came out of a side door.

Their gazes met. His pulse picked up at the sight of her, decked out in a red dress, so pretty it made his chest hurt. She shook off her surprise and beckoned for her mother.

"I know you're still in uniform," Wanda Sue said before crossing the room, "but we'd love for you to stick around."

Actually, he kept a change of clothes in the squad car. He could change after the ceremony. Slipping into an empty chair in the back row, he didn't have to wait long. The ceremony started, and when he saw Faith again, his breath hitched.

She'd done something to her hair. It curved around her face, bringing attention to her lovely features. And the color? A little lighter than usual? He couldn't look away.

She walked with ease, posture straight as she followed her children up the aisle. When she turned at the front, their gazes locked, and once again he was overwhelmed by her.

What was happening to him?

Soon Grace and her brother made their way toward the groom and the vows were exchanged. After a drawn-out kiss and raucous response, the ceremony ended. Everyone rose, giving Roan time to slip out and retrieve his spare clothes. He quickly changed, returned his uniform to the car and came back to find drinks being served and guests lined up at the buffet.

"Roan, what are you doing here?"

He turned to find Faith at his side. Her soft floral perfume enveloped him. Her face shone in the overhead lights. His gaze fell to her lips, and he had a difficult time answering. Finally, he snapped out of it.

"Your mom called to ask me to pick up the bouquets. Once I got here, she convinced me to stay."

"Thanks. We were all sure there'd be no hiccups."

"Disaster averted."

She smiled, then shook herself. "Are you hungry? There's plenty of food."

"I could be persuaded to eat."

She grinned and they crossed the room together.

"Where are the girls?"

"At their grandparents. I have some time before I need to pick them up." He glanced at her. "How are you?"

"Better now that things went off with only one hitch."

"Not stressed-out?"

The last time they'd talked, the topic had been all the busyness in their lives, how they were each juggling so much. He had a feeling she was putting on a brave face.

She laughed. "Oh, I am."

"You're handling it well."

"Practice. Lots and lots of practice."

He chuckled. "Oh, I have some good news."

She tilted her head.

"Kaylie was asked to be part of the dance troupe marching in the Christmas parade. Her teacher is impressed with her natural talent."

"She must be over the moon."

"She is." He paused, reached out to finger a stand of her hair. "Thanks for the suggestion."

She shrugged, but Roan could read the pleasure in her eyes.

When they reached the end of the line, Grace called Faith over, and he was left alone. Thinking that maybe this hadn't been a good idea, he turned to leave when Roy Harper blocked his path.

"Running out?"

"No, sir."

"Good. There's more food here than we can eat, and that's including those Matthews boys."

Roan nodded. Roy had given him a job when he'd first come to town, and he owed the guy. But the speculative gleam in his eyes put Roan on edge.

"Gotta ask, how are things going with Faith?"

"Come again?"

"You know, with the house. Heard she had furnace issues."

He tried to mask his relief that Roy wasn't asking about them like they were a couple. Which they weren't. And why did his mind go there in the first place? He still wasn't convinced they should get involved, for a multitude of reasons, but enjoying Faith's company overrode his reluctance.

"Faith needs to be independent, but, like all of us, she could use a little help once in a while."

"Glad I could be of assistance."

Roy chuckled. "Sure that's it?"

"What more would it be?"

Roy gave him the once-over. His brows drew together. "Been like a daddy to her since Earl's stint in prison, and after, when he took off for parts unknown. She's a special one, our Faith is."

He couldn't agree more. And he didn't miss the unspoken warning.

Before he could respond, Roy was called away for pictures. Shaking his head, Roan wondered again why he'd decided it was smart to hang around for the reception.

He'd eaten, made small talk and decided to leave when the DJ called everyone's attention to the couple's first dance. He should escape now, but Faith came into his peripheral vision, and it was like his shoes were nailed to the floor. She had a dreamy smile on her face as the bride and groom danced to a love song. Before long, the DJ asked others to join the couple.

The people between them filtered away. He found himself moving in Faith's direction. She waited. For him to make the first move? He held out his hand and she took it, and soon they were swaying to the music.

"You look beautiful tonight," he said, his breath fanning the hair by her ear.

"Thank you," came her breathy reply, hitting him right in the solar plexus.

He leaned back. "I like what you've done to your hair."

"Really?" Her face lit up at the compliment. "I haven't tried anything new in a long time."

"You should do it more often."

Her smile spread. When had this woman started to affect him so? Probably the night he'd fixed her furnace and they'd begun talking about single parenthood.

They twirled around the room as the song

changed to a more upbeat tempo. Faith laughed and he was caught in her spell. Did he want to find a way out?

He and Catrina hadn't dated long before getting married. He'd been swept up in her larger-than-life personality. It had been okay for a time, but once the children came, he'd gone into protective mode. She'd accused him of going overboard, but after his own family experience growing up, this was his way of showing his love. How could keeping his family safe not be the height of his devotion to them? Catrina had bristled, and they'd gone downhill from there.

From the first time they'd met, his connection to Faith had been tangible. Initially, he'd thought it was because they could be a sounding board for each other as single parents, but later he'd realized it went deeper. Had much more substance. He let his guard down around her, which he'd never done with another person. So why wasn't he embracing that fact instead of questioning it?

Her eyes were luminous under the soft lighting. He wanted to take a chance with her. Open up more. But what if she shot him down? Proved Catrina's point that he was so overprotective, he'd drive her away?

A slower song changed the mood of the

room. They danced in silence, drinking in the moment. Soon, they had drifted to the sidelines, where the lights were even dimmer. She gazed up at him, happiness reflected in her gaze. Before he even realized what he was doing, he lowered his head. Her lips parted. He grew closer, his heartbeat loud in his ears, drowning out everything else. He wanted to kiss her right now. Right here. He was inches away, so close he could feel the whisper of her breath against his lips. Until another dancing couple jostled him. His head snapped up.

"Roan?" Faith looked confused.

He didn't know what to say. He'd almost kissed her in front of her entire family. What would they think, when he and Faith hadn't even figured out this growing attraction between them? He wasn't sure what he wanted, or needed, going forward. Could he trust loving again? Risk being hurt? He should figure it out first before giving Faith mixed signals.

"Sorry. I, ah…should go."

Her face dropped. "Right now?"

"The girls are waiting."

She nodded, her face closed off now.

"Thank you for coming," came her very polite reply.

"Faith…" What did he say?

"I think we know where we stand," she said, blinking rapidly.

Did they? He wanted to say more, but the right words wouldn't come to him.

"I'll see you later?"

She nodded, then turned and disappeared into the swirl of dancing couples.

A range of emotions he hadn't felt in a long time swept over him. Regret. Uncertainty. Unmistakable attraction. Hope. All because he'd almost kissed Faith. Again.

And she'd walked away.

CHAPTER ELEVEN

"It's LIKE Y'ALL don't think I can be as sneaky as the rest of you," Wanda Sue crabbed to the Matchmakers Club as they watched the wedding celebration from the sidelines.

Gayle Ann kept her thoughts to herself. Actually, Wanda Sue had done her part well. Still, no point giving her friend a big head.

"How do you think I got Earl to marry me in the first place? A little misdirection goes a long way," she went on to say.

Bunny's mouth dropped open at her friend's revelation. "You never told me that."

"I wasn't proud of it and then, after things fell apart, it was plain embarrassing."

"Figures. Earl never was the kind of man to see through a scheme."

"Unless it was his own," Wanda Sue griped, disgust heavy in her tone. "But this time it's for a good cause."

"Looks like some movement on the Roan and Faith romance front," Alveda said as the four women hovered beside the dance floor.

Wanda Sue scanned the room. "That dance looked mighty intense between them. Wait? Where'd they go?"

Gayle Ann searched with the others. Neither Faith nor Roan could be found.

"That's strange. They were here a minute ago." Wanda Sue took another quick look before facing her friends. "I know Faith has spent time with him, but overall she's been mum. Which means things are good and she doesn't want to jinx it by sayin' a word, or things are bad and she just doesn't want to talk, period."

Gayle Ann nodded. "At least you got him here."

"See. Told you my plan would work."

Alveda snorted.

"I asked the florist to hold off on the delivery of the bouquets. This room already had the arrangements delivered, so Grace didn't realize the bouquets were missing. I faked a little panic when I called Roan and asked if he could be a dear and pick them up, since the floral shop is near the station. He jumped right to it."

Gayle Ann's lips quivered. "I couldn't have come up with a better scenario myself. I'm impressed."

Wanda Sue beamed.

Harry sauntered up to the group. "Have I missed anything?"

"Progress report," Gayle Ann said.

"So far so good," Wanda Sue chimed in.

"Really?" the judge said. "Because I just saw Roan leave. Faith went into the bridal changing room."

Silence fell over the women before they all started speaking at the same time. Wanda Sue and Bunny took off in one direction, Alveda in the other.

"Something I said?"

"What could have happened?" Gayle Ann asked.

"Cold feet?" Harry hypothesized.

Gayle Ann stared at him.

"I noticed them on the side of the dance floor, caught up in each other. Then, it was like a switch flipped and they parted ways."

Disappointment swept over Gayle Ann. "And yet it seemed to be going so well."

"Doesn't mean we can't meet our goal. Perhaps a little strategizing will help?"

"I suppose."

"In the meantime, I hate to see you so glum." Harry held out his hand. "Would you care to join me for a spin on the dance floor?"

Surprised by the offer, Gayle Ann hesitated. Her heartbeat picked up a notch. It had been years since a gentleman had asked her to dance.

Harry's brows rose, and with an unusual shyness, she took his hand, feeling her face flush. "Why, thank you."

He grinned at her. "The pleasure is all mine."

THE NEXT MORNING, armed with a bracing cup of Sit A Spell coffee, Faith unlocked the back door at the Put Your Feet Up office. She'd managed to drop the kids off at school and day care in record time. Probably because she hadn't slept well. She'd lost the battle and risen at dawn.

Flipping on the lights, then the heat, she walked the short hallway to the office and tossed her purse on the desk.

All night she'd wondered why Roan had acted so strangely. Yes, it would have been awkward if he'd kissed her—because there was no doubt that's what he was going to do—in front of her family and friends. She could understand hesitating because of that alone. But there was something in his eyes. Some sort of uncertainty that didn't bode well for her. Before she could find out why he'd wavered, he'd announced he should go, leaving her behind with a deep sense of embarrassment. Did he think she kissed just anyone in public? Would give away her affection like it was nothing? It seemed like he was more interested in appearances than being swept up in the emotion.

She stopped in her tracks. Could it be that he didn't want anyone to know they were spending time together? Was he concerned about her past making him look bad?

She pressed a hand against the sharp pain spearing her chest, hoping she was wrong.

Or maybe he just wanted to be neighbors. Made sense. Another single parent to talk to? Absolutely. Romance? Obviously not. Yes, the one kiss they'd shared had been unlike anything she'd ever experienced. Explosive. But if Roan was unsure—he'd certainly appeared that way—then she couldn't trust her future to him.

She wanted a man who made her a priority. Who put her first. Not that the children weren't important, of course they were. But romance should be special. Not an afterthought.

When her family had all retreated into themselves after Daddy got arrested, she'd acted out, searching for acceptance elsewhere. She'd barely even believed love existed, at least for the middle child who was so frequently overlooked. Then she'd settled for Lyle. She would not put herself in that kind of position again. She deserved a man who loved her to distraction. She wouldn't settle for less ever again. No matter how much her feelings for Roan were growing.

Tired of the direction of her thoughts, she turned on the computer, retrieved messages from the answering service and pulled up accounts for next month's billing. She hadn't gotten too involved in her day's work when the back door opened and Grace breezed down the hallway to the office.

"You're early," Grace commented as she shrugged out of her coat.

"I'd be worried if you were here first," Faith replied.

"I did hate leaving Deke." Grace went up on tippy-toes and squealed. "I'm married."

Faith shook her head at the very un-Grace-like behavior. Guess she'd cut her normally pragmatic sister some slack since she was so happy.

"Sorry. Don't mean to rub it in."

"Go ahead. You deserve it."

Grace claimed a seat on the chair across from Faith. "Down to business."

"I'm dying to know what's up."

"I got a call from Donna Smith, owner of the Nugget B and B."

Faith frowned. "What did she want?"

"She's ready to retire and is putting the inn on the market. She wanted to give us first dibs if we're interested."

"Interested in owning a B and B? We help facilitate vacation excursions. We don't offer lodging."

"But we also book cabins for Uncle Roy. Rentals at Gold Cabins have gone up in the last year. People have noticed."

"I did update the website and I tweaked the search function."

"Plus, tourist traffic has picked up in Golden. We have to strike now."

"Strike?"

"Add to our business portfolio. Corner the market on vacation rentals in town."

Faith took a deep breath. "We don't know anything about running a bed-and-breakfast."

"So we learn."

"Grace, you're an attorney with a busy practice here in town. When are you going to have time to operate a B and B?"

"That's where you come in."

Her eyes went wide. "Me?"

"With all the improvements you've made

running our business, I know you can do this."

Fear, plus seeing the determination and confidence in Grace's eyes, made Faith mute. Her sister wanted her to run an inn? At the thought of the new responsibility, her mind went blank.

"It's not like this will happen overnight. We need to look into the inn's financials, which you can handle. Then there's the sale price, offers, inspections, you know the drill."

"No. I really don't."

"Mama and Nathan will be in on the decisions too. As a Harper owned business, we'll figure it out."

"Have you told them yet?"

"Just briefly last night."

"And?"

"They were speechless."

She knew the feeling.

"Faith, you aren't the same woman who finally decided to divorce Lyle and start a new life. I had my reservations when you first began working here—"

"Gee, thanks."

"—and you've far surpassed my expectations."

To be honest, Faith hadn't known how running the administration part of the family business would turn out. She'd come to love it. But expanding?

"I told Mrs. Smith not to worry, that you're more than capable of handling the transition."

Faith held up a hand. "Wait. She questioned my ability?"

"At first. Once I informed Mrs. Smith about you going to business school, her initial reaction changed, so it isn't a make-or-break issue."

Make-or-break? Like that was even a consideration?

She wouldn't let her past cast a shadow over her present. Before, she'd always been in trouble, only thinking about herself. And her ex-husband? A liability. Until she'd turned her circumstances around. Had people's opinions changed since she'd diligently worked to improve her life and that of her children?

"I asked Mrs. Smith to email me with all the pertinent information. When I get it, I'll forward it to you. It'll give you a chance to read it over, come up with an analysis. And when I come back from the honeymoon, we'll make a decision."

"You do realize Christmas is almost here and I have two children who are ridiculously excited about the holidays."

"I do. But they have a supermom who can do it all."

She heard her own mantra echo in her head. *You are a strong, capable woman. You are a present mom. You can finish what you start.* She froze.

"No one can do it all," she said.

"But together, we have a chance."

Faith stared at her sister. She didn't want to disappoint Grace, since she'd been the one to keep Put Your Feet Up running after Daddy went to prison and held the family together, such as it was then. Now it was Faith's turn to put in the hard work.

The back door opened again, bringing with it a chilly draft and the crisp winter air, as Mama breezed into the office.

"My goodness, it's nippy this morning." She stopped unbuttoning her coat when she saw Grace. "What are you doing here? Don't you have to get on the road?"

"I needed to talk to Faith before I left. You know, about the B and B."

Wanda Sue glanced at Faith as Grace brought her up to speed.

"Are you sure it's a good idea to have Faith handle this? The children will be out of school for the holiday break soon. And she's been busy with the Donovan family."

Was her mother questioning if Faith could take on more responsibility? Faith's intention had been to have Mama work less, but was that doubt written all over her face? Faith couldn't ignore the hurt swirling in her chest that maybe not everyone thought she could do her job and more.

"Faith will be fine," Grace said. "And we don't have to make any moves until after the first of the year. Mrs. Smith swore she'd keep this potential deal quiet until we give her an answer."

"So there's time to really think this through," Mama said.

Faith's back went up as it always did when she was hurt. If anything, proving to the people of Golden that she was more than her past made her want to accept the challenge. Her own mother had doubts, for Pete's sake.

She'd been slowly figuring out who she wanted to be and what she wanted out of life. Having people look at her as a success was high up on her list. She wanted the satisfaction of proving to them, and herself, that she was capable. She wasn't a screwup. Maybe she never had been. She'd just been lost. Now that she had her bearings, she could proudly put one foot in front of the other.

But then she thought about John and Lacey. *If I do this, what will it cost?*

Grace grabbed her coat. "I have to run. We'll be visiting Deke's family in Florida after the cruise, but I'll be back before Christmas." She rushed around the desk to kiss Faith's cheek as she rose. "I can count on you?"

Faith nodded.

Grace rushed off, ecstatic.

Wanda Sue went quiet.

And Faith wondered if pride had gotten her into trouble once again.

ROAN PRESSED AT his temples for the fiftieth time that day.

Folding his big frame onto a small stool in front of the teacher's desk, he inhaled the memorable scents of chalk and glue, bringing him back to his school days when he hadn't always been the best student. Not because he wasn't smart—he'd just had other things on his mind and lost interest easily. He draped his heavy jacket over his legs, waiting for Mrs. Walker to continue with the conversation that wasn't going well.

"Your daughter is not the teacher."

He frowned. "Come again?"

"She insists on correcting me anytime the subject of Christmas comes up."

"She's a little…excited this year."

"She informed me that adults can't touch the Elf on the Shelf when I was discussing the tradition with another student."

"Technically, you can't."

Mrs. Walker blinked at him from behind her dark-framed glasses.

"I read the rules," he explained, then cringed, sure he was going to be reprimanded.

"Still, she shouldn't be talking back to me."

"You're right."

Mrs. Walker nodded. Subject closed. "Please remember to bring a healthy snack for the class party next Wednesday."

The directive was burned in his memory.

Once she waved her hand in dismissal, he jumped up and hightailed it out to the car. The cold air had him rubbing his ungloved hands together. Why did he keep forgetting to keep a pair with him?

At the thought of gloves, he recalled the pink pair Faith had loaned him at the park. Which then led him to think about the epic blunder on his part last night. And how the night had ended.

When he'd gone to pick up the girls, Emmie had wanted to stay at her grandparents' house. After the way he'd left things at the wedding reception, he hadn't been in the mood to argue, so instead, he'd made sure to praise her gingerbread house. Once Emmie had calmed down, he'd gotten them home, only to sit at the kitchen table staring out into the dark night, waking up this morning with a hollow feeling in his chest.

As he drove out of the elementary school parking lot, he tried to gather his scattered thoughts, with no luck.

He eased into traffic, his next stop the middle school a few blocks away. Kaylie had called and left a message on his phone, asking him to pick her up. She'd sounded subdued, which made Roan all the more worried.

When he stopped at the light, an SUV the same color as Faith's crossed on the green.

Faith.

The other reason he was out of sorts today.

Why had he hesitated to kiss her? At this point, there was no denying the attraction between them. An attraction that had been there from day one. Was that the problem? Was he feeling guilty about moving on after Catrina's death, even though their marriage had been over? Or was he using Catrina as an excuse? If he didn't move on, then he could protect his and his daughters' hearts from breaking. It sounded reasonable.

Until his gaze fell on Faith, and before long, all he wanted to do was spend time with her. Kiss her. Create a future? He still wasn't sure he trusted in love.

His folks' example had been disastrous. Eventually his mom took off, leaving his father to rule with an iron fist. Roan and his brother did their best to live with him, staying out of his way to reduce the damage, but it had been soul crushing. At eighteen, Roan had struck out on his own, finding odd jobs here and there until he discovered the ski patrol, which then led to his spot with the tour.

Where he had rushed into marriage with Catrina. Had he really loved her, or had he loved the idea of having a life unlike his own parents'? How did he know if what he was feeling for Faith could lead to love? He wanted it, but was he seeing clearly? There was so much more to consider this time.

The light changed and he drove on, coming up to Kaylie, who stood by the road alone. She opened the door and slid in.

"Hey, honey. Did you have a good day?"

Kaylie stared out the window as he pulled into traffic.

"Just came from a teacher meeting. Emmie's trying to take over the world again."

Silence. Okay, he'd try again.

"So, what do you want Santa to bring you for Christmas?"

His first clue to trouble was sniffling coming from the direction of Kaylie's seat. Then came whimpers, which soon turned into full-out sobs. Terrified that something bad had happened to her, Roan turned into the first parking lot he could find and put the car in Park, twisting in his seat to face her.

"Kaylie? What's wrong?"

"I… Hate… School," came her halting explanation.

"But you're doing good in your classes. You've made friends."

The sobs grew louder and more drawn-out.

"All the… Girls… Hate me," she sputtered.

"That can't be right."

The sobs came faster now.

"What happened?"

"Diandra won't… Talk… To me."

"I'm confused. Weren't you talking to her on the phone last night?"

It took a few minutes before the intensity of her tears subsided. Kaylie wiped her eyes and took a steadying breath. "She did. But then the two girls who got in trouble for shoplifting came back to school today. They're telling lies about me and pulled Diandra into their group." She turned to him, her face miserable. Heartbreak shone in her eyes. "I thought she was my friend."

He ached for her. How could these girls not see how sweet and good-natured Kaylie was? He supposed it didn't matter. They were getting back at her for the shoplifting incident. He racked his mind for the right thing to say, but what did he know about mean adolescent girls? For all his bluster about protecting his girls, he couldn't fix this. So he pulled his daughter into his arms and stroked her hair. "I'm sorry."

"You didn't do anything."

"Except have an awesome daughter."

Against his chest, Kaylie snorted. At least that sounded familiar.

"I could tell you that things will get better in time, but I doubt you'd believe me right now."

She sniffled. Hugged him tighter.

"Do you want me to arrest them?"

She jerked up. "Dad!"

He shrugged. "It was just an idea."

"That wouldn't help anyway."

The sedan went silent as Kaylie moved back to the passenger seat. He kept the car running, heat pumping around them, while he waited. For what, he wasn't sure.

"I bet none of those girls got asked to be in the Christmas parade after only a few dance classes," he said.

"None of those girls are in dance."

"Even if they were, they couldn't hold a candle to you."

He noticed her slight smile and the ache in his chest eased.

"It'll be all right," Kaylie finally said.

"*You* will," he agreed.

She spied him out of the corner of her eye. "You have to say that, Dad."

"Maybe, but I mean it."

She squared her shoulders. "Are we going to Grandma's house?"

"Yes." He reached over and squeezed her shoulder. "Are you really going to be okay?"

"I don't know."

He nodded, then straightened in his seat and put the car in gear to head to the Jessups' house.

After they'd driven half a mile, Kaylie asked, "What did Emmie do now?"

"Corrected Mrs. Walker's views on Christmas."

"Uh-oh."

"Yeah."

Kaylie sighed. "Sometimes I wish I was more like Emmie. More like Mom."

He turned to give her a quick glance before focusing back on the road. "In what way?"

"They always believe in themselves. Emmie's only six and goes after what she wants,"

"Which is not a good idea when she's contradicting her teacher."

"Okay, bad example. But Mom? She knew what she wanted and went for it, even if the people around her didn't like it."

He pressed his lips together.

"Sorry," she said in a quiet tone.

"You aren't wrong. She had self-confidence in spades."

She let out a long sigh. "I just wish I didn't let what other people think bother me so much."

"Kaylie, you did the right thing by walking away from that shoplifting situation. No matter what those girls think."

"I know. I just wish it didn't hurt so much."

Roan scowled. "I still want to arrest them."

Kaylie chuckled. "Thanks, Dad."

He pulled into the driveway of his in-laws' house, not relishing the conversation he'd have with his youngest. They went in to find Emmie and Laurel in the kitchen.

"And then," Emmie was saying to her

grandmother, who stood at the island chopping vegetables, while the little girl drew a picture at the table, "I told John that you can't make a puppy love you unless you pet it all the time and sneak it snacks."

"That's not how it works," Roan said, shrugging out of his jacket to drape it over the back of a chair. The kitchen was warm, a tasty meal cooking in the oven, as he joined his daughter at the table. Kaylie had disappeared, probably to lick her wounds.

"Well, I'll show him when we get our puppy."

He froze. "What puppy?"

"Grandma said we can get a puppy."

He glanced over the table at Laurel, hoping his pointed expression told her he wasn't agreeing to this.

"We were just talking," his mother-in-law hurried to say.

"Just talk," he said directly to her, then turned back to Emmie. "Besides, until you behave in class, you aren't getting any special privileges."

"I do behave. Mrs. Walker is wrong."

"She is your teacher. You need to respect her."

"But all the kids come to me about Christmas stuff." Emmie pouted. "I have to tell them the truth."

He stifled a smile.

"Emmie, I'm glad the students like you, but you have to let Mrs. Walker handle the classroom."

She shrugged. "Okay."

No way was her concession that easy.

"See." Laurel said from across the room. "Emmie understands." She chuckled. "Catrina was a handful at that age too."

At her mother's name, Emmie perked up. "Did Mommy have a puppy?"

"She did. We named her Scout."

"Where is Scout?" Emmie asked.

"Well, um, your mother outgrew her, so we had to give her away."

Roan knew that meant Catrina had lost interest and left her parents with the responsibility of owning a dog.

"That's sad," Emmie said, changing out one crayon for another color. "When you get us a puppy, we'll name it Scout II."

"How sweet," Laurel said, her eyes going misty.

"Emmie, no dog," Roan countered. "Not right now anyway."

She laid down her crayon. "But why not? Miss Faith let John keep his dog."

"What they do at their house is different from what we do at ours."

Emmie's face slowly turned red. "Then I want to live there. Miss Faith is nicer than you."

Laurel's barely hidden gasp reached his ears. Mentioning Faith right now would not only make Laurel more upset, it would escalate the already mounting tension.

"We'll talk about this at home." Roan picked up the crayons. "Get your things so we can leave."

Emmie jumped up and ran to her grandmother. "When you bring the puppy over, we'll have a party," she said, then ran from the room.

Roan rose and picked up Emmie's drawing. "Next time you promise Emmie a gift as big as a puppy, please talk to me first. I don't want her disappointed if it doesn't happen."

"I don't see the big deal. Who cares if they have a dog?"

"That's not the point. I'm trying to teach Emmie life lessons. I can't give her everything she asks for."

"Are you trying to say I spoil her?"

There was no way to be diplomatic about this, so he said, "Yes."

Laurel reared back. "What a terrible thing

to say. If Catrina was here, she wouldn't let you talk to me that way."

Roan walked to the island. Measured his words. "Laurel, I've often told you and Gene how grateful I am that you've helped me with the girls. And I know how much you miss Catrina. We all do."

Laurel brought her fingertips to her lips as if to keep from bursting out in a sob.

"But Emmie's getting more headstrong every day. She needs boundaries. Discipline."

Her voice subdued, Laurel said, "Catrina was a free spirit, and she did fine."

Until she had to make a point to Roan and in the process, it took her life.

He couldn't back down now. "Please stop, Laurel. I need to deal with Emmie. And right now, she needs to hear the word *no* more often."

Laurel drew herself up. "We'll do things your way."

Again, the answer came much too easy, but he wasn't going to fight it.

"Thank you."

He turned to leave when Gene walked into the room.

"Why is Kaylie moping around?"

"Friend troubles. We're working on it."

"Why won't you let her hang around with

her classmates?" Laurel accused. "What's the harm? Catrina was always involved in activities."

"This has nothing to do with me keeping her from friends."

Laurel wiped her hands on a dish towel and came around the island. "Why don't you let me talk to her."

"I've handled it," Roan said, hating the command in his tone, but Laurel didn't always listen. Trying to walk a fine line with his in-laws was wearing on him, and he didn't want to make a complicated situation worse.

"Fine," Laurel sniffed.

Muffling a groan, Roan rounded up the girls and drove home. Both daughters were quiet, which concerned him in opposite ways. Kaylie was still hurting, but Emmie was plotting. He knew it in his bones.

As he pulled into the driveway, he noticed Faith's dark house. Like his mood. He hadn't realized how much he looked forward to the cheery lit windows greeting him.

Where was she? He'd really love to get her take on his daughters' problems. Or maybe it was just that he wanted to see her sunny smile. He liked her positivity. Needed it to rub off on him. But after the way she'd walked away from him last night, would she even talk to him? He didn't like the idea that she was upset with him.

Faith seemed to have chipped away a small area of the ice around his frozen heart.

With a sigh, he shut off the engine. Looked like he wouldn't get any parenting advice tonight. He was on his own.

CHAPTER TWELVE

ROAN EXITED THE glassblowing shop on Main Street, his last stop of the afternoon. The sun was setting behind the mountaintops. Lamppost lights clicked on, emitting a soft glow. His stomach growled over the aroma drifting from Smitty's Pub, a hangout frequented by locals a few blocks away.

His Christmas shopping was officially finished. Once he wrapped the gifts he'd ordered for the girls online or picked out here in town, he'd have done his Santa duty. He couldn't wait to see their faces when they opened the presents he'd selected.

He really had to thank Faith for the change in him. Her Christmas exuberance was catching, no matter how much he tried to humbug his way out of the traditions his daughters loved. There was something about Faith, a sense of hope that drew him in. Yes, she was a beautiful woman, but her inner beauty shone with an intensity he couldn't help but be drawn to. Even when she was uncertain about her place in life, she'd gone after what she wanted and was moving ahead, one step at a time. He hadn't really analyzed the similarities in their lives too closely but could see that while she was making progress, he'd wallowed in being stuck. Wasn't his reluctance to have a merry Christmas proof of that?

Somehow Faith had made him see there was more wonder to life than he'd allowed for. Due to her influence, this year the girls would have happy memories instead of the gloomy holiday they'd had previously.

His pace slowed when he noticed Mrs. M. and Alveda standing on the sidewalk outside the shop. Were they waiting for him? As he approached, both women wore identical grins that sent a warning down his spine.

"Good afternoon, ladies."

"Just the man we wanted to see," Mrs. M. said.

"He is perfect for the job," Alveda remarked.

Now he was getting nervous.

"Faith needs your help," Mrs. M. informed him.

"Is she okay?"

Alveda chuckled. "Depends on how you look at it."

What did that mean?

Mrs. M. continued. "You know she's taken over the candlelight stroll this weekend?"

"She mentioned it."

Even though they hadn't spoken since the wedding, she was always front and center in his mind.

"There was a bit of a… Let's just say…"

"Her stroll bombed," Alveda finished.

Mrs. M. shot her an appalled glance. "You could have been more diplomatic."

"I'm just speaking the truth."

Roan pressed two fingers against his temple. "Ladies, could we take a few steps back?"

"Right," Mrs. M. said. "From what we heard—"

Alveda cut in, "Myrna at the coffee shop has her ear to the ground."

Mrs. M. rolled her eyes. "Anyway, it seems the stroll ends up at Sit A Spell for beverages and cookies. Myrna overhead a few of the women lingering outside the coffee shop complaining about the lackluster delivery. Apparently they were expecting Grace and were very disappointed with the quality of this year's candlelight stroll."

Roan frowned. If these ladies knew the gossip, then the news had probably gotten back to Faith. He and Faith had had enough conversations about her overcoming her past for him to know this had to be killing her. How was she handling it?

Mrs. M. cut into his thoughts. "The last stroll is this evening. I believe you can assist her."

Alveda nodded.

His gaze moved up the street to the Put Your Feet Up office. In the weakening rays of the late afternoon sun, he noticed light streaming out of the front window. He did owe her an explanation for his reaction to their almost kiss at the wedding. And a thank you for his new attitude toward the holidays. But would she welcome his presence?

"What did you have in mind?" he asked. It couldn't hurt to hear them out.

"Are you familiar with Golden history?" Mrs. M. asked.

"I've read about it."

"Then you know the story of Archibald Tremaine?"

"Sure. He was the first lawman in this area."

Alveda poked Mrs. M. in the side with her elbow. "See, he is our guy."

"Let me finish," Mrs. M. griped.

"Well, hurry it up. By the time you finish, the stroll will be over."

Roan hid a grin from the bickering friends.

"As I was saying, legend has it that one day while Sadie Banks walked the newly established town of Golden, a runaway horse nearly ran her down. She froze in fear, but Archibald, out on patrol, had seen the danger and swiftly came to her aid. He swooped her out of the path of the horse, saving her life.

"Sadie twisted her ankle when Archibald yanked her to safety. He gallantly lifted her in his arms to take her to the doctor who'd set up shop in town. Sadie looked up at him to give her thanks, but the words died in her throat. They locked gazes, and it is said that in that very instant, they fell hopelessly in love."

"And started the line which now leads all the way to the current Tremaine family," Alveda finished.

He'd heard the story, but not this romantic version.

"Your point?"

"Faith is reenacting Sadie. She needs an Archibald or the stroll will tank again," Alveda stated bluntly. "And if the people on the stroll leave bad reviews, Put Your Feet Up can kiss any future holiday-themed tours in Golden goodbye."

He wasn't sure how to react. Were they trying to set him up? But for what?

Mrs. M.'s eyes narrowed as if she was reading his mind. "We asked Brady to play the starring role, but he had to go down to Atlanta. Evan is on duty, so he can't step in either."

"What about Carter Tremaine?" Roan asked. "It's his family history, and the way he works the Chamber of Commerce to bring more attention to Golden, his stepping in would make sense."

Both women went quiet.

Alveda snapped her fingers and said, "He and Lissy Ann have some important function tonight. He wouldn't be able to cancel last minute."

Convenient.

"Which leaves me?"

Mrs. M. pounced. "Yes. You're Faith's friend, aren't you?"

Okay, they got him there. He didn't want to see Faith fail.

He glanced down at his leather jacket, sweater and jeans, and said, "I don't think my clothes are appropriate for the time period."

Mrs. M. perked up. "Not to worry. Buck at the Jerky Shack has a fringed leather jacket that would have been worn at the time. You can borrow it. Your jeans and boots are pretty worn, so they'll pass as authentic, especially once it gets dark outside."

"Get him to throw in a cowboy hat and you'll fit the bill," Alveda added.

Seems they had this all planned out. Time to throw a wrench in the works. "And if I refuse?"

Mrs. M. moved closer and placed her small hand on his jacket sleeve. "Roan, she truly needs your help. You're part of the town now, and if there is one thing the town of Golden does with excellence, it's helping our neighbors."

Darn if the pleading in her eyes didn't get to him. He couldn't tell if he was being played or if her request was sincere. He glanced at Alveda, and she wore the same expression, like she had faith that only he could solve the problem.

Yeah, he'd go with their request being sincere.

"I'll do it." He chuckled when they both grinned. "The Jessups took the girls to the ornament decorating at the community center. They'll be fine without me."

Mrs. M. squeezed his arm. "Of course, they would never be fine without you. You're a good father."

"And a good neighbor," Alveda piped in.

When Kaylie had asked if they could go with their grandparents, he'd hesitated, until she handed the phone to him with Laurel on the other end. Did he trust his mother-in-law not to play games? Not really. But she'd promised not to let the girls out of her sight. For the sake of keeping peace in the family, he'd agreed to let Gene and Laurel take the girls and later have a sleepover.

Mrs. M. gave him the once-over. "Now, let's turn you into a mountain man."

He dropped off his bags in the car, then joined the women as they walked down the block to the Jerky Shack. When he heard the plan, Buck was more than happy to loan Roan his coat.

Roan tried it on. It was heavy and carried the scent of smoke. He faced the women. "Well?"

Mrs. M. tapped a finger on her chin. "Something is missing."

A smile spread across Alveda's face and she raced across the room. Next thing Roan knew, a cowboy hat had been dropped onto his head.

"Are you sure this is accurate to the time?"

"Honestly, all the folks will care about is you showing up as Archibald."

Once he got the final stamp of approval, the three made their way up Main Street to Put Your Feet Up. A group, consisting of eight women and two men, stood outside the office. Roan lingered in the back, waiting with the women who had talked him into this scheme.

Moments later, Faith walked out the door, dressed in an old-time calico dress, cape and bonnet, a wan smile on her face. Her hair had been swept back; her cheeks were red from the chilly mountain air. She was beautiful, no matter what time period she inhabited.

Cleary, participating in the stroll wasn't her cup of tea. She straightened her shoulders, but before she could speak, one of the ladies asked, "When are we going to get started?"

Another followed with, "You said something about hot cocoa and cookies."

"Right now," Faith answered. "With refreshments to follow."

She smiled widely, from ear to ear. "Welcome, one and all. You're in for a treat tonight." She nodded toward the group. "Each of you holds a battery-operated candlestick. Just click the bottom and it will light up."

One by one, each candle came to life.

"Wonderful. Now to start, let me introduce myself. My name is Sadie Banks."

"It says on the brochure that your name is Faith Harper," corrected an older woman.

Faith blinked.

"Excuse me, Miss Banks." Roan took the

hat from his head and said with a drawl that he hoped came off as authentic, "Heard you were giving these fine folks a tour of our fair town. Mind if I tag along and add my two cents?"

Faith's surprised gaze met his over the group. When she sputtered, the curious crowd turned to see who had spoken. Roan bowed.

"Evening, ladies and gents. My name is Archibald Tremaine, local lawman in these parts."

The crowd twittered with excitement.

"I know who you are," one woman said. "You saved Miss Banks's life."

His gaze locked with Faith's. "Indeed I did."

"Oh, my," came a loud whisper. "This is even better than last year."

Roan kept his gaze on Faith. She'd hidden her surprise at seeing him well, but he hoped her silence didn't mean she'd rather not have him tag along. She gauged the response of the crowd before a genuine smile curved her lips.

She matched his drawl when she said, "Why, Mr. Tremaine, I would be humbled if you would join us."

Alveda leaned in and whispered, "Good work."

The crowd parted as Faith walked toward

him and slid her hand into the crook of his elbow. He plopped the hat back onto his head. His chest puffed when Faith shook her head at him and said in a low voice, "I don't even know what to say."

"Why, Miss Banks, your thanks would be plenty."

She chuckled, and off they went to the first stop on the tour.

For the next hour, Faith recited her prewritten lines to the members of the group. Once in a while, Roan would insert a bit of history he remembered reading when he first moved to town. The banter between them, however, wasn't staged.

"Miss Banks, you sure know a fair bit about our town."

"Likewise, Mr. Tremaine. You've added your colorful commentary to the history, as well."

"I can't help but be bold, what with such a pretty woman on my arm."

She playfully swatted his shoulder with a twinkle in her eye. "You do say the sweetest things."

The women in the crowd ate it up.

He didn't have to rehearse with Faith. Everything he felt for her was genuine. She'd gone along with this crazy ruse, so did that mean she was no longer upset with him? He sure hoped so, because he couldn't remember when he'd had a better time.

By the time they made it back to Sit A Spell at the end of the stroll, the crowd was ready for a hot drink and sweets.

Faith faced the group. "Thank you so much for—"

"One last thing." Mrs. M. held up her hand. "I heard there was some sort of reenactment of the time Archibald rescued Sadie."

The crowd clapped.

"I… Ah…"

Faith's astonished gaze flew to his as if to say, *What do we do now?*

Roan frowned at Mrs. M. *Now* he was being played, but he didn't deny that he kinda liked the idea.

He leaned close to Faith. "Might as well give them their money's worth."

She rolled her eyes. "Fine."

Moving away from the group, Faith stepped to an open area beside the coffee shop that was normally scattered with tables and chairs during the day. She waited until Roan moved to the other side of the shop and forced a frightened look on her face. "The horse…"

As quick as he could, Roan raced to her side and swept her into his arms. Her arms circled his neck. When he stopped before the onlookers, he didn't lower her to the ground, instead savoring the feel of her in his arms.

She jerked her head to signal, *drop me*, but he only grinned. Finally taking the hint that he wasn't letting go, she said, "Mr. Tremaine, how can I ever thank you for saving my life?"

"How about a kiss?"

The voices of the women in the crowd rose in excitement.

"Are you kidding me?" she whispered.

"Hey, I did save your tour," he whispered back.

She glared at him. "Okay, but—"

Her argument was cut off by him pressing a kiss to her lips. She froze, then just as quickly went soft in his arms and kissed him back.

The crowd cheered.

After a long moment, when the people seemed to vanish as the kiss grew more heated, she broke away, pushing at his chest to signal him to let her down. Once she had her feet on the ground, he clasped her hand in his and they both took a bow.

"I must say," one woman remarked, "this was the best candlelight stroll Golden has ever staged."

As Myrna invited all the guests into the store for drinks, he faced Faith.

"Sorry. I got caught up in the moment."

"It's okay." After a second, she grinned. "It was a fun moment."

"Yeah?"

"Yeah." She stood on her toes and brushed her lips against his. "Now we're even."

He couldn't deny the pleasure sweeping though him. Only Faith had the power to make him feel this way.

"I didn't know it was a contest."

"Harpers hate to lose."

With that, she lifted her skirts and marched up the sidewalk to the office. He couldn't help but watch her go, marveling over how well the night had gone. How she'd kissed him in return. A real, honest kiss, not one staged for an audience. He was happy, an emotion he hadn't experienced in a long time. Could it last?

He liked Faith. Okay, more than liked. But he was reticent by nature. What if they rushed and it all fell apart? He didn't think he could live through that again. Did he dare to try?

He turned to find Mrs. M. giving him a thumbs-up, followed by Alveda sending him a wink.

Yeah, he'd been set up from the get-go.

FAITH CHANGED OUT of the costume, thankful to be back in her jeans and a soft sweater. Tonight had been surprising, to say the least. She'd expected to slog her way through the stroll, only to be waylaid by Roan. She shouldn't be shocked—he did have the ability to keep her on her toes.

She knew the previous night's stroll had been a disaster. This morning she'd brainstormed some ways to make it better, never in a million years thinking that Roan would be the one to salvage her less-than-stellar performance. It was like he'd ridden in on a metaphorical horse to save the day.

She chuckled at her own whimsy. But, yeah, he had managed to save the tour and had given them a high bar to match next year. Grace was never going to believe her when Faith explained what had happened. She was still taking it all in herself.

Especially the kiss. Impromptu and totally welcome. Okay, maybe it had started out for show, but when their lips touched, there was no going back. After his reluctance to kiss her in front of people at the wedding, what had possessed him to kiss her at the end of the stroll? Not that she was complaining, mind you, but she was still confused.

Shaking off her strange mood, she flopped

into the chair behind the desk. Since the kids were spending the weekend at her mother's so she could concentrate on the stroll, Faith opened a folder on her desk. She should go home, beat after a weekend of performances, but she was also curious about the proposal Grace had forwarded to her.

She was focused on the numbers and adding a few notes when a tapping came against the glass at the main door. She jumped, then realized it was Roan. Lifting one end of the counter separating the room, she crossed into the foyer area and unlocked the door. The scent of woodsmoke slipped in along with a gust of cold air.

Roan ducked in, hunched into his jacket. "I saw the light on. It's late and I wanted to make sure you're okay."

"Because it's your duty as the local lawman?"

He chuckled. "Something like that."

"C'mon in."

He was big, rugged, and his cologne smelled amazing as he brushed by her. Her face heated up when she thought about kissing him earlier. Would he bring it up? If he did, what would she say? *Thank you?* How lame.

She locked the door and led him into the office.

"I was just going over some business," she told him.

"On a Saturday night?"

"The kids are with my mom, so I'm taking advantage of the quiet."

He paused in the motion of removing his jacket. "So I'm interrupting?"

On the contrary, he was making her blood rush.

"No." She straightened the papers and closed the file. "I'm finished."

He placed his jacket over a chair. "Good, because I wanted to talk to you."

She nodded, suddenly jittery inside.

"I feel like I owe you an apology and an explanation."

Curious, she hid her reaction. "About?"

"My behavior at the wedding."

"Roan, I—"

"No. Let me do this."

She crossed her arms and met his gaze.

"First of all, I think we got our signals crossed at the wedding. About me not kissing you."

True, she'd been conflicted and hurt. Thought perhaps the idea of kissing her bothered him in some way when she thought things were going so well between them.

Her stomach clenched. "Then what do you want?"

"I like you, Faith. Like this attraction between us."

A heavy silence fell over the room. "But?"

"Catrina and I rushed into marriage. I guess I'm afraid of this thing between us ramping up too soon."

Faith didn't think a person could control the timing of attraction, but she let him finish.

"I worry that because of my failed marriage and how I grew up, I'll make mistakes. I don't want to do that to you or our kids."

"You aren't the only one with a failed marriage. And you know I was a troublemaker when I was a kid because of my home life."

"Which means we should go slow. I really want to see where this attraction takes us, Faith, but I also want to make sure no one gets hurt."

She didn't think slow would matter with the feelings that were growing steadily inside her.

"Is that what you're worried about? Getting hurt?"

He seemed to hesitate. "My parents didn't model what a healthy marriage looked like. And once I realized Catrina and I were in trouble, I could see that we never had a solid foundation."

"Okay. You're careful. Nothing wrong with that."

His gaze pierced her, sending goose bumps over her skin. "So I'm not sure where that leaves us."

She rounded the desk and sat on the edge, mere feet from where he stood.

"Are we dating? In a relationship? I don't expect you to ask me to marry you on the spot, Roan."

His shoulders lowered. Relief crossed his handsome face. *Sheesh.* Was she that much of a bad risk?

"You're great, with me and the kids. You've made Christmas something to look forward to this year." He sent her a devastating grin. "I'm enjoying where we are right now."

But not in the future? She couldn't deny the letdown.

"Relax," she assured him. "We're simply single parents who need sounding boards."

He sent her a sheepish grin. "I do tend to be overprotective of the girls."

This was good. Move away from the relationship topic and focus on the children. Much safer.

"I understand. John is still upset about his

father remarrying. I'm trying to find the right balance with him."

"We both agree that it's all about giving the kids the best Christmas ever."

"Quite a turnaround."

"It was pointed out that I could make my girls happy and it wouldn't be the worst thing."

She worked for a convincing grin. "So we're good?"

"Yeah. I mean, are you?"

"Yes. We focus on the children and whatever else is meant to happen will happen."

"I'm glad you agree. I don't want our time together to be awkward. So, slow it will be."

She shrugged, as if this topic didn't make her want to curl up in the corner and cry. It was clear Roan wasn't interested in moving ahead in the romance department, if he ever would be.

He glanced outside, then back at her. "So, are you ready to head home?"

She pushed off the desk. "Yes. Let me get my coat and we can go out the back."

She led him down the hallway, then flipped off the office lights as they exited the building. She tried not to react when Roan stood close to her while she locked the back door. It was best he didn't recognize her reaction to him, so she covered by saying, "It's gotten cold tonight."

When they reached her SUV, he watched her get in. "See you tomorrow?"

"Sure," she replied.

He made sure the vehicle started, then waved when she pulled away, driving home to a dark and cold house.

Her chest ached. Maybe she wasn't meant to have happy-ever-after. She should just focus on being a mom and accept that no guy would ever love her the way Archibald Tremaine had supposedly loved Sadie Banks.

No matter how much fun they'd had tonight, Roan wasn't ready for serious. Maybe he'd never be. It seemed to Faith the kind of love she wanted only happened in books. She'd be much better off if she remembered that.

CHAPTER THIRTEEN

ON THE TUESDAY night before Christmas, John walked into the kitchen as Faith had her head in the pantry collecting ingredients for the cookies they were going to make for the Operation Share party after the parade on Friday.

"I'm ready, Mama."

Faith glanced over her shoulder as she rummaged around. "To bake?"

"No. To talk about Daddy."

Slowly turning, Faith read the serious expression on her son's face. She'd been trying to draw him into discussions about life changes, but he'd shut her out, either playing with the puppy or closing himself off in his room. Why now? Not that she was complaining.

She placed a bag of flour and sugar on the counter. Then she pulled out a chair at the table and pointed. John climbed up and she took the seat next to him.

"What's going on, John?"

"Daddy's not going to be my daddy with you, is he?"

Her heart pinched at his solemn expression. "No. I'm sorry, he's not."

John picked at the hem of his shirt. "But you'll always be here, right? Even if you get married?"

She reached over and pulled her son into a hug. She kissed the top of his head, drinking in the little boy smell, and then let him go to peer down at his face.

"Yes, John. I'll always be here. Nothing could take me away."

Almost nonchalantly, he said, "Daddy is always away."

"You know he drives a truck. He has to travel."

He grabbed her hand and held on tight. "But you won't drive a truck, right?"

Her voice cracked when she answered. "I have no desire to drive a truck. I like working at the office."

"I like it too, because we get to play there after school."

"You do." She framed his face with her hands. "I love having you with me, no matter where I am."

"You promise?"

"I promise." She brushed his bangs from

his forehead. "Is that why you've been so quiet? Because you thought I might leave you?"

He nodded.

"Sorry, buddy. You're stuck with me."

He grinned. "Even if you marry Emmie's dad?"

"What?" she sputtered. "Whatever gave you that idea?"

He shrugged. "We hang around with her family. A lot."

"That doesn't mean Mr. Donovan and I will get married. We're neighbors."

Disappointment flashed over his features, but as soon as Rocky—the name they'd settled on for the puppy—barked, John raced into the living room. Apparently a puppy trumped trying to marry her off to the next-door neighbor.

For a brief moment, Faith pictured what that would look like. Family dinners, with lots of laughter around the table. Sitting before the fire on cold nights like tonight, huddled under a blanket. Summer cookouts. Attending school events together. Watching the children grow up. All wonderful, but the vision that made her throat thick with emotion? Roan, his eyes only for her. Kisses every morning and night, and a few in between. Hopelessly happy with a man whom she not only liked but also admired. The man who made her insides jittery and her spirits soar.

But he wanted to take things slow. Did that mean he didn't have the kind of feelings for her as she did for him? She closed her eyes against the sting and the beautiful image went up in smoke.

Shaking off her melancholy, she got back to work and lined up the rest of the ingredients on the counter to make snickerdoodles. She pushed up the sleeves of her plaid flannel shirt and had just leveled off two cups of flour in a measuring cup when the doorbell rang in short, constant bursts. Rocky started barking and the kids' voices rose. She wiped her hands on a towel and rushed to the foyer, just as John was reaching for the doorknob.

"John, wait. You don't open the door until—"

Too late. He twisted the knob and the door flew open. Emmie stood on the porch, wringing her hands in distress.

Faith hurried over, hiding her dismay. "Emmie, honey, what's wrong?"

"Daddy forgot all about the cookies. We have to bring them to the party at the community center. If we don't, Mrs. M. is going to be mad at me."

Faith ushered the little girl inside. She

placed her hands on Emmie's shoulders. Leveled her voice. "Mrs. M. won't be mad at you."

"She will. Operation Share is important, and if I don't bring cookies, all the kids won't have any." Her voice hitched and her eyes started to well. "Daddy forgot," she repeated in a heartbreaking tone.

Faith gave her a quick hug and directed the kids into the living room. Once they were distracted by Rocky—who knew he'd come in handy?—she found her phone and speed-dialed Roan. He answered on the second ring.

"Donovan."

"This is Faith. Emmie just showed up on my doorstep. She's upset."

"I'll be right there."

Faith stood by the door, and within minutes, like a repeat of a movie scene, Roan and Kaylie were running across the yard.

She opened the door wide and he stepped in, bringing the crisp air with him, Kaylie fast on his heels.

"Is this about the cookies?" he asked, a troubled glint in his eyes.

Faith nodded, closing the door behind them as he strode into the living room.

Emmie hovered by the fireplace, clearly upset by her father's transgression. She rubbed a finger under her nose as he went straight to her and got down on one knee, resting his elbow on top.

"Emmie, we've talked about this. You can't keep running away every time you aren't happy."

"This time is different," she sniffled. "You forgot, Daddy. Miss Faith is making cookies with John, so I thought she could make extra for us."

"Be that as it may, I was getting ready to go to the store to buy the ingredients when Faith called. I had it under control."

"Not until I reminded you," Emmie accused.

"Yes. You're right." He ran a hand through his hair. "But we still have plenty of time to make cookies. The party isn't for three days."

The little girl didn't seem to be buying it, so Faith stepped in. "I just started baking," she said. "I have plenty of ingredients to make a few extra batches, if your dad wouldn't mind us working together."

Emmie's face lit up. "Are you sure?"

"That's what neighbors are for."

"Yeah, but not to get married," John piped in.

Faith closed her eyes and hoped her face

didn't reveal her discomfort. Or the heat she felt spreading over her cheeks.

When she chanced a look his way, she couldn't decipher Roan's expression. Was he aggravated with her for offering to help? Or about John's remark? Not wanting to know, she turned and headed to the kitchen to preheat the oven.

"I'm sorry about this," Roan said moments later as he joined her. "I really was on my way to the store. I picked up snacks for Emmie and John's class party tomorrow but forgot the cookie dough."

She picked up the measuring cup and dumped the contents into a bowl.

"If you don't want our help, I can watch the girls while you run out." She turned and waggled a finger. "But no premade packages. You have to make them from scratch."

"Who cares how I make them as long as they're made?" He crossed his arms over his broad chest encased in a dark blue Henley shirt, the color of which matched his eyes. "Is this some kind of Christmas rule I don't know about?"

"No, but Emmie will remember the time her dad almost forgot the cookies for a good cause, but then at the last minute he saved the day."

He looked amused instead of angry. "You have it all figured out?"

Relieved, she let out a laugh. "Hardly, but as I told you, I vowed to make this Christmas special for my children. I thought that's what you wanted, too?"

He didn't respond, his facial expression similar to a few weeks before, when he wasn't happy about all the Christmas hullabaloo.

She forged ahead anyway. "How did you forget?"

"We had a lot of calls today. Things usually heat up before the holidays."

She didn't understand the parameters of his job but knew this time of year wasn't happy for some people.

"So, you messed up one thing."

"Not one."

When she glanced his way, he flinched.

"I still haven't taken Emmie to see Santa so she can give him her list," he confessed.

Faith added sugar to another bowl. "Can't the Jessups take her if you're busy?"

"We've had some issues. I need to keep some boundaries with my in-laws."

Seeing his closed-off expression, Faith didn't push the topic. Sheesh, conversation tonight was extremely tough.

"I know all about boundaries," she said.

"In my case, I have to make excuses for why Lyle isn't around, why the kids don't see him often." She cut a stick of butter in half and placed it in a cup, then put it in the microwave to melt. "Tonight John finally told me why he's been so upset about his father getting married. Seems he's afraid I'll leave him too, like he feels Lyle has done with us. I had to assure him that would never happen."

He frowned. "Is that why he made the wedding comment?"

The microwave dinged, and she concentrated on taking the butter out as an excuse not to answer the embarrassing question. Scraping the butter from the dish with a spatula, she folded it into the sugar.

"My point is, children need to feel secure," she said.

"And mine aren't?"

She stopped midstir, hearing the outrage in his voice. She chanced a look his way. "I didn't say that. I'm sorry if I came off judgmental."

He remained rooted to the spot.

Aware of the tension in the room, she put down the spoon and asked, "Roan, what's going on?"

He pushed away from the wall. "I'm the dad who is letting his girls down."

"No, you're not. So you forgot about the cookies. No one is perfect."

"But they need to be able to depend on me."

"And they do. You're there for them. For the important things." She grabbed his arm and pulled him over, his boots clomping against the floor. "Help me while we talk."

"What do I do?"

She handed him a teaspoon. "Scoop up the batter, roll in sugar and drop little balls on the pan."

He stared at the utensil, then at her. "That's it?"

"It's easy." She chuckled. "Anyone can do it."

He didn't look swayed but started to place round blobs of batter on the sheet.

Faith retrieved another bowl from the shelf to start the chocolate chip mixture. "I've watched how close you and Kaylie have become, and it's sweet. Emmie?" Faith shook her head. "That child will take some time settling into your new family dynamic, but she loves you. That's all you, and the girls, could ask for."

He finished filling the pan. "Sometimes I think it would have been better if the Jessups had taken over."

Faith gasped.

"Sometimes." He turned to lean against the counter, crossing his jean-clad legs at the ankles, and watched the children playing with the puppy. "But then I remember how I grew up and think, no, even as a single parent, I'm doing better—the best I can."

Faith put the pan in the oven and set the timer. "Then quit beating yourself up."

A grin curved his lips. "Is that what I'm doing?"

"Sounds like it to me." She slid the bag of flour and the empty bowl in his direction. "Get busy. It'll take your mind off your problems."

He chuckled and soon followed the chocolate chip cookie recipe she recited from memory.

"Seriously," she said. "Kaylie and Emmie couldn't ask for a more wonderful dad."

"And John and Lacey are fortunate you're their mom."

"We're a mutual admiration society, aren't we?"

He caught her gaze. "I wouldn't want to be in the club with anyone else."

Faith savored his remark but had to keep reminding herself that Roan wasn't ready for a relationship. Right now they were parents, first and foremost, no matter that Faith wished for more with the man who made her pulse race and had her dreaming of forever.

Before long, the sugary sweetness of baked goods permeated the kitchen. Two batches were already cooling on a rack before being transferred to the plastic holiday containers Faith had picked up at the store. The children came in to taste-test and announced the bakery delights a big hit.

"Daddy, do you have a Christmas dish to put them on?" Emmie asked.

Faith bit her lip. She could offer one of hers but waited for his response.

His forehead creased. "Kaylie, wasn't there a dish in the box of Christmas stuff in the garage?"

She perked up. "I think so."

"We'll look when we get home," he said. "It'll be one of your mom's dishes."

Emmie clasped her hands together under her chin.

As the kids hurried back to the movie they were watching, Faith started cleaning up.

"There you go," she said. "You're a hero."

He rolled his eyes, snatching a cooling cookie from the rack to sample, but he couldn't hide the satisfaction on his face. He took a bite, then held it out in front of him as he chewed. "Not bad."

"Of course not. I used a Harper family recipe."

He munched away, clearly impressed with himself.

Shaking her head, she placed the bowls and utensils they'd used in the sink as it filled up with warm sudsy water. She tossed him a towel to dry.

"You have crumbs." She pointed to the vicinity of his chin.

"Where?" Roan swiped, but a few remained.

"Let me."

Faith stepped closer and reached up to brush the stray cookie crumbs away. When her fingers touched his bristly chin, she couldn't deny the shot of pleasure that zinged up her arm. Her eyes met his and she froze, scorched by the heat in his gaze. Unable to resist, Faith went on her toes and softly pressed her lips against his. This move might not be smart, but after sharing their thoughts and working in close proximity in the warm kitchen, she couldn't stop herself.

His hands found their way around her waist and she savored his warmth when he moved closer. "I thought we weren't going to do this," he whispered against her lips.

"I went with the moment," she said in a husky tone she barely recognized.

He leaned in and another kiss exploded between them. Faith knew she was playing with fire, that it might be a long time, if ever, before Roan would want a serious relationship with a woman. But if they didn't take a chance, they'd never know. She had to try to convince him otherwise, didn't she?

Laughter filtered in from the living room. With a drawn-out slowness, Roan broke the kiss. His hands remained on her hips.

"What are we doing?" he asked, his voice raw.

"Giving in to the attraction between us?"

"I need to focus on the girls." He stepped back. "And we decided to go slow."

He'd made that decision, so was he reminding her, or himself?

As she opened her mouth to ask, Emmie ran into the room with a book in her outstretched hand.

"Daddy, come read to us."

He shook his head, as if trying to dispel what was happening between them, and dropped his gaze, taking the book from his daughter. Faith caught a glimpse of the cover and recognized it—one that featured a mouse family decorating for Christmas. John had brought the book home from school, and they'd already read it three times.

"Please, Daddy?"

Faith knew her cheeks were red but shrugged. The heated moment between them was gone. Now he had his wish, to focus on the children. Not on Faith or them as a couple, which might never be.

Emmie grabbed his hand and tugged him into the living room. He dropped onto the couch as the children surrounded him. Kaylie, with her feet tucked under her, curled up on the other end. Emmie and John sat at his feet. Lacey climbed up on the cushions and tucked herself into Roan's side.

Her heart nearly burst from her chest. Could this scene be any more adorable?

As Roan opened the book and started to read, Faith tucked her hands in her jeans pockets and rested a shoulder against the wall near the kitchen. The children were mesmerized from page one.

"Voices, Daddy," Emmie commanded as more characters came alive in the story.

Faith bit the inside of her cheek when Roan's voice went into falsetto or dropped down into a deep bass, depending on the dialogue. The children laughed, resulting in Roan growing more animated. And he was worried he wasn't doing enough for his girls? Didn't he realize that this was what they wanted? For him to be silly, and overprotective, but always showing his love? If anything this Christmas, Faith hoped he saw just how much his daughters loved him in return.

Just like she did.

As the thought popped into her head, her smile faded. She placed a hand over her thudding chest when it occurred to her that she had totally lost herself to this man and he wanted to shut down any talk of a serious relationship. When had she fallen so completely for Roan? Sometime in the past month when they'd relied on each other to get through the ups and downs of single parenthood? When he'd made her hope for second chances? She'd been taking steps to be more confident in her personal life and had made great strides. But this? She'd never expected to fall in love at Christmastime.

Hot tears stung her eyes.

This was not good. Roan didn't want anything stirring between them. Could she hide her feelings going forward? Pretend she was okay with the crumbs he tossed her way? Over time, it would wear her down. Maybe even destroy her spirit.

What did she do now?

FAITH DROPPED JOHN and Lacey off at school the next morning, then headed into the office. Grace was back from her honeymoon and had texted that she wanted to talk about the possible B and B purchase. There was plenty of time before John's class party, so Faith spread out the reports she'd created since studying the proposal.

She tried to calm her nerves. Would Grace agree with her assessment? Even though she hadn't graduated with a business degree yet, she'd applied much of what she'd already learned in classes to her analysis. Pride filled her. She'd taken on the challenge and was succeeding. She hoped her sister felt the same.

Conversely, she was still dealing with the bombshell revelation from the night before. It had been so hard to say good-night to the Donovan family without letting Roan read her emotions. As hard as she'd tried, he'd regarded her with a look that had her shaking in her boots. Had he figured out the depth of her feelings for him? But how? She hadn't let on. No, she was simply overreacting. At least she hoped so.

No more kisses. No more being alone with Roan. The temptation was too strong, and she obviously had no control when it came to the man. She'd be pleasant, neighborly and heartbroken. Nothing more.

She dropped her head to the desk and lightly banged her forehead a few times.

The back door opened. Grace hurried into the office, unbuttoning her coat along the way.

"After spending a few days in Florida, I forgot how cold it was here."

Faith smoothed the black wool skirt she'd paired with a red turtleneck sweater and knee-high boots, a professional look for today's meeting. "They're forecasting snow for Christmas."

Grace's eyes lit up. "That would be a treat."

"I've had to keep from watching the weather reports so John doesn't get too excited if he hears the news."

Grace held up her hand. "Fingers crossed."

Faith tilted her head. "Enough chitchat. How was the cruise?"

"Romantic," came her sister's immediate reply. "The water was the most gorgeous shade of blue. The food was superb, the stateroom sublime. And Deke surprised me with a special gift every day."

Faith chuckled. Before Deke, Grace had been the least romantic person she knew.

"And visiting his family?"

"Actually, lots of fun. When he and his brothers are together, it's like watching a comedy show. Throw their mother into the mix and it's downright entertaining." She hung her coat on a rack in the corner and rubbed her hands together. "How are things here?"

"Good. The candlelight stroll was a hit."

Grace grinned. "I heard."

Faith grew wary. "Heard what?"

"That none other than Archibald Tremaine put in an appearance. Apparently it was all Sadie Banks could do not to throw herself into his arms."

"I did no such thing."

"Mama heard it from Mrs. M., who was there and related the entire incident, and she called me with the news."

Faith rolled her eyes. "I was giving the people their money's worth."

Grace winked. "Good job, sis." She placed a hand on her hip. "After the positive reviews on our website, you and Roan are going to have to re-create those characters again once word gets out."

She nearly groaned out loud. Faith had read the reviews as well but knew there was no way she could put herself in that position again. Since he obviously wasn't looking for something serious, keeping him at arm's length was best for her state of mind.

"We'll debate that issue at another time," Faith said. "I have to get to John's party later this morning, so let's get down to business."

Grace took a seat across from her. "What did you think?"

"I did a comparison of similar businesses. The asking price is in line with current sales."

"That's what I thought."

Faith picked up a pen and tapped it on the desktop to control her nerves. "I went over the financials Mrs. Smith sent to you. I do have a few concerns."

Grace leaned forward. "Such as?"

"First of all, there haven't been any renovations to the property in years. The place is dated and would need a capital investment to upgrade and make the inn more attractive to travelers."

"That makes sense."

"Revenue is down. Perhaps due to the dated business model? Hard to tell."

"I think once Mr. Smith passed away, Donna lost interest."

Faith went on, "The room rental prices haven't been raised in over a decade. I went on the website. It's very hard to maneuver, and the comments from guests weren't favorable."

"So we'd have some work to do."

"Most definitely." Faith slid a piece of paper across the desk. "Some initial projections. As you can see, we'd have to work with the bank on funding. But because of the current state of the inn, we might be able to offer a little less than the asking price."

Grace nodded. "Our company financials are good." She looked up. "Due to your diligence, I have to say. Faith, since you took over, you've steered the company into a much healthier position. We're actually making money."

Faith reveled in her sister's praise, which didn't come often and was hard-earned, and handed her another report. "And if we make upgrades at the inn, I believe it'll be a moneymaking proposition in about a year."

Grace sat back. "You've really thought this through."

"I have. And the business plan I drew up reflects all of this. We have enough capital for the down payment and renovations, but we'll need Mama and Nathan with us if we decide to apply for a loan."

Looking back down at the numbers Faith had spent hours crunching, Grace pursed her lips. It was all Faith could do to keep from shifting in her seat.

"But after we get the place up and running, it will make money, correct?" Grace surmised.

"Yes."

"Okay, then let's hold a company meeting and get their input. Nathan will probably go along with it, as long as he doesn't have to run the place. And Mama will have a new project to focus on."

When a serious gleam filled her sister's eyes, Faith tamped down the sudden panic, her old go-to position.

"Deke and I want to make an investment in the inn if we decide to buy it. We may not need to get the bank involved."

Faith's eyes went wide.

Grace shrugged. "We've both been frugal."

"I didn't expect this, but it will move the bottom line from red to black faster."

"If we do invest, I'd like Deke to become one of the company officers."

"Are you kidding? Since he started working with us, our tours have doubled. He deserves a place at the table. And I can't see Nathan or Mama disagreeing."

With a smile, Grace took the file from the

desk and flipped through the remainder of the research Faith had put together.

"Very thorough."

Faith beamed. It had taken so long to believe in herself; now it was wonderful to have someone validate her hard work, especially her sister.

Grace returned the file.

Faith took a breath and said, "I want you to know that if we decide to do this, I'm fully committed. Yes, my children always come first, but I'll give one hundred percent."

"I never thought otherwise." A sly twinkle shone in her sister's eyes. "But that won't leave much time for hanging out with Roan."

She went still. Where had that come from?

"He's got a busy life, and once I get involved with this new investment, we probably won't see each other much."

"Really? Because I got the impression you two were hitting it off."

Keeping from squirming was becoming next to impossible. "More like we've become a sounding board for each other regarding parenting. Other than that, we're just neighbors."

"*Hmm.* And why don't I believe you?"

Her voice went flat. "Grace, just leave it alone."

Never one to give up, Grace asked, "What's going on?"

The fact that Grace was an attorney meant Faith would be bombarded with questions until Grace was satisfied with her answers.

"Let's just say he's not in a hurry to get tangled up in a committed relationship."

"Because he lost his wife?"

"Yes. He wants to do his best for Kaylie and Emmie, which excludes dating at this point."

"Admirable, but when I saw you two at my wedding, I hoped maybe…"

Faith swallowed hard, then said, "He has his priorities. I'm not one of them."

Sorrow washed over her sister's face. "Oh, Faith, I'm sorry."

"Look, between my family and work, I have more than enough in my life to keep me busy. I'm not going to press the issue on this. Or regret something that isn't going to materialize."

Her mind flashed back to the domestic scene in her living room last night. The children mesmerized while Roan read them a story, making voices to go along with the characters. He was so good with them, it had brought tears to her eyes. Couldn't he see that he didn't have to put all areas of his life in separate categories? He could be a good dad and still fall in love again.

She couldn't change Roan's attitude on this—stubborn man—nor was she going to beg for a little of his affection. Either he would love her or he wouldn't. Yes, it hurt, but she wasn't going to wallow. She had a life. As much as she wanted Roan in it, she needed to accept his viewpoint and continue with the plans she'd set in place before they'd become neighbors.

"It's fine, Grace. Better to know now than down the road when the children are more invested in the relationship."

The truth hurt, but this was where they stood right now.

Grace didn't look like she believed Faith. "You're really okay with this?"

Faith pushed back her shoulders. "Yes. Now, let's discuss a few more items and then I have to get to John's school."

Her sister opened her mouth, presumably to argue, but closed it when she read Faith's face. The decision had been made. Roan didn't want romance. Faith did. Now she had to figure out how to get through the holidays without anyone knowing her dreams had been dashed.

CHAPTER FOURTEEN

"Our plan is working," Gayle Ann said under her breath to Alveda as they filled stockings full of small gifts in anticipation of the Operation Share party. The community center was a beehive of activity with the date of the party fast closing in. Harry organized the gift-wrapping table while Bunny put colorful tablecloths in place. Wanda Sue approached from the kitchen.

"What did you do now?" she asked Gayle Ann.

Gayle Ann's hands flew to her chest. "Me?"

"Stop with the innocent act. How on earth did you get Bill Barnes to give up driving a float in the parade? He's done it for twenty years now."

Gayle Ann shrugged. "It was easy. His daughter moved to Atlanta, taking the grandbabies with her. When his wife mentioned they'd have a short holiday visit because he'd committed to the parade, I assured her I had another driver lined up. She couldn't thank me fast enough." She proudly held her head up. "And I did."

"Let me guess," Alveda said. "Roan?"

"Exactly. We already knew Faith would be on the float. Another way to get them in the same place at the same time."

"But what if he says no?"

Gayle Ann shot her a don't-be-silly look.

"I don't know." Wanda Sue's face fell. "Faith changes the subject when Roan's name comes up. Ever since the candlelight stroll."

The vague sense of unease washing over Gayle Ann made her pause. "But they were marvelous together."

Bunny sidled up to the group. "Who's marvelous?"

"Faith and Roan."

"We know that." Bunny rolled her eyes.

Wanda Sue wouldn't budge. "I swear something is off."

Not to be left out, the judge made his way over, catching the tail end of the conversation. "I have to say, the more I see Faith and Roan together, the more I think we're doing a good thing."

Quick to agree and stop the negativity, Gayle Ann said, "We always do good things."

"Sure, as long as it benefits you," Alveda teased.

Her eyebrows rose. "In what way?"

"Interfering. You live for it."

Gayle Ann sent her friend a wily grin. "I'd argue, but you're right."

Alveda chuckled over the din of volunteers readying the center for the party. Voices echoed off the walls and the tempting scent of cinnamon rolls drifted from the kitchen.

"What makes you think there's a problem?" Bunny asked.

"On the way over, I dropped by the market to get the supplies on the list for the party," Wanda Sue explained. "I ran into Betty Barnes and she told me the good news, how they were leaving town this afternoon. It had Mrs. M.'s fingerprints all over it."

Gayle Ann beamed.

"Then I called Madge at the school office, and she confirmed that Mrs. Walker would recruit a driver. Emmie's teacher, as a matter of fact," Wanda Sue said.

Gayle Ann held her ground. "So far I don't hear a problem."

"Well, here it is. As I drove by the school and stopped at a red light, Laurel was getting out of her car. She saw me and waved, a very satisfied smile on her face, before she sauntered inside."

"Think she'll mess up our plans?" Alveda

asked. She flinched at Wanda Sue's *What do you think?* look. "We probably shoulda asked her to join us from the start."

"She wouldn't have gone along with us. She still wants Roan to mourn Catrina, like she does." Gayle Ann had all the sympathy in the world for the woman. How horrible to lose her daughter in her prime. And while she didn't want to denigrate Laurel because of her deep loss, someone had to rally for the Donovan family—who needed Faith so they didn't fall apart at the seams.

"Do you think she'll come between them?" Bunny asked Wanda Sue.

"Faith's confidence has risen since she took over administration at the office. But it's very possible Laurel might say something to play on her doubts about not being able to hold on to a romantic relationship."

"Should we do something?" Bunny asked.

"Short of crashing a kindergarten party, there isn't much we can do," Harry advised.

"Faith may be confident at work, but I'm not so sure she's on firm footing when it comes to love," Wanda Sue said. "Maybe things aren't going as smoothly between her and Roan as we originally thought."

"That is one area we can't control completely," Harry said, his voice serious. "No matter how carefully we chart our course, we can't make them feel anything for each other if it's not there to begin with."

Gayle Ann wouldn't be deterred. "I refuse to believe they can't make it work. Christmas is just days away. They'll see what a gift they are to each other. I'm sure of it."

"And if they don't?" Alveda asked.

"Then we'll come up with another plan."

The group went silent. Gayle Ann clasped her hands together to keep her nerves from showing. Faith and Roan belonged together. She'd stake her reputation as leader of the Golden Matchmakers Club on it.

ROAN GLANCED AT his watch. Faith was running late for the kindergarten holiday party. He expected her to breeze through the door any minute now. Then on the heels of that thought, he frowned. Hadn't he wanted some space from the alluring woman? He shouldn't be thinking so much about her, yet here he was, his mind on an automatic loop with Faith front and center.

His distress increased. Who was he kidding? He still couldn't get their last kiss out of his mind. What was he doing?

"Daddy, you haven't seen my pictures."

Roan left his sentimental thoughts and looked down at Emmie, who smiled up at him.

"You're right. Lead the way."

Emmie took his hand and, with one last glance at the door, he trailed behind his daughter.

When he'd left Faith's house last night, she'd been quiet. Withdrawn. He'd chalked it up to being tired after a busy day and then a marathon baking session, but the shadows in her eyes gave him a bad feeling. She'd handed him the wrapped cookies and sent them on their way, but the itch at the back of his neck hadn't diminished. He wished she would get here so he could make sure he wasn't jumping to conclusions over nothing.

His gaze fell on John, who sat by himself at a small table, happily drawing a picture. If there was trouble in the Harper household, wouldn't he sense it by the boy's behavior? Unless Faith was hiding something, which was a leap. She'd been transparent since day one.

Emmie stopped before a bulletin board showcasing a dozen papers. It was all a jumble of colors, until Emmie pointed out her masterpiece.

"Mrs. Walker said to do a Christmas picture. Do you like it?"

He leaned in closer to the art display, examining his daughter's talent. It featured a house. There were two large stick figures, adults he figured, and four smaller. Outlining the house were messy dots in different colors. Christmas lights? One figure was off to the side, alone.

"Nice, Emmie."

"Do you recognize it?"

"The night we turned the Christmas lights on at our house?"

She bounced up and down on tiptoes. "Yes. We had so much fun." Tugging on his arm, she indicated that he move closer. He crouched down and sat back on his haunches, following her finger as she pointed out the scene.

"There's you and Miss Faith, Kaylie, John, Lacey and me."

"I figured that out." He pointed to the one figure separate from the group. "Who's this?"

Emmie wrapped her little arms around his neck and whispered in his ear, "Mommy. I didn't want to leave her out, even though she wasn't there."

Roan tried to swallow around the tightness in his throat. Emmie was a sensitive soul, even if she was also headstrong.

"Is it okay? That I drew Mommy?"

He pulled her into a tight hug. Inhaled. "Of course, sweetie. We should always remember Mommy."

Emmie pulled back and grinned at him. "I know Miss Faith isn't my mommy, but she sure is nice."

Roan rose, wisely not taking up that comment.

A few more parents arrived, and Emmie took off to play, leaving him staring at the drawing. Wondering if Faith's insistence on celebrating the holiday at full tilt was why Emmie felt secure in creating this scene. What would Catrina have thought about all this? For all her stubbornness and having it her own way, she'd delivered memorable holidays for the girls. Would she approve of how they'd moved forward? How he'd put aside his less-than-ecstatic attitude toward the holiday and worked to make this Christmas merry?

He rubbed his palm across his chest, trying to suppress the ache there. There was no going back in time, but if he could… Would he have done things differently?

"Another of Emmie's drawings?"

Roan nearly jumped at the voice directed toward him. Turning his head, he spied his mother-in-law. "Laurel. I didn't know you were coming today."

"And miss Emmie's first school Christmas party? I never missed any of Catrina's events."

Roan hadn't mentioned the party, so Emmie must have filled her grandmother in. He didn't know whether to be frustrated or understanding that she'd shown up.

"She's quite an artist," Laurel said as she moved toward the board. Her smile slipped when the meaning of the scene before her became clear.

"She's all caught up in the holidays this year," Roan explained, covering for Emmie, not sure how this was going to play out. "We have plenty more drawings at home, taped on the refrigerator."

"She's moving on," Laurel said in a voice Roan barely heard. "Before long, she won't remember Catrina at all."

Roan sympathized with the woman's pain over the realization. For the first time, he truly appreciated how much the loss of her daughter affected Laurel's actions. And all their decisions, really.

"We made sure to put out as many of Catrina's holiday decorations as we could. Unfortunately we never found the rest of the boxes from the move. I think they must have been misplaced."

Laurel continued to stare at the drawing.

"I'm sorry her things were lost. They meant a lot to Kaylie, and I'd hoped to make sure Emmie knew where our traditions came from."

Laurel's eyes were misty when she met his gaze. "So you haven't just forgotten her? Moved on?"

He hadn't expected how his marriage would end, never would have wished any harm on Catrina. There would always be a special place in his heart for the mother of his children. Not even time could dim her larger-than-life influence over all of them.

Voice tight, he said, "No. In fact, we've talked more about Catrina this month than we have since the accident."

"That must explain all of Emmie's questions. I wondered what had prompted her curiosity."

"I encouraged her to ask you about her mother. She needs a lasting legacy, and I think you need to share memories you've kept locked up inside since she passed."

Laurel's surprise shone on her face. "You did that?"

"Contrary to what you think, I want to re-member the good things Catrina, the girls and I shared. No one can ever take her place. I don't want that."

She nodded, reaching out to run a finger over the picture. "But it's clear you're moving on. All of you."

"I'm realizing that time doesn't stand still. But it doesn't mean we leave the past behind. We embrace those memories as we journey on."

Laurel nodded. There was an edge when she asked, "So, Faith?"

"We've been neighbors for a month. Only ran into each other here and there beforehand." He paused. "I don't know, Laurel."

Which wasn't entirely true. He thought about Faith at odd moments in the day. Pictured her smile. Savored the laughter they shared. She'd made the perfect holiday for her kids because she wanted them to be happy, and that had overflowed to him and the girls. But he'd been honest when he told her he didn't want to hurry into a serious relationship. Things were finally turning around for him and the girls, so there could be no distractions.

"You know that Catrina and I rushed into marriage," he finally said.

A small smile curved Laurel's lips. "We

advised her to take more time when she told us you were engaged."

"Shocker," he replied in a dry tone.

"You know Catrina. Once she made her mind up there was no stopping her."

"Yes, I remember."

Laurel's shoulders lifted as she drew in an audible breath. "Kaylie speaks highly of Faith. Said Faith is the one to encourage her to go back to dance." She paused. "I have to be honest, Roan, I still have reservations."

"Because of her past or because you don't want her taking Catrina's place?"

"I don't want anyone taking Catrina's place." Her voice wavered. "What I want is my daughter back."

Roan knew that, but there wasn't anything he could do to change the circumstances. "Listen, I have the girls to think about now, so I will always take them into consideration first when making decisions."

"So that means you won't be dating Faith?"

"That means any relationship has to be on the back burner. I need to be there for Kaylie as she navigates middle school. And Emmie? She's too headstrong. I need to keep an eye on her."

"Which we can do, as a family. Gene and I are always there to help."

"Thanks, but I need to spend time with Emmie. Make her understand she can't do what pleases her on a whim."

Laurel scoffed at his concern. "Catrina did that all the time and she grew up just fine."

Had she? Having spent years with Catrina away from her parents, he could argue that point.

"We've talked about this. I'm afraid I'm going to stand firm about redirecting Emmie and making her see she has to think before she leaps."

From the shift in her gaze, Laurel seemed to realize she'd said too much. "You're right."

Why did he think she didn't really mean it?

"I'd appreciate it if we're all on the same page," he said.

"Absolutely," Laurel responded quickly. Much too quickly for his peace of mind. "And speaking of that, I'd hoped we could work out our Christmas schedule. The girls will want to wake up surrounded by presents, and since I'm making dinner, perhaps they should spend the night."

She hadn't listened to a word he'd said.

Roan closed his eyes and muffled a groan. If he didn't put his foot down now, Laurel might continue to reverse his wishes. "The girls will be sleeping in their own beds on Christmas Eve," was all he said.

Emmie finally noticed Laurel's arrival and beelined across the room. "Grandma! You're here."

Laurel caught her in a hug. "Where else would I be?"

Emmie pulled from her arms and beamed. "Do you like my picture?"

"It's very…festive."

"Daddy put the lights on our house and John's house. We had a party and everything." His daughter sighed. "I love Christmas."

Laurel shot him a look he couldn't quite decipher, just before Emmie expressed an interest in showing her grandmother the other projects scattered around the classroom. Laurel reached over and patted his arm, a touch of affection usually missing in their relationship. "You're doing the right thing."

He was, wasn't he? For the girls, most definitely. So why couldn't he get rid of that hollow feeling?

He was just about to follow Emmie and Laurel to view her other displayed work when Mrs. Walker marched up to him. "Mr. Donovan. Just the man I want to see."

He winced. Was he in trouble? Mrs. Walker only seemed to have one tone—strict.

"How can I help you?"

"It seems we have a situation."

He glanced around the room, searching for danger.

"Not a police matter," she assured him. "The driver of the kindergarten float for the Golden Christmas parade backed out last minute. Is there any chance I can recruit you to fill in?"

Roan had Christmas Eve off and had planned to watch the parade with Emmie while Kaylie danced with her class. "You can't find anyone else?"

"No so far." Her voice softened. "Please consider helping."

"What does it entail?"

"Driving a pickup truck with a decorated trailer attached. The route in straight down Main Street, so it shouldn't be too difficult to navigate."

Emmie popped up beside him. "Daddy, you have to do it."

He glanced at his daughter. Figured she'd overhear. "But what about watching the parade with you?"

"Emmie can ride along on the float," Mrs. Walker cut in, probably hoping to persuade him by adding an incentive. "I'll make sure there are adults with her so she'll be safe."

"Please, Daddy, please?"

He let out a sigh. Kaylie would understand, wouldn't she? The studio was video recording the girls as they danced down Main Street and posting it on their website, so he'd still be able to see Kaylie's performance. "How can I say no?"

Emmie hugged him. Mrs. Walker sent him a rare smile and turned on her heel to return to her desk, which was covered in wrapped gifts and homemade treats.

Shaking his head, Roan went to join Emmie after she ran off to tell her grandmother the exciting news. How like her, to finagle her way to get what she wanted. Not through malice, but because she was truly excited about the upcoming parade. But what about Kaylie? How did parents live with the guilt of making one child happy while disappointing another? He was stuck in an untenable position and hated every second of it.

At that moment, Faith rushed through the door, shrugging off her coat, her expression harried. His gaze moved over the outfit she wore, over her hair framing her flushed face and how bright her eyes shone. There was something different about her today, a new vibe he couldn't put his finger on.

When was he going to listen to his own directive and stop thinking about her?

Faith searched the room before her gaze collided with his. When she sent him a soft smile, he felt as if he'd just had the breath knocked out of him.

Was he in love with Faith?

The truth was like a bell sounding above his head. Why was he only now realizing it? *Because you don't want to get hurt again.* Because this time, his feelings were more intense than the connection he'd had with Catrina, and he had much more to lose.

FAITH SLIPPED ON her game face. She'd known Roan would be at the party, but she hadn't expected to have her heart skip a beat when she saw him. The man affected her so, especially since he'd put the skids on a romantic entanglement.

Still, he looked eye-catchingly good in the dark green sweater and black slacks. His hair was neatly combed, although she preferred the windswept look, and his eyes were a deep blue. Even though he was across the room, she wondered what he'd do if she walked up to him and…

Like a bucket of water thrown on an out-of-control fire, her musings came to an abrupt halt when Laurel walked into view. Faith blinked and turned to hang her coat on a wall hook.

"Mama."

Her attention moved to her son, who'd run up to her. She knelt down for a quick hug.

"Sorry I'm late," she whispered.

"It's okay. We haven't started the party yet."

Letting out a breath, she noticed the other parents milling around the classroom. The children's festive decorating came in the form of red and green paper chains draped from one wall to the other, construction paper cut-out Christmas trees with scrunched up tissue glued on to resemble ornaments, and gingerbread people hanging beside the alphabet stretched out over a whiteboard. Looked like art hour had taken precedence this month.

John tugged at her hand. "Come see what I'm making."

Feeling Roan's stare on her, she brushed off the urge to fix her hair, and let her son lead her to a desk with a piece of paper and crayons scattered on top. "It's Rocky," he pointed out. Faith leaned in to inspect the artwork.

The dog stood beside a misshapen Christmas tree.

"What a good likeness."

John's chest puffed out.

"Are you going to add Lacey and me?"

"Yep. And Emmie, Kaylie and her dad." He smiled up at her. "And Grammie and Aunt Grace and Uncle Deke and Uncle Nathan and…"

"I get it. The Harper clan."

John tilted his head. "I don't think I can fit the rest of Golden on this paper." He scowled before his eyes lit up. "I need another." He sped away to find more paper.

"Christmas energy," Roan commented as he strode up to her.

His intoxicating cologne enveloped her, making her stomach dip at his presence. His eyes sparkled, as if there was a secret between them. Keeping her face composed, she smiled, not allowing herself to be affected by this man who was fast taking control of her emotions.

"I was wondering where you were," he said.

"I had a meeting."

"Explains the outfit."

She looked down at her clothes and frowned. "What's wrong with my outfit?"

"Nothing. You look great." His wry grimace saved the slipup. "I guess I'm used to seeing you more casual."

"Well, get used to this because I'll be dressing up for work from now on."

He looked confused. "You said you're usually not busy this time of year."

"I had an interesting proposal come across my desk. This morning I had a meeting with Grace to discuss our options."

She sounded professional. Confident. Like a woman who didn't need the attention of a man who hadn't decided where he wanted this relationship to go.

"During the holidays?"

"Getting a jump start. After the first of the year we'll go back to normal, and I'll be diving into this new development if the family agrees."

Even if the B and B deal fell through, she'd still find opportunities to fill her hours in order to stay away from her handsome neighbor.

"That's…ah…great. I assume you'll be putting your business skills to work?"

She lifted her chin. "I will."

This project was an important step. It was more than just melding it into the already established company that Faith ran well. This was a chance to show everyone that she'd become a changed person, that she had the ability to tackle bigger things. That she was committed for the long run.

"So life will be different."

"It will." She infused enthusiasm into her tone. "Kaylie has dance now, and I'm sure Emmie will find an activity to keep both you and her busy. Plus, you're all getting into a routine now that your shift rotation has changed."

"We have been making dinner a priority at our house. The girls and I have been cooking together. Kaylie loves finding new recipes."

Wasn't that what Roan had told Faith he wanted? Growing closer to his family?

"Since my children will be spending more time at the office after school, I'm thinking we'll all be too slammed to socialize."

"Emmie will miss seeing John after school hours."

She nodded, wishing he'd admit to missing her. But that was a pipe dream. Better to concentrate on the good news before her instead of what-ifs. Roan had made it perfectly clear he wanted to devote his time to his family, so Faith would devote her time to her career. An even trade-off, right?

Clapping came from the front of the room. Everyone gave Mrs. Walker their full attention.

"Thank you all for being here today," the teacher greeted. "The children have been excited to show you their projects and to share this party on our last school day before the holiday vacation."

Excited murmurs broke out among the children.

"In a few minutes we'll get the festivities underway, but first I have a very important piece of news to share."

The adults exchanged nervous glances.

Faith refused to look at Roan, even though she could feel his warmth as he stood close beside her. Yeah, her noticing every little thing about him had to stop.

"It seems our original driver for the kindergarten float had to cancel last minute. Mr. Donovan has kindly agreed to take over."

The children cheered him.

"Now, for those of you who have already volunteered to join the float, please see me if you have not gotten an elf outfit yet. We need Santa's helpers at the parade staging area early Friday morning."

As chatter broke out, Faith grinned. "Way to fill in. It's a place of honor."

"Driving a float?"

She held back a chuckle. "You haven't heard about the parade of '06?"

Interest gleamed in his eyes. "I'm almost afraid to ask."

"Mrs. Rodgers, who'd been a bus driver for as long as anyone can remember, volunteered to steer the float that year. Unfortunately, she didn't take into account the crowds lining the street or the limited view from her position in the truck. Near the end of the route, she took a turn too soon and went up the curb, nearly crashing into the front of the dress shop. The float got stuck and, if I remember correctly, a tire bounced off."

Disbelief crossed his face. "Was anyone hurt?"

"Thankfully she wasn't going fast. The few people on board were fine and those on the sidewalk scattered. I'd say the only injury was to Mrs. Rodgers's pride."

Roan shook his head. "Golden sure does have its share of stories."

She laughed. "These days, the town council vets all drivers. In your case, I'm sure they'll make an exception since you serve and protect Golden."

"Now I'm nervous."

She patted his arm, realizing her mistake

when pleasant tingles shot up her arm. "You'll do fine."

His gaze moved to her hand. She quickly pulled away.

Blinking as he returned his attention to her, Roan asked, "Do you have your elf outfit ready?"

"I bought it months ago when Mrs. Walker first asked for volunteers. Parents sign up six months in advance to participate in the parade."

"What about Lacey? Who will she be with while you're on the float?"

"Mama, along with Grace, Deke and Nathan. Lacey really got into the Thanksgiving parade on television this year, so she'll love seeing us live on a float." Faith paused, leaned in and conspiratorially asked, "Are you wearing an outfit?"

His eyes went wide. "Sure, jeans, sweatshirt and boots."

"C'mon, that's normal, everyday wear."

"Uh-huh, but I'm not an elf."

She lifted her hands, palms up. "And I am?"

"Given how you've made everyone feel special this season, absolutely. I think you are."

She tried not to let his words make her face

heat, but couldn't deny the delight warming her.

"Since I'm driving, Mrs. Walker told Emmie she could ride on board. Mind keeping an eye on her for me?"

"Of course. I'm sure she and John will want to stand next to each other the entire route."

"Thanks."

Then a thought flashed in her head. "What about Kaylie? Won't she be disappointed you'll miss her going by with her fellow dancers?"

"She was kind of bummed we weren't technically participating in the parade, so I think she'll be happy once she finds out we all have a place, at least." He frowned. "I hope anyway."

"I can get Nathan to video her when she goes by."

"That would be great. Even with the studio also recording them, I'll take whatever I can get. And I'm sure Laurel and Gene will take lots of pictures." He paused. "Between you and me, I've already seen most of the routine a half dozen times when I've gone to pick her up at practice."

"She's a good kid."

"She is. I've been grateful for your help with her."

Her pulse went galloping away again at his words. His very kind words.

Their conversation faded as the party kicked into full gear. The students took turns reciting portions of *The Night Before Christmas* and sang a song. After a standing ovation, Mrs. Walker invited everyone to sample treats the parents had supplied, spread out on a long table. Faith was nearly run over by the stampede of kids.

She clasped her hands together and chuckled. Ah, those carefree days of youth. When looking forward to Christmas was the high point of the entire year. When everything seemed possible. That little girl had to be inside her somewhere, because as an adult, Faith still loved the magic of the season.

"Are you hungry?" Roan asked.

She started and looked his way. "No, but that doesn't mean John won't try to get me to sample something."

"Emmie insisted on cutting up the apples into slices herself. Under strict supervision, of course."

"John was more excited about the little gifts he got for all his classmates than the brownie bites I fast-tracked in the kitchen."

An awkwardness flitted between them until their children ran up with plates of fruit and vegetables, chips on the side for good measure.

John held out a cookie. "Here, Mama."

"Thank you."

Emmie scowled up at her dad. "Daddy, you didn't sneak anything yet, did you?"

"No, ma'am. I was waiting for you."

The children shared their bounty before running off to play with friends, leaving them alone again. Well, as alone as you could be in a room full of people.

"So, ah, nice party?" Roan asked before munching on a carrot slice.

"Your first?"

"Catrina always did the honors."

"Glad to see you stepping up. Emmie is beside herself, and I'm sure Kaylie is pleased you're making the season merry."

"Thanks in large part to you."

"No, you put forth a good effort, Roan. From now on the girls will know you're there for them and they can count on you for everything. They won't miss so much time with me and my kids at all."

Was that disappointment flashing over Roan's face? Why, when he'd made sure to insist on spending time with his girls to the exclusion of seeing where the sizzling attraction between them led?

He shifted. "Unless Emmie decides to stop by your place unannounced."

"She's always welcome, but I'll make sure to bring her right home. I know how much you're looking forward to your new family dynamic."

His eyes flashed when he met her gaze before he looked away. What was up with him?

Emmie's voice rang from across the room. He waved at his daughter. Hesitated. "I should see what she wants."

Faith smiled. "The party seems to be winding down anyway."

Roan nodded and left. She did her best to ignore the regret simmering under the surface. *Is this what it would be like between them now? Discussing parenting? Chatting about the weather or town events?* It was what Roan wanted, so she'd have to do her best to adhere to his wishes.

She walked around some of the children to get to the desk where John had been drawing and picked up his picture. How like her son to want everyone in his drawing, jamming the people he loved into the Christmas scene. And appropriate that her and Roan's stick figures were nowhere near each other in the rendering.

"Hello, Faith."

Faith tore her gaze from the artwork to find Laurel standing before her. Her stomach dropped. The woman had a secretive smile on her face.

"Hello, Mrs. Jessup."

"Lovely party."

"It was."

"Your mother couldn't make it?"

She cleared her throat, hating that this woman made her so jumpy. "I was under the impression just parents were invited."

"I make it a priority to be at Emmie's events. Kaylie's too."

"How fortunate for them."

"It is. We're there for each other."

What was she getting at?

"And the holidays?" Laurel asked in a much too neutral tone. "Where will you spend them?"

"Most likely at Mama's house."

She nodded. "Gene and I will be making new traditions. We're the only family Roan and the girls will ever need."

Point taken. They were a family. Faith was not part of that category. Nor would she ever be.

"I hope you have a nice Christmas, Mrs. Jessup. Enjoy your family."

"Same."

Faith crossed the room to bundle up John and collect his goodies before heading home. She tried not to let the other woman's words bother her but gave up when the pain in her chest only grew. Mrs. Jessup had zeroed in on her soft spot and managed a direct hit.

She'd never have a family with Roan.

Why, when she finally fell in love for real, did it have to be with a man who didn't return her feelings? She could almost swear she heard someone say *Bah Humbug* in her ear.

CHAPTER FIFTEEN

On the morning of the parade, Roan dropped Kaylie off to meet up with her dance team—wearing a red, sparkly outfit and a matching headpiece—before continuing to the staging area. She gave him a distracted kiss on the cheek before hurrying off. And here he'd been worried she'd be miffed because he wouldn't see her dance troupe perform.

After dinner the night before, he'd brought up the subject about driving the float. Kaylie wasn't the least bit upset. Instead, she'd chatted on about how Diandra had finally seen the light and dumped the mean girls in class. Kaylie had her best friend back and asked if they could spend time together over the holiday school break.

It occurred to him that he must be doing something right.

Emmie, on the other hand, hadn't slept a wink last night, so pumped to be part of the town festivities. He hoped she didn't collapse from too much happiness once this was over.

Before the float parking area grew crowded, Roan checked the tires on the trailer, not wanting a replay of the '06 debacle. Then he checked the hitch to make sure it was attached properly.

The float had been decorated to resemble a classroom, with a banner reading Golden Elementary along either side.

Emmie chatted nonstop while he worked. How happy both his girls were today, a far cry from the holidays last year. This season started a new chapter in the Donovan family. They were more willing to talk about Catrina. And his girls weren't looking at him like a man they barely knew, but like the father who spent quality time with them. When they'd first arrived in Golden, he hadn't known if change was possible. But they'd worked through the difficulties. Tackled the major problems. And he found his love for both Kaylie and Emmie had grown in leaps and bounds.

Still, he continued to be protective of them, something he'd never let up on. The world could be a scary and dangerous place. Hadn't his own childhood taught him that lesson? He would shield them with his life, if necessary. But now joy had filtered through the worry, and he found himself rushing home at the end of the day to see their smiling faces.

If he could sort out his feelings for Faith, life would be…complete.

"Daddy, look at the reindeer," Emmie shouted from the side of the trailer.

He followed her pointed finger to see six horses, sporting reindeer antlers, along with jingling bells, being led to where he assumed Santa's sleigh was waiting.

"I would love to pet one," she said, longing in her voice.

"If you listen to Miss Faith when she gets here, maybe we can stop and see them after the parade."

Her eyes lit up. "Really?"

"Yes, but you have to behave. No running off."

"I promise, Daddy."

Still, her riveted attention on the horses didn't set him at ease.

As the parents began to arrive at the parade staging area, Roan found himself on the lookout for the one woman who wouldn't leave his thoughts. For a guy who didn't want to rush things, when had he fallen for Faith? Each day, the lines grew a little blurrier, and his reservations about engaging in a relationship seemed less critical.

After hearing about her elf outfit, he couldn't wait to see it in person. Maybe tease her a bit. He did love when her cheeks turned red over a compliment. Or how she gave as good as she got when they bantered.

No question about it, he loved her.

It didn't matter when it had happened or how he'd subconsciously tried to sabotage his feelings. He wanted to see what a life with Faith would entail, and the only way to get there was to tell her.

People wove in and out of the crowd. Some wore costumes while others bundled up against the chilly wind. Clouds scuttled across the sky, allowing the sun to peek out now and then. In the distance, Roan could make out the strains of the high school band warming up. He'd have to keep Emmie close by so she didn't take off to check out the surroundings. In this crowd, he could easily lose sight of her.

In the past month, the Donovans had settled into family life. Sure, there were some bumps in the road—there always would be. But it was a long way from the beginning of the holiday season when he'd thought his girls were better off forgoing Christmas rather than stirring up sad feelings. Emmie listened better and Kaylie was back to her sunny self, acting like an eleven-year-old instead of trying to be the adult in the house. He had Faith to thank for that.

Faith. She had the biggest heart of anyone he knew. Hadn't she accepted his family with open arms when they really needed it? In return, he'd worked behind the scenes to make sure to support her. Fixing faulty furnaces. Listening to her concerns. Chopping firewood. Encouraging her efforts whenever he could. He understood how hard it was raising children alone and wanted to make sure she had everything she needed to succeed.

And now you miss her.

He did. More than he'd ever imagined. He still carried plenty of baggage from his childhood. And yeah, he'd closed down after he and Catrina had split. Was that what had prompted his fear of moving forward? Getting hurt? He wasn't ashamed to say it was selfish, and he'd rather avoid the pain. But distance from Faith didn't seem to be working. Yes, he'd told her he wanted them to take their time, but he was wrong. And now she was treating him like any other friend she might be working with on a project. Did he blame her?

"Daddy, lift me up. I want to find the perfect spot to stand with John."

Shaking off his depressing thoughts on this

happy occasion, he lifted Emmie up onto the float.

He stuffed his hands in his pockets to search for his gloves but came up empty. He'd forgotten them again. Rubbing his hands together, he blew a misty warmth over his frigid fingers, wishing for even the pink pair with pompoms Faith had loaned him that day in the park.

"Next time remember your equipment," Brady said as he rounded the truck. He hadn't forgotten his hat or thick gloves to fight the elements. "Heard we might get snow later today."

"Hey, I had two girls to get ready and out the door this morning."

Brady handed him a steaming cup of coffee. "Why not ask your neighbor for help?"

"Because she has her own kids to worry about. Plus, she has to be here soon too. Busy morning all around."

Brady shook his head. "I thought you were a smart guy when Pete hired you. Now? Not so much."

Roan reared back. "Meaning?"

Pointing an accusing finger, Brady said, "You'd be lucky to get Faith Harper to go out with you."

Something that felt like jealousy expanded in his chest. "And you know this how?"

He shrugged. "I was in the friend zone with her in school. She's smart, funny and pretty. You, my friend, are letting a good thing get away."

"Why are you bringing this up now?"

Brady chuckled. "You've got it bad, my friend, and I decided to take pity on you today and make you see the light." He held up his cup like he was making a toast, then took a sip. "Consider it my Christmas gift to you."

Had not wanting to rush into a relationship been the perfect excuse not to open up his heart again? Roan had to admit, the icicles keeping him from feeling had melted since Faith came into his life. So why on earth had he thought distance would be the answer?

"Dude, if you don't tell her how you feel, some other guy is going to have the courage to swoop in."

He scowled. "You?"

"Nah. But someone…" He trailed off before strolling away like he hadn't just dropped a bombshell.

"Daddy," Emmie called from the trailer. "When is John going to be here?"

"Soon."

Which turned out to be right now. Faith

hurried toward the parents huddled together, holding John's hand while he jogged alongside her to keep up. "We made it," she announced.

Dressed in a cute elf outfit of a green sweaterdress and a wide black belt, black leggings and ankle boots, and wearing a jaunty, red hat with a jingle bell at the point, she personified the holiday. As always, she took his breath away. He needed to tell her how he felt. Soon.

Walking over, he helped John up onto the float to join Emmie. "Need a boost?" he asked her.

"I can manage."

"You look very…elfy."

She curtsied. "That's what I was going for."

"You do bring out the spirit of Christmas," he said.

"Which is exhausting." She sighed. "I'll be happy for a few days off during the kids' school break. All too soon I'll be back at the office to focus on the new project I mentioned."

"Your family agreed?" He offered what he hoped was an encouraging smile.

"Yep. I'm in charge starting January 2."

"Wow. That's fast."

"I'm sure we'll wave at each other from across our front yards," she said.

Would they? What if she got so busy she realized she'd dodged a bad relationship? Went out with another guy, like Brady suggested?

An official-looking man walking by with a megaphone yelled, "T minus ten minutes, people. Get in place."

She nodded to the truck. "Keep us safe."

"I will. And you keep an eye on the kids. Especially Emmie. She's on holiday overload."

"I will."

She climbed aboard without his help, and he had no excuse to linger, so he got in the truck cab and started the engine.

They were lined up in order. The mayor led, seated in a convertible Cadillac with the top down so she could wave and yell out greetings to her constituents. From what he could tell from driving in earlier, the townspeople were out en masse, lining Main Street on both sides. There were lawn chairs and blankets spread out, marking spots as folks visited and purchased popcorn or soft pretzels from the vender carts set up along the route. Everyone was in great spirits on this overcast Christmas Eve morning.

Next came decorated Jeeps from the local

car club, dogs bounding about on leashes representing the veterinarian clinic, a gymnastics class doing flips to the oohs and aahs of the crowd, then Kaylie's dance class. Next came the band, playing Christmas tunes. Along the way, volunteers handed out balloons and red or green beads.

Finally the floats followed, homemade decorated trailers pulled by a cavalcade of pickup trucks, representing different businesses in town. Deep North Adventures featured outdoor enthusiasts pretending to zip-line across the length of the trailer. Hot Air, the glass-blowing shop, featured a mosaic of stained glass windows. When the sun managed to make a spotty appearance, colors reflected on the damp street as the float moved. The hospital, fire station and other municipal entities had joined in making their floats welcoming.

Santa would bring up the rear, sending good tidings to all the boys and girls lined up along the curb. When Roan checked the rearview mirror, he could see Emmie and John interact with the crowd. If they waved to the bystanders any harder, they'd dislocate their little shoulders.

He kept his attention ahead of him, not willing to go off track and create a scene. But as he drove, Brady's words echoed in Roan's head. Once the holidays were over, he had to reconsider what he thought he wanted for his family, and what they needed as a whole. And hope he could make Faith happy, not to mention John and Lacey.

Forty minutes later, he steered the truck and trailer to a clear spot at the end of the parade route, a few blocks from the community center. He stepped out of the cab, backing up against the truck as chaos ensued. Parents were milling about, picking up their children as they jumped down from floats. People who had marched along the route were heading for their cars. Voices rose, and music still blared from certain floats, making it difficult to hear. A man who had driven the float ahead of Roan asked for help disconnecting the trailer from the truck. Roan made sure it was done properly before waving off the other man's thanks.

He sidestepped a few running teens, then maneuvered over to the float. He stopped short when Gene grabbed his arm to pull him aside. What was he doing here at the end of the parade route? Then the anxious expression on his face registered and made Roan's heart pause.

"We can't find Emmie."

All sound and movement around him

dimmed as he froze. "What do you mean? We didn't have plans for her to go home with you."

"We didn't, but after the parade ended, we came to take pictures while she was still aboard the float. We got some good shots, then one by one, the parents started helping the children down. She waved and said she'd be right there, but a few minutes passed and we couldn't see her. We walked completely around the float, but she was gone."

Emmie was…gone? No. Faith was watching out for her like he asked. She had to be.

"There must be some mistake."

Laurel hurried to them, her face white. She shook her head at Gene.

Wanting answers, Roan tried to ignore the searing pain in his chest just as Faith walked his way with John. Her smile faded when she took in their desolate expressions.

"What's wrong?"

"Emmie wandered off," Laurel managed to say.

Faith's mouth dropped. She turned her head to look behind her, then back. "But I saw her heading right to the Jessups."

"Somehow we missed her," Gene confirmed.

Faith glanced back at Roan, fear in her eyes.

"I asked you to watch her," he said, fear lacing his tone, making it sound like an accusation. "And now she's missing."

FAITH WINCED AS if she'd taken a physical blow, trying not to let Roan's words wound her. But they'd hit the intended target. Emmie was gone? How had that happened? And did he honestly think she just let Emmie wander off on her own? No, she'd watched Emmie navigate the crowd. At least she thought Emmie had reached her grandparents. Could she have been mistaken?

Uncertainty hit her anew. Had she messed up? She reran the scene in her mind. No, Emmie had been in her sights the entire time she grew closer to the Jessups.

"We were starting to follow behind her," Faith explained, her insides shaking. The panic on Roan's face was frightening, especially since this wasn't the first time Emmie had taken off on her own. She could be anywhere.

"You didn't see her?" she asked Laurel.

The woman shook her head, clearly so distressed she couldn't speak, but accusation shone in her eyes, as well.

The crowd was still thick with revelers running to and fro. Which way did they begin to search? Where would Emmie have meandered off to?

The hard line of Roan's mouth made her feel worse than she had seconds ago. He was blaming her, she knew. But he was wrong.

She felt a hand on her shoulder and turned. Mama was holding a jabbering Lacey, the two unaware of the drama playing out before them. "We came to collect you. Lacey wants to ask John all about being on the float."

She took John by the shoulders and led him toward her mother. "Can you take John? Emmie took off and we need to find her."

Mama paled. "Of course." She reached out for John's hand. He looked close to tears himself, having heard the adults' entire conversation. "I'll take them to the community center."

"We'll get Kaylie and bring her there too," Gene said, taking Laurel by the arm.

Faith turned to ask Roan what they should do now, but he was a few feet away, already searching the area around them.

"Call your friends," Faith told her mother. "Get the word out. Someone is bound to see her."

Mama pulled her phone from her pocket, already on the job. When Faith turned, Roan was stalking through the crowd, calling out for Emmie.

Faith bounded into the revelers, looking for a little girl with blond curls. She caught up with Roan, placing a hand on his arm.

"I don't need your help," he snapped, dread washing off him in waves. "I called Brady."

His words hurt, but she'd break down later. "Yes, you do need me." She raised her voice over the din of the crowd. "Mama will get the word to the town grapevine and call me if anyone has seen Emmie."

"And if they don't?"

Her stomach twisted. "They have to."

Roan turned on his heel, continuing to call Emmie's name. They covered the entire area, but Emmie was nowhere to be found. By the time they were near the community center, the crowd had thinned, but still no sign of the little girl.

"Let's go back to the float," Roan said. "Maybe she got turned around and went back there."

They retraced their footsteps, but no Emmie. Roan paced, until he pulled his phone from his pocket and stared at it, like he was willing it to ring.

Faith still kept her gaze moving all around her, hoping Emmie would roam back in their direction. Tell them a story about her great adventure. Could Faith live with herself if something horrible happened to Roan's daughter?

"I told you I didn't want to get caught up in Christmas fever," Roan railed, his words tight and controlled. "If I hadn't let us get carried away, we wouldn't have come here today and Emmie would be home where she belongs, safe."

"C'mon, Roan. You couldn't keep your children from experiencing the holidays, no matter how hard you tried."

"But I would have tried anyway."

"And they would still have found a way to celebrate."

"How do you know? Just because you've bought into Christmas doesn't mean we all have."

"Because they're children. And it's hard to get through December without mentioning the holidays."

"I wish I hadn't let you encourage them. Get their hopes up."

She stared at him. Yes, he was scared, so she let his criticism slide.

He stalked around the float, his face red now.

"I promised to protect them," he said, still searching around them.

"And you have."

He shot her an icy look. "Not since I let my guard down."

Guard down? Was he talking about her?

Her phone rang. She covered one ear and placed her phone against the other.

"Mama?"

"She's been spotted. Walking toward the park."

She hung up and grabbed Roan's arm. "The park."

"That's half a mile from here."

"Let's go."

They took off at a dead run.

WITH FAITH KEEPING up her speed beside Roan, they tore down Main Street. Stubborn woman wasn't giving up in this quest to find Emmie, even when he'd undeservedly blamed her for the incident to begin with.

With each step, he could barely breathe as fear replaced the oxygen, but he pushed on. His daughter needed him.

A few shopkeepers watched them run by, questions on their faces. Myrna from the coffee shop saw them and pointed north, yelling, "That way. I tried to get her to stop here, but she ran off."

Not far from the park, Roan spotted Emmie

standing on the sidewalk alone, her face scrunched up, her shoulders hunched like she was trying to hide herself. She started to walk to the park entrance, then abruptly halted and turned to walk back down Main Street, then pivoted yet again.

"Emmie," Roan called, as they grew closer. The little girl's eyes went wide when she saw him, and she started running in his direction.

When they drew close, Roan got down on one knee and held out his arms. Emmie detoured around him and ran straight into Faith's arms. He shook his head, then watched his daughter throw her arms around Faith's neck and hang on. What the heck?

Faith looked over Emmie's shoulder at him, surprise etched on her face. She rubbed one hand up and down Emmie's back while holding on tight with the other.

Emmie finally broke the embrace, tears streaking her cheeks. "I knew you'd find me," she told Faith. Then she faced Roan, eyes downcast. "I'm sorry, Daddy," she said in a voice he could barely hear.

When he tugged her into his embrace and held on for dear life, she started crying in earnest. Roan muttered sweet words in her ear. She finally calmed down, rubbing her finger under her nose when he put some space between them. He lightly grasped her upper arms. "What were you thinking?"

"I was walking to Grandma and Grandpa when I got pushed out of the way." She sniffled. "Then I saw Santa and his reindeer and decided to follow him."

"But why not wait until you reached Grandpa and Grandma, so they could go with you?"

"Because it was important. I had to talk to Santa right away." She reached into her pocket and extracted a folded, rumpled paper, then unfolded it so Roan could see words scratched on the page. "This was my last chance to give Santa my Christmas list. He's coming tonight, Daddy. I had to make sure I put this in his hands."

Roan wiped a shed tear from her face.

Faith moved closer to the little girl. "I'm sure Santa knows what you want for Christmas, Emmie."

She glanced at Faith. "The list isn't for me. It's for Daddy. I want to make sure Santa gets my wish to make Daddy happy again."

Roan's heart nearly cracked in two. All this drama for him?

Determination etched Emmie's face now that the fear was gone. "I asked you to take me to see Santa before now, but you never made time." She dodged his gaze. "I even tried to get John to help me mail the letter, but it didn't work out."

This was all his fault. He thought the tradition silly, never realizing his daughter would go to great lengths to deliver the letter. For dad and daughter, it was supposed to be the other way around.

"But then I got mixed up in the crowd, Daddy. I thought maybe they brought the reindeer to the park so they'd have room to run around before they fly in the sky tonight."

Unshed tears shimmered in Faith's eyes. He couldn't deny the heat behind his own, but he blinked the moisture back. She took a few steps away and made a phone call.

Roan cleared his scratchy throat and stood, taking Emmie's tiny hand in his. "I think it's time for you to visit the jolly old man."

Emmie giggled. "Daddy, you're silly."

He couldn't stop his slow smile if he tried.

"Maybe, but I also happen to know where he is."

"You do?" she asked in wonder.

"I do. Let's catch him before he gets too busy tonight."

She beamed up at him and his chest seized. Had he ever seen her so happy as she skipped along beside him? As if her actions hadn't aged him a dozen years?

He said silent thanks. He had his daughter by his side. She was in one piece and not nearly as distressed as she might be. If asked, he'd admit to being more shook up than her. But she was safe. He'd deal with her headstrong ways another day.

"I let Mama know everything is okay," Faith said as they headed toward the community center. She must have lost her hat in the mad race to get to Emmie. She pushed her hair from her eyes as she related the news. "She'll let everyone know."

He nodded, unsure what to say. She knew he'd lashed out because he was afraid for his daughter, right? Her relief when they'd found Emmie matched his own. But the way she pulled into herself, the way her expression was closed off, gave him pause. Why did he get the feeling something irreparable had happened and he might be unable to fix it?

CHAPTER SIXTEEN

As SOON AS they entered the community center, adrenaline kicked in and Faith began to shake. She dug her fingers into her thighs to keep from giving in to the surge of relief and residual fear. Roan's family surrounded them, making sure Emmie wasn't any worse for wear. Faith stepped aside, allowing Kaylie and the Jessups to get in their hugs and questions.

Faith glanced around the room, her gaze stopping on Mama as she bounced Lacey in her lap while John silently watched the reunion from beside her. She was surrounded by Mrs. M., Alveda, Bunny Wright and Judge Carmichael, who were all here for the Operation Share party. Faith walked over to join them.

She bent down to kiss Mama's cheek. Made sure her voice was even when she spoke. "Thanks for the heads-up."

"I'm relieved you found her," Mama said,

her face still drawn. "Everyone was so worried."

"What got into that girl?" Alveda asked, looking a little worse for wear.

"She followed Santa," Faith explained, "but got turned around and headed in the wrong direction."

Mrs. M.'s eyes were soft as she watched the family bond. "At least they're all safe and sound."

"And just in time for the party," Bunny said, clapping her hands together as if to snap them all out of their funk. "Folks are starting to arrive. Let's celebrate."

Faith looked over her shoulder to see Roan leading Emmie to Santa. The guest of honor had a special area set up in a corner of the room, with an enormous chair and eager elves waiting to get to work.

Emmie would get to deliver her list after all.

"Mama can we stay and help hand out gifts?" John asked, a little more color in his face since his friend had arrived at the center in one piece.

"We'd love it," Bunny answered him. "And Faith, can you help me lay out the desserts?"

Avoiding her mother's gaze, she went to the kitchen. Mama was sure to notice her distress, even as Faith tried to hide it. She didn't want to talk about what had happened or what it meant for their relationship with the Donovans. Mama would get the truth out of her later. Right now she was too raw to talk.

She took the plates from the refrigerator as Bunny handed them to her. The older woman asked, "Are you okay?"

"I'm happy we found Emmie."

"Thank goodness you were by Roan's side."

She might have been by his side, but he'd made it clear he didn't want her there.

After a few trips back and forth to the kitchen, the spread was finally laid. More folks arrived, their voices echoing, cries of excitement resonating as the children glimpsed Santa waiting for them. In the background, Faith could hear Santa's deep *ho, ho, ho.*—

"Faith."

She froze at Roan's voice. Met his gaze and forced a smile. "Did Emmie accomplish her mission?"

"She did."

"I'm so glad."

He nodded. Did he feel as awkward as she? They both spoke at the same time.

"I wanted to—"

"Thank you—"

Her skin felt itchy, and she forced a light tone to her voice because Roan was serious instead of angry. "For what?"

"Searching with me for Emmie."

"I wouldn't have rested until I knew she was safe."

"But I shouldn't have been so tough on you."

"You're right." She paused. Straightened her shoulders. "If it had been John or Lacey who disappeared, I would have been terrified. Out of my mind. Just like you. But I didn't do anything wrong here, Roan, and it wasn't fair for you to blame me."

"It's because of you we found her." Lines of concern stretched between his eyes. "It was your quick thinking to get the word out that made all the difference. Otherwise, who knows how long we would have been searching until we found her."

"Exactly." Hot pressure burned behind her eyes. "After all the time we've spent together, you should have known I would never do anything to hurt you or your children."

"I…" He seemed at a loss as to what to say next.

Her voice cracked as she voiced the decision she'd made on the walk back to the community center. "It's better we don't see each other after the holidays."

He rubbed his jaw. "Wait. Are you—"

She cut him off. "I need to check on my children."

Turning, she crossed the room. It would be better for everyone if she stayed in her lane, taking care of her family and keeping busy at work. For all she'd accomplished moving forward after the bad decisions she'd made in her past, she wouldn't let anyone make her feel like she'd taken ten steps back. Even if it was the man she'd fallen hopelessly in love with.

ROAN WATCHED FAITH walk to her mother and say something into the other woman's ear. Wanda Sue nodded, her eyebrows angled as if she didn't like the conversation. Faith spun around, shoulders stiff and gait jerky, then exited the community center, never looking back. Was that it? Was it over between them?

She was right. In that moment, he had blamed her. All he could think was that *he* should have had an eye on his daughter, so he'd placed his guilt and fear on Faith. Was there any way he could make this up to her?

He went to the table where Emmie held court with Kaylie and her grandparents. He had a lot of work to do with his youngest, but he had his family all together. Why didn't it feel complete without Faith?

"Roan," Laurel said, sidling up beside him.

Weary after the events of the day, he nodded in her direction, readying himself for a lecture about what a bad dad he was.

"I owe you an apology."

Surprise made him take a step back. "For?"

Laurel bit her lip, then said, "Not listening to you. Not realizing that Emmie was getting out of control. I didn't want to face the truth, but today…"

"I know you never wanted anything like this to happen."

"But I bucked you at every step. Thought I knew better." The expression in her eyes was desolate. "I was wrong."

Words he'd never thought he'd hear. But he found himself grateful. "And now we come up with a plan."

"We?" Hope slowly replaced the pain on her face. "You'll still let us have a place in her life?"

"Of course. Why would you think otherwise?"

She placed a hand on her chest. "This is so overwhelming. I didn't want to compare her to Catrina…"

"But she's exhibiting the same behavior?"

Laurel nodded.

"We'll do everything we can for Emmie, while showering her with love."

Laurel nodded. Seemed to consider her next thought. "Emmie said Faith was there when you found her."

"She was."

"I should thank her too." She hesitated. "Faith did watch Emmie get off the float, Roan. Kept her eyes on Emmie the entire time she walked to us. It's not her fault Emmie got lost in the crowd and wandered off."

"I know that. Now."

"Does Faith?"

After his accusation, of course not, but he was determined to show her otherwise. He was tired of believing only he could protect his daughters. That he couldn't move on because of what had happened between him and his ex. Not being united in their decisions had been at the root of their issues, and instead of learning from it, he'd carried his pain and regret into the next season of his life. He had to actually trust his daughters, his in-laws and especially Faith, who deserved a man who loved her without reservation. He wanted to be that man.

If he'd discovered anything today, it was that letting Faith down was unacceptable.

FAITH BARELY GOT in the door when Rocky ran for her, jumping and barking, eager to play.

"Down, buddy."

As if on autopilot, she plugged in the tree lights and got a fire going, Rocky on her heels. As the log crackled and popped, she sank to the floor, pulling the fluffy puppy into her arms.

"You're kinda growing on me," she told him as he licked her face. She croaked out a chuckle, and the sound surprised her. Even though she hadn't wanted a puppy right now, she couldn't deny how his presence added joy to her family. Guess Lyle had been right about this one thing. She buried her face in the puppy's soft fur, taking a few minutes to unwind.

Mama had told her she'd drop the children off after the party. There was dinner to prepare, cookies and milk to place out for Santa, then after the children went to sleep, presents to carry downstairs and place under the tree. Yet Faith still sat with the puppy, stroking his fur as the flickering flames mesmerized her.

She didn't expect to get much sleep tonight, not after the way she'd left things with Roan. Things would never be the same between them. How could they? She'd done the right thing by walking away. She finally believed in herself and needed to be with a man who felt the same.

With a deep sigh, she rose to fill the puppy bowl, then opened the refrigerator door to peer inside and decide what to fix for her hungry family. The doorbell startled her out of her doldrums.

"Coming," she called out as she headed to the foyer, Rocky again at her feet.

She hurried to the door and yanked it open, but it wasn't her mother on the other side.

Instead, Roan stood on the porch, Lacey in his arms, surrounded by Kaylie, John and Emmie. The frigid wind should have made her shiver, but she was too dumbfounded to register the freezing temperature.

"What are you all doing here?"

His eyes were solemn. "We took a family vote."

She stared at him, confused.

"We're going to spend Christmas Eve together," John said.

"But…"

Kaylie held up a bag Faith hadn't noticed. "We have dinner."

Emmie held up a dish. "And cookies. Santa said it was okay to bring some home."

"Are you going to let us in, or are we going

to freeze out here?" Roan asked, his expression hopeful.

"Right." She stepped back as they all trooped into the foyer.

"Can we talk?" Roan asked, transferring Lacey into her arms when the child reached out for Faith.

Faith grabbed hold of her daughter, who carried the scent of Mama's perfume.

"Or if you'd rather, I can take the girls home."

"No. The children will be disappointed."

Roan pulled something red from his pocket. It jingled as he handed it to her. "You lost this."

"My hat."

His grin was bittersweet and tender, with a twist of regret in the corners. "No self-respecting elf goes without one."

They went to the kitchen to unpack the food. Faith's stomach twisted. Roan had brought his family here? Surely they had other plans. And what did he mean by a family vote?

Roan took plates and glasses from the cabinet, Kaylie found utensils and John and Emmie ran off into the living room to play with Rocky.

"I didn't expect all this," she said, still flustered by this impromptu visit.

"But you deserve it."

She didn't respond—because really, what could she say? Roan placed the glasses on the counter. "Your mom said she'll see you tomorrow."

When her daughter started squirming, Faith put Lacey down. Kaylie claimed the toddler's hand to lead her into the other room. Faith was ready to ask Roan more questions when John started yelling.

"Snow! Mama, it's snowing."

She and Roan hurried into the living room just as the children and the puppy ran outside, leaving the door wide-open.

"Not again," Roan muttered, taking up the chase.

Faith grabbed her coat and followed. As she stopped on the porch steps, sure enough, in the late afternoon gloom, snowflakes drifted from the sky.

"I knew it," John yelled, jumping about, trying to catch the elusive flakes. "I told you we'd have snow."

The children ran about, making a game out of trying to snatch the Christmas Eve flurries.

She made her way to Roan's side. To her surprise, he took her hand. The warmth made her heart kick up a beat, but the questions still lingered.

His devastating smile floored her as he caught her gaze. "I'm kinda slow on the uptake."

What? Oh… "Gloves." She searched her pockets, pulling out a pair.

He chuckled. "That's not what I meant."

She stared up at him. "What then?"

He took both her hands in his. "Remember when I told you that I didn't want to rush into a relationship?"

How could she have forgotten?

"I was wrong."

Nerves fluttered in her stomach.

"After my marriage fell apart and then Catrina passed, I closed up inside. Decided I was the only one who was capable of taking care of my kids, even though I clearly needed help. I also decided falling in love again wasn't in the cards, but I should never have put all of that on you, Faith. I'm sorry for not believing in you when Emmie disappeared. You're a great mom and you've had a positive influence on my children's lives." He paused. "My life."

She didn't trust herself to speak.

"You've made this the best Christmas the girls and I could have ever expected. I thought rushing a relationship would cause problems, but, Faith, I can't stay away." He slid one hand from hers and palmed her cold cheek. "It's not that I can't take care of my family alone, Faith, it's that I don't want to."

Her nose stung as her eyes filled with tears.

"The girls love you."

She swallowed hard.

"I love you."

Tears streamed down her cheeks.

"No response?"

"Oh, Roan." Throwing caution to the wind, she threw her arms around his neck and kissed him with everything in her being. To the soundtrack of their children running while dodging snowflakes and Rocky barking and chasing after them, Faith pulled back. Spoke from a deep and sure place inside her. "I love you too."

"Good, because this whole neighbor thing is going to get old fast."

"What are you saying?"

"I didn't need Emmie's Christmas list to make me happy, Faith." He framed her face in his warm hands. "You've already given me more joy than I could imagine."

Then he kissed the tip of her cold nose. She trembled, not from the cold but because he loved her.

"No matter how you look at it, it seems we've been a family for a while now." He squeezed her hand. "I don't see that changing."

Sheer delight overwhelmed her. She kissed him again, knowing this was just the beginning of many merry Christmases to come.

THE COMMUNITY CENTER had cleared out, leaving only the Golden Matchmakers Club. The party had been a hit, if smiles on the faces of happy children were the measure for success. Volunteers had cleaned up in record time, hurrying off to their warm homes on this Christmas Eve, but Gayle Ann had asked the club members to stay behind.

"So?" she asked Wanda Sue.

The group sat around a table, expectant expressions on all their faces.

"When Roan asked if he could take the children home, he alluded to both the Harper and Donovan families having the best Christmas ever."

"I knew it!" Gayle Ann crowed. "Our plan is a success."

Alveda rested her elbows on the table. "Two matches in a row. Who knew we had it in us?"

"I think we owe it to the vision of our fearless leader," Harry said, eyes on Gayle Ann. She sent a smile his way.

"Thank you all. So much," Wanda said, her eyes misty.

"Well, with another happy couple together, I'm all in," Bunny said. "And ready to convince my nephews to take the plunge."

"I did wonder about them," Gayle Ann said in her most cagey voice.

"Adam could use a little meddling in his love life." Bunny's eyes sparkled with humor. "If we all agree, how about making him our next project?"

Ayes chorused around the table.

Gayle Ann narrowed her eyes. "I may have just the right woman in mind for him."

"Do tell," Bunny said.

"When we meet after the holidays."

"You're gonna make us wait?" Alveda crabbed.

"We've done enough for today, so let's all head home and spend time with our families."

Everyone gathered their belongings, the women moving toward the door. Harry stopped Gayle Ann by placing a hand on her arm.

"Something you wanted to say, Harry?"

A small wrapped box with a red bow sat

on the table. He slid it her way. "Seems Santa left a little something for you."

She blinked furiously. "But…"

"He knows all about your big heart."

She couldn't quite cover her shock. "I don't know what to say."

"Thank you will do."

She picked up the box, her heart racing. "Thank you, Harry."

He nodded, a satisfied smile on his lips, then held out his arm so she could place a hand in the crook. Together, they walked out into the star-filled night, just as flurries scurried about in the air.

At this time of year, how could anyone not believe in second chances?

* * * * *

For more romances from USA TODAY *bestselling author, Tara Randel, and Harlequin Heartwarming, visit www.Harlequin.com today!*

HARLEQUIN SELECTS COLLECTION

19 FREE BOOKS IN ALL!

From Robyn Carr to RaeAnne Thayne to Linda Lael Miller and Sherryl Woods we promise (actually, GUARANTEE!) each author in the Harlequin Selects collection has seen their name on the *New York Times* or *USA TODAY* bestseller lists!

YES! Please send me the **Harlequin Selects Collection**. This collection begins with 3 FREE books and 2 FREE gifts in the first shipment. Along with my 3 free books, I'll also get 4 more books from the Harlequin Selects Collection, which I may either return and owe nothing or keep for the low price of $24.14 U.S./$28.82 CAN. each plus $2.99 U.S./$7.49 CAN. for shipping and handling per shipment*. If I decide to continue, I will get 6 or 7 more books (about once a month for 7 months) but will only need to pay for 4. That means 2 or 3 books in every shipment will be FREE! If I decide to keep the entire collection, I'll have paid for only 32 books because 19 were FREE! I understand that accepting the 3 free books and gifts places me under no obligation to buy anything. I can always return a shipment and cancel at any time. My free books and gifts are mine to keep no matter what I decide.

☐ 262 HCN 5576   ☐ 462 HCN 5576

Name (please print)

Address   Apt. #

City   State/Province   Zip/Postal Code

Mail to the Harlequin Reader Service:
IN U.S.A.: P.O. Box 1341, Buffalo, NY 14240-8531
IN CANADA: P.O. Box 603, Fort Erie, Ontario L2A 5X3

Get 4 FREE REWARDS!

We'll send you 2 FREE Books plus <u>2 FREE Mystery Gifts</u>.

Both the **Romance** and **Suspense** collections feature compelling novels written by many of today's bestselling authors.

FREE
Value Over
$20